This novel is a work of historical fiction. Some names which appear on these pages are fictitious. Any name resembling a living or deceased person is purely coincidental. Some events and stories discussed are fabricated. Most of the locations and trail history come from memory of living on the Southern Shore and volunteering on the East Coast Trail Association, and hiking on the trail since its inception in 1994.

ISBN 978-1-7777964-0-2

A story about the marijuana trade in the 1980s in rural Newfoundland before it became legal in Canada.

WORKING CAPE RACE

A NOVEL

By Chris Ryan

Dedication

I dedicate this book to these individuals who have made a difference and improvement in the lives of many people in our Province. And who are responsible for bringing thousands of hikers and tourists to our beautiful Province.

Randy Murphy-President of the East Coast Trail Association 1995-. Without the drive, guidance and leadership abilities of this man, the award-winning East Coast Trail would not be what it is today.

Ed Delaney-Trail Operations Manager, overseeing the physical building of the trail 1997-.

It was and is a pleasure to work alongside these dedicated men. Thank you for the work you have done to give the Province of Newfoundland and Labrador a world-class hiking trail. And to anyone who has served on the East Coast Trail Association board, on committees, trail clearing or as a custodian.

INTRODUCTION

Come along for an adventure as small-time drug dealers Rory O'Ryan and Butch Hynes from Cappahayden, Newfoundland, who are on the run on the Southern Shore from the Royal Canadian Mounted Police for twelve days. They make their way from Goulds to Cape Race Road in Portugal Cove South. They travel on coastal paths used for centuries before roads and cars. These paths would become the foundation for the East Coast Trail. Some of their travel consists of an ATV and a canoe. They befriend an Irish Setter on their travels.

CHAPTER ONE

Butch did not have a car, and he didn't know how to drive. He figured he could steal a car and learn to drive or find someone who owned a car and use theirs. Either way, Butch had to get a car. He didn't have the money or the income to get a car loan. He figured he could talk Rory into buying a car. Why not? They were hitchhiking or paying one of their buddies to drive them from Cappahayden to St. John's or the Goulds to pick up their weekly supply of weed and hash. He could offer to help Rory with the monthly payments.

But how to start the conversation with Rory was something Butch knew he had to time correctly. And the time was now. They were walking along the highway in Middle Pond, north of Bay Bulls, where they had been dropped off after hitching a ride out of St. John's with their stash of drugs. Middle Pond was mostly cabins belonging to people from St. John's. It was the middle of nowhere. As they walked along, the breeze rattled the scrub and twigs in the ditch. Butch was nervous as a cat, wondering how to start the conversation. Finally, he thought, fuck it, here goes.

"Rory, this is bullshit, me and you hitchhikin' or bummin' a ride up and down the Shore once or twice a week all for the sake of a measly few thousand dollars. Why don't we buy a car?"

"Butch, yer off yer head. Where are we gettin' money to buy a car?"

"Rory, we're both gettin' the pogey. Yer makin' a few dollars every week sellin' a little weed and hash. Between the two of us, we could do it. Wouldn't it be nice to jump in our own car, head to town when we wanted? We could see places like Signal Hill and Cape Spear. Sure, I've never been to the Avalon Mall; it must be open fifteen years. They says it's huge. Rory, ya loves to read. We could go to the library every week or two. We wouldn't be hitchhikin' in the cold, snow, and rain."

"Good idea, but who'd give us a loan to buy a car?"

"Rory, we both got bank accounts at the Credit Union. I'm sure they'd consider it. If we don't try, we'll never know."

A few months ago, Rory thought about the day when they opened their accounts at the Fishermen's Credit Union in Witless Bay. Witless Bay—he'd been scared witless, embarrassed as he'd never been inside a bank or a credit union, he didn't know what to do. He had given the teller a hundred and forty dollars. She looked at him as though he had two heads. She asked him where he worked to have that much money. He could feel himself shaking, he told her, he'd saved it up. She'd congratulated him on being so frugal. Butch had put in a hundred bucks; he tried to hide it from the teller when he had trouble signing his name. Butch lived from unemployment check to unemployment check, drinking and smoking most of it. He was hungry all the time; his father never kept much grub in the house. Butch always said that he would never be hungry again when he could afford to buy his own food. Butch's mother had taken off when he was ten. His father was out fishing or on the booze. Much like Rory's father. Rory's mother was dead, which was bad, but not as bad as having your mother fuck off on you.

"Let me think about it for a while."

The sound of their boots tramping along took up the silence. The conversation had gone much better than he'd expected. Usually, Rory just blew him off. Rory was the type who always wanted to come up with ideas. He'd have to leave it with Rory for a few weeks to think it over; Rory was never one to make a quick decision, but he always made the right decision.

A few weeks later, Rory said to Butch, "I've been thinkin' about what ya said about buyin' a car." He took a puff of his cigarette and watched the smoke rise towards the blue sky. "I gotta agree with ya. It would be nice to have a set of wheels. Next time I'm into the Credit Union, I'll mention it to one of the tellers. I have no idea what's involved in gettin' a car loan. They might wanna' co-signer."

"What's a co-signer?"

"Someone with a steady income who signs the car loan for ya and vouches for ya that ya'll pay it back."

"Rory, yer father must have good credit."

"Butch, I doubt it. He never had a loan or credit card in his life. Everythin' he buys, he pays cash for it."

"Any chance he would lend us money to buy a car?"

"Doubt it. He only has enough to get 'im through the winter. Not only, but I also wouldn't feel good about takin' money from me, ol' man. What if somethin' happened and I couldn't pay 'im back?"

"What's goin' to happen to ya that ya wouldn't be able to pay 'im back?"

"Butch, who knows? What if I never got me job back at the fish plant in Fermeuse?"

"All ya do is worry. Why wouldn't ya get yer job back at the plant?"

"Who knows, Butch?"

"Rory, ya gotta give up worryin' about everythin'. Yer goin' to put yerself in an early grave."

"Well, Butch, I try to be mature. Not like you, livin' day to day with not a worry in the world." Rory threw his cigarette butt to the ground and screwed it into the dirt with his heel. Butch was pissing him off. He couldn't help being stupid, not getting any further than grade seven. He didn't always have to be at Rory like a woman, even if they had been together since they were kids. Although if Rory had a sister, she would probably grind him as Butch did. He had no sisters or brothers, and neither did Butch. Rory could imagine no one else in the old grey saltbox except him and his old man. What the eyes don't see, the heart doesn't grieve for.

CHAPTER TWO

Rory paid his buddy Brock White to drive him and Butch to St. John's. On the way back, Rory asked Brock to haul into the Credit Union. Rory had a few dollars gathered up he wanted to deposit; Butch, as usual, had nothing. The Credit Union was empty, not a person being served when Rory walked in.

After putting a few dollars in his account, he asked the teller about the car loan. He shuffled his feet and coughed.

"Miss, could you explain to me what is involved in gettin' a car loan?"

"Sure. Give me a few minutes to do your deposit first. And I'll explain the steps involved in getting a loan."

The young woman looked up, gave him a quick smile, and finished counting the money. She handed him back his bank book and said, "Well, Rory, you've either have to have some past credit history, or you most likely will need a co-signer. How much are you applying for?"

"I don't know. I wants to buy a car."

"A new car or a used one?"

"Used. I don't got the income to afford a new one."

"Okay, come with me."

She led Rory to an office at the back. Rory took the seat in front of the desk. She took papers from a drawer and sat behind the desk.

"The first thing is, I need to know where you work. And what your income is."

"I works at the Bonavista Cold Storage fish plant in Fermeuse. I spent one summer at Aqua Fisheries LTD in Aquaforte."

"So, are you from Fermeuse?"

"No, I'm from Cappahayden."

"And you have decided to do your banking this far from home."

"Well, the Scotiabank in Trepassey is a fine drive from Cappahayden. And I'm in town at least once a week. So, I figured I may as well use the services of this business."

"Yes, that makes sense. Thank you for your business. How long have you been working at the fish plant in Fermeuse?"

"I started workin' there when I was fourteen."

"My! That's young to be working."

"Well, it was either go to work in the plant or go trappin' cod with me ol' man. I couldn't go fishing. I gets sea-sick on the wharf."

The woman smiled and made another quick note on the pad in front of her. "How old are you, Rory?"

"Nineteen. Born on October 3, 1962, miss."

"So, you've been working for five years."

"Well, only in the summer months. I was in school 'til I was sixteen. Finished grade eleven with honors."

"How much do you make?"

"Well, every two weeks, I usually gets a check for around four hundred and fifty dollars."

"That's good money for a young man to be making. How many weeks do you usually work each summer?"

"I usually starts in May, finishes up in late September."

"I guess you collect unemployment insurance in the winter."

"Yes, I gets the pogey all winter."

"Excuse me?"

"We calls unemployment the UIC or the pogey." Rory was uncomfortable saying this to her. Snotty bitch.

"I see you only have two hundred and eighty dollars in your savings account. I would have expected more."

"Well, miss, ya see, I gotta buy me own groceries. And me ol' man wants seventy-five bucks every two weeks for board."

"My God, Rory, that's a lot for board."

"I agrees, I pays that much, or I can find somewhere else to live. There are not a lot of places to find to live in Cappahayden. Me and me buddy Butch Hynes are talkin' about movin' to Toronah one of these days."

"You are, Rory? Well, in that case, I don't believe we can give you a loan."

"Why, Miss?"

"Well, there is a high risk if you leave Newfoundland, you won't pay off your loan."

"No, no, no, Miss. We have been talkin' about goin' to Toronah since we were fifteen. I may never see Toronah. I'm a homeboy, I loves livin' in Cappahayden. I loves to hunt. I loves to go troutin'. I loves anythin' to do with the woods. So, for me to leave and go to Toronah and leave it all behind, I don't think I will ever do it." He'd do it quicker than the time she took to put on them fake eyelashes if he got the chance.

"Okay, here is where we are. I'll look over your application in the next few days to see if you qualify for a loan. There are two things you must do. You may need a co-signer. You have to find someone with good credit to co-sign. Look around for a car you might be interested in buying. So, we'll have a ball-park price range of how much you'll need. Oh, one more thing. Do you have a driver's license?"

"No, Miss, I don't."

She looked up from the pad and gave a half-smile, her expression was edged with impatience.

"Well, my advice to you is to contact the RCMP in Ferryland and inquire about getting your driver's license. As you know, the RCMP take people out for their road tests in rural Newfoundland."

"Yes, hon. I'll drop in and see 'em on me way home. I gotta drive past the detachment anyway."

"Okay, Rory, leave this with me for a week or so. I'll call you when I hear something about it. Give me your phone number."

"Well, we don't gotta phone in our house." He could feel the heat rising in his cheeks, he knew they were red. She gave a sigh, and her head tilted sideways as though she were suddenly tired.

"I makes a run to the city almost every Friday, miss. I can drop in next week and check on it. If you needs to get a hold of me, you can call my grandmother's house. She lives in Port Kirwan." Rory uncrumpled a piece of paper in his pocket and presented it to her. "Here's her name and number, leave a message with her. I'll warn you now, she's deaf as a haddock."

"Excuse me."

"Sorry, she's a little deaf on the phone. I drops in and sees her every second day or so."

"Okay, I'll call if I need to get in touch with you. So, Rory, get the ball rolling on the things I mentioned to you."

Rory left the building; his shoulders relax as he went through the door. Trying to speak correctly to a townie was draining. He didn't want to sound like a buck bayman. When Rory got in, Brock turned on the engine; the gravel crunched beneath the tires as they pulled out onto the Southern Shore highway.

Butch lit up a cigarette, he leaned towards Rory in the front seat. "What did she say, Rory?"

"Said I will most likely need a co-signer."

"They don't need that. If 'em people are good enough to give us money to buy a car, me and you will be good enough to pay it off."

"Butch, it will be my car."

"Now, Rory, don't go gettin' on like that."

"Like what?"

"Sayin' it will be yer car."

"Well, Butch, I'm takin' the loan out in my name."

"Yes, I knows. But we will be sharin' it, won't we?"

"Not likely, Butch. Ya can't drive, and ya destroys everythin' ya puts yer hands-on."

"Now, Rory, don't go gettin' high and mighty on me. I'm not the only one in this car who can't drive."

"Yer right, I'm gettin' me license soon. Missus told me; she wants me to get me license if she gives me the loan. I'm sure the car insurance company will want it."

"Rory, who d'ya think will co-sign for us?"

"Ya mean co-sign for me."

"Whatever."

"I dunno. I knows the ol' man won't. I won't even give 'im the satisfaction of askin' 'im. Fuck 'im. Nans old-age pension check isn't enough to cover it. I dunno, Butch. I gotta ask around."

Brock hauled into Crane's Ultramar gas bar on the corner of the Witless Bay line. Butch wanted a six-pack.

"I'm sweatin' like a bull. That was the most nervous thing I ever did in me life."

"Rory," said Brock, "when I got my car loan at Scotiabank in Trepassey, me oldest sister signed for me. And she only makes minimum wage at Fahey's old age home in Fermeuse."

"Yes, Brock, but she was still workin' full time. That's what they wants when they gives ya a loan. I knows no one workin' full time who's goin' to sign for me. Sure, everyone on the Shore is on the pogey in the winter. I'm a bit nervous about it. She mentioned I only had two hundred and eighty bucks in my bank account. I guess she figured I should've had more. I told her by the time I gives the ol' man his seventy-five bucks for board every two weeks, buys a few groceries for meself at Leo Kavanagh's food store in Fermeuse, buys a tub or two of baccy to roll me smokes, that's it for the pogey check. But if I gets this loan."

"Ya, mean we gets the loan . . ."

"Butch, shut up. It will be my loan and my car, not ours."

"Okay, b'y, don't blow a gasket."

"I'm not blowin' a gasket. I gotta tell ya somethin' ten times 'fore it sinks into yer thick skull!

"Okay, Brock," Rory said restlessly, "back to yer car loan." Brock was watching the road ahead carefully. "When did ya get it, and how much a month d'ya pay?"

"I got it about ten months ago. I pays one hundred and twenty-five dollars a month on it. Took it out for three years."

"How much does insurance cost?"

"Wasn't cheap, Rory."

"No beer, for me, Butch. I wants to stop at the RCMP detachment in Ferryland on the way home to inquire about gettin' me license."

Butch and Rory had done everything together since they were kids, trouting in the summer and winter, catching rabbits in the fall of the year, getting rides on horse and pony sleds in the country when their fathers went cutting logs or firewood. Rory was getting fed up with Butch. His father always said Butch was trouble, even when he was a youngster. Butch lit another cigarette, he told Rory to crack open the window. He had an idea, but he needed a car for it. No use telling Rory about it, he'd flip out. It was weird all the same, keeping something from him. If it worked out, Rory would be part of it anyway, on the road, heading for Toronto.

CHAPTER THREE

A blonde female RCMP officer looked up briefly from behind a desk when Rory walked in. She got up and walked into a back room. A male officer, six feet in height, walked to the front counter, his name tag said: "Constable Jack Campbell."

"Good day, officer," said Rory. "I'm inquirin' about gettin' me driver's license."

"And you are?"

"I'm Rory O'Ryan from Cappahayden."

"You're Max O'Ryan's son?"

"Yes, sir, I am."

"How old are you?"

"I'm nineteen."

"Do you know how to drive?"

"No, sir, I don't."

"Do you have a car?"

"No, sir."

"So, why do you want your driver's license?"

"Well, I applied for a loan taday to buy a car."

"At the bank in Trepassey?"

"No, sir, at the Fishermen's Credit Union in Witless Bay."

"So, why do you want a car if you don't have a driver's license?"

"Well, sir, I either have to hitchhike or pay someone to drive me back and forth to St. John's whenever I haves to go."

"How often do you have to go to the city?"

"Well, officer I . . . uh . . . I goes once a week. No, sir, about once a month.'

"Why would you be going to St. John's once a month?"

"Well, sir, it breaks up the monotony. Stuck on the Shore all winter makes for a long winter.

The officer tapped his pen on the desk. "What year were you born, son?"

"I was nineteen on October 3."

"So, you were born in 1962."

"Yes, sir."

"Okay, give me a minute." He picked up a clipboard and studied it.

"I'm looking at my schedule for road tests. I do road tests once a month. I have an opening three weeks from today. I'll take you out right after lunch. Say around one fifteen."

"Sounds good, sir. What's involved in this test?"

"Well, young man, not a lot. We leave from the detachment, drive the length of Ferryland. We go down by Bernard Kavanagh's buildings and do a little parking. Straight parking and parallel. I'll set up cones for the parallel parking."

"Sir, I have to be honest with you. I have never driven in me life."

"Well, son, you have three weeks to learn."

"Thank you, officer, see you in three weeks."

Rory walked to the car feeling content.

"How'd it go in there?"

"Good, Butch. I goes for me road test in three weeks."

"I wouldn't learn in that short a time."

"We know Butch, we all knows yer not the brightest bulb in the house."

Brock started up the car.

"Go fuck yerself, Rory. Smart as ya are."

"Brock, interested in teachin' me how to drive?"

"Sure, why not?"

They drove in silence for a while.

"Butch," blurted Rory. "I for gotta tell ya: the pretty little buxom blonde cop that was recently stationed here on the Shore was in the office when I was in talkin' to the cop at the counter about gettin' me license."

"Man, she's gorgeous. I wonder if she's single or married." Butch stretched out in the seat and yawned.

"Butch, don't get too excited. Most women in the RCMP are lesbians."

"How would ya know that, Rory?"

"Actually, I don't. I knows the two women Mounties that were stationed in Trepassey were lesbians. And me buddy in Bay Roberts tells me almost every time they gets a new female cop they're lesbian."

"Rory, I don't give a fuck if she's lesbian or not. She's one hot lookin' piece of ass. Shag it, I could be a lesbian for a night."

"Butch, ya foolish bastard!"

One thing about Butch, he was good for at least two laughs a day, even if they were on him.

"Rory," Butch said, after a silence, "What are ya goin' at tanight?"

"I'm readin' the history of Cuba. After the revolution in '59."

"What about you?"

"Well, I got to make some splits and bring in the firewood when I gets home. Have to feed the horse and cows. And let's not forget the hens and the noisy fuckin' rooster."

"What's wrong with yer ol' man he can't do it?"

"He's in bed with the flu. He has it bad, he's almost after coughin' up a lung."

CHAPTER FOUR

"Hey, Brock," said Rory as he got in his friend's car.

"Rory. Ya wanna' drive from here or start somewhere on the highway?"

"I'll start drivin' by Chance Cove Park, Brock. I gotta few bags of weed with me. Hope ya don't mind."

"I don't have a problem with it," said Brock, starting the engine, a swirl of dust rose as he turned onto the road. "If we gets caught with it, it's yers and all yers. I don't even know ya have it with ya."

"Okay, no problem."

They switched seats at Chance Cove Provincial Park.

"Now, Rory, adjust yer seat. Check yer rear-view mirror and the ones on the sides of the doors, seatbelt."

"Brock, I never wore a seat belt in me life."

"Well, yer drivin' my car . . . so put it on! Okay, haul her down in drive. Take yer time, ease her out. Okay, easy, easy yer doin' good. The speed limit is fifty miles an hour; a scattered place, it's a little higher. So, try and stay close to the speed limit."

"Brock, me hands are sweatin'. My neck is killin' me."

"That's 'cause yer nervous—ya have to relax."

"Turn down the radio. I can't think."

"Ya'll have to get used to the radio bein' on when yer drivin'."

"Brock, I wants to go see Perry Flannigan."

"Why?"

"I fronts 'im a few bags of weed every week or so. He owes me a few bucks. I'd like to get it off 'im, give 'im what I got with me."

The boys reached Trepassey in thirty-five minutes. Flannigan's house was on the Lower Coast, at the mouth of the harbour on the north side. His mother told Rory Perry was still asleep and to come back in twenty minutes.

Twenty minutes later, Rory was back at Perry's door.

"Perry, why the hell are ya at in bed this time of day?"

"Had a late night over at Outer Limits, Fred Lee was playin'."

"Ya got my money."

"Yes, but it's buried in Portugal Cove South."

"Why the fuck did ya bury it? And in the Cove?"

"Well, Rory, I wasn't walkin' around the harbour with three hundred dollars on me. I couldn't bring it in the house and have the old lady findin' it."

"I have to agree with ya."

"That means I got to bring ya to get it and bring ya back?"

"Yup. If ya wants yer money."

"Did ya bring me a few more bags?"

"Yes, but yer not gettin' it 'til I gets me money. Where d'ya have it buried?"

"On the beach behind Victor Ward's garage."

When they came to a curve in the road, Perry said, "slow down, haul in here." The car slowed to a stop beside the beach, Perry got out. "Go for a run while I digs it up. A car parked here will bring the attention of the locals."

The boys set off on a five-minute tour of Portugal Cove South.

"Brock, did ya know Alexander Graham Bell was shipwrecked in Portugal Cove South around a hundred years ago?"

"Who the hell was he?"

"The fella who invented the telephone. I remembers me grandfather tellin' me when I was young."

Five minutes later, Perry was back in the car.

"Perry," Rory said, "Why'd ya bury it here?"

"Well, the main reason is, it's easy to bury in the sand. Ya don't need a shovel."

"Yes, but yer right out in the open for people to see ya."

"Now, Rory, d'ya think I'm stund. I only comes here when it's dark. This is the first time I ever came here in daylight. Here's yer money. Three hundred. Thirty ten-dollar bills. It's all there, no need to count it!"

"I always counts money when someone passes money to me. Here's three more bags. This is better than the last stuff I gave ya. I wants a hundred and twenty-five bucks a bag. I finds a single draw gives ya a buzz for much longer than the last batch."

"Hope there is a little more than an ounce for that price."

"Perry, an ounce is an ounce. Ain't it pay week and all at the plant."

"Yes."

"Drop me back at the house." As Perry was getting out, he said, "See ya next weekend or whenever. Try not to be so damn early from now on."

"Brock," said Rory, when Perry had gone into his house, "thanks for bringin' me to Trepassey."

"No problem."

"Did ya know Amelia Earhart visited Trepassey?"

"Who the fuck is she? One of the strippers at the Beaver from Montreal?"

"No, Brock, she was the first woman to fly across the Atlantic. She was a passenger on a plane that flew from Trepassey to Wales. Back in the late twenties. A few years later, she flew a plane by herself from Harbour Grace to Ireland, the first woman to do it. She did it five years to the day after Charles Lindberg made the first solo flight across the Atlantic.

Brock, where did that come from?" Rory suddenly wanted to punch Brock in the face. If he did, there would be no more rides into town or driving lessons. He lit up a smoke, hoping Brock wouldn't notice his hands were shaking.

Brock grinned. "Just sayin'."

"She was probably a dyke."

Rory slept for two hours when he got home.

CHAPTER FIVE

When he got up, he strolled outside for some fresh air. Butch was walking up the road across from Rory's house. Rory joined him.

"Rory, how was yer first drivin' lesson?"

"Best kind. Took me time. Dropped in and got me money from Perry."

"Did he have all yer money?"

"Yes, every cent."

"Man, he sure is a good fella to have sellin' weed. He sells everythin' ya gives 'im and always has yer money."

"Yer right, but remember, Butch, Trepassey is boomin'. The Fishery Products Limited Plant is goin' two shifts twelve months a year, with five or six draggers goin' in and out the harbour non-stop. There's lots of money goin' around Trepassey. They got three nightclubs rockin'. Ya wait and see, give Perry a few more months, he'll be sellin' a pound of weed a week or more."

"Which means we'll be able to afford a decent set of wheels."

"Butch, don't go romancin' about the car I'll be buyin'."

"Rory, where we goin' tanight?"

"Petrel, Medicine Jar is playin' there."

"Where they from?"

"Butch ya knows 'em. They're local. We heard them at the Soundbone last spring. Ronnie Harte from Witless Bay, Leonard Doyle and Aly Hearn from Petty Harbour, Teddy Lee from the Goulds is on the drums. Fred Power is the lead singer. They're good! Fred Power is a great singer, he does a wicked job on Bob Seger's 'Down on Main Street.' He also does an awesome job on Rod Stewart's 'Hot Legs.'"

"How we gettin' down there?"

"I guess we'll hitchhike or find someone goin' down the Shore."

"Okay, meet ya at the pool hall around eight."

The boys hitchhiked down the shore. The Petrel was crowded, the dance floor was rocking. The band was loud and good.

"Rory, get me a Screech and coke. To hell with it, make it a double."

"Now, Butch, don't go wanderin' off and not buy yer round when it's yer turn."

"I will don't worry."

"Butch, ya never buys a round when it's yer turn. Yer always on the other side of the club playin' pool. Or outside tryin' to bang someone's daughter in the back seat of a car."

"Not my fault, the women likes me. Got anythin' on ya?"

"Yes."

"Gimme a draw."

"What happened to the bag I gave ya the other day?"

"Half smoked left the other half home. Hopin' to get the rest of the week out of it."

When the band announced the last song for the night. Rory said to Butch.

"Butch, c'mon. I got us a run home."

"Who's it with?"

"Perry Flannigan's buddy. He's leavin' right now, headin' for Trepassey."

"I'm not leavin' yet. And I don't like how the crowd from Trepassey drives. You'd swear most of 'em raced in NASCAR."

"Ok, ya'll be stuck in Witless Bay all night."

"Fuck it, worse places to be stuck."

"Listen, Butch, if ya can't get a run, find Joe Walker, tell 'im yer my buddy. He'll take care of ya. Don't dare tell 'im yer a Habs fan. He won't have anythin' to do with ya if he knows yer a Habs fan. He lives on Fisherman's Road; the locals call it Birchy Hill. Yellow two-story house with two green sheds."

"Ya wanna' get outta here?" Butch asked the girl he'd been charming all night.

"Okay. Where we goin'?"

"I dunno. Why not go for a walk? We could go to the swimmin' pool by the ballpark."

Later, he walked her home. She lived at the bottom of Birchy Hill. He walked up Birchy Hill; he eyed the yellow house with the green sheds. There was a light on in the shed. He walked up the long gravel driveway, knocked on the door. Said hello in a low, quiet tone. A huge man with a full beard, bigger than himself, opened the door.

"Hello, what the fuck d'ya want this hour of the night?"

"I'm Butch Hynes, Rory O'Ryan's buddy."

"So what?" said Walker.

"I missed me run up the Shore. Rory told me if I couldn't get a run home to come here and tell ya who I am. He said you'd take care of me."

"He did, did he? Do I look like a bloody babysitter? Do ya see a motel sign in my yard?"

"No problem, mister."

Walker laughed heartedly. "I'm only fuckin' with ya. Come in, b'y, have a beer."

Butch walked cautiously through the door. "Sure . . . thanks."

"What d'ya want, Labatt's Blue or Molson Light?"

"I prefer Molson. If yer low on Molson, Labatt's will do. Neat shed ya have. TV, fridge, dartboard. Ya even gotta CB radio and a police scanner."

"Yes, b'y, I loves me shed. Me and the missus, Beatrice, don't get along too well.

So, I spends all me time out here away from her."

"That's too bad, sir."

"Don't call me, sir. Joe's the name."

"Sorry, Joe, I don't wanna' be nosy. If you and the missus don't get along, why are ye still together?"

"Yer askin' some pretty personal questions. Good thing we

just met."

"Sorry."

"I don't mind. Well, here it is, I'll tell ya. We have two young girls, Louise and Hannah. Hannah is the younger one. She talks an awful lot and is nosy as bejesus, she might ask ya when ya shit last. Louise is reserved and shy. Hannah is like me, and Louise is a carbon copy of her mother. So, we agreed to stay together as a family 'til they're old enough to understand. Another eight or ten years or so, and hopefully, I'll never see her again."

"Joe, that's too bad. Where's yer woman from?"

"She's a Tobin from St. Michael's."

"Isn't Tobin a Witless Bay name?"

"Yes, it is. That's life, it could be worse. I could be stricken with cancer or some other life-threatening disease. I'm healthy, and my girls are healthy, that's what matters."

"So d'ya sleep out here?"

"Usually only on the weekend if I have a few too many. The missus has a problem with drunken men. Her father was a boozer. She despises alcohol and anyone who drinks it."

"Great, ya can have a few beers, and ya gotta comfortable, warm spot to crash. You plannin' on stayin' here in the shed tanight?"

"I was goin' to. I'll go on in the house out of it and let ya have the bunk."

"Gee, that's nice of ya."

"Well, I'm not doin' it for you, I'm doin' it for Rory. He's a good head. Does me a lot of favours. I guess he told ya I likes a draw and an occasional trip on acid when I can get it."

"Yes, he mentioned it to me one time. What's yer favourite acid?"

"Purple micro-dot. I find it the smoothest on the guts. I don't appreciate Rory talkin' about me and me habits."

"Don't worry, Rory and me are best friends. Whatever he tells me, I never repeats it. Rory's news is my news, and my news is Rory's news. I sells a bit of weed and hash meself."

"Well, Butch, or whatever they call ya. Where the fuck did ya get a name like Butch?"

"Bit of a story, Joe."

"Well, I got lots of time. So, how'd ya get it?"

"Me mother had a brother, who had a butcher shop in St. John's. I looks like 'im. So, everyone called me the butcher. It got shortened to Butch later on."

"Stupid nickname if ya ask me. I've heard worse nicknames on the Shore. Sure, most of the Bottle Nosers in Bay Bulls got a nickname, and half the Gamy Birds in Witless Bay also got nicknames."

Butch asked Joe. "Ya watch hockey?"

"Yes, Leafs fan, have been since I was a kid.

"Well, Joe, Rory warned me not to tell ya who my team is."

"Don't tell me yer a fuckin' Habs fan."

"Yes, and like you, have been since I was a kid."

"By the Jesus. Rory, what a cocksuckin' prick to send a fuckin' Habs fan here, worse fuckin' fans in the world. Especially this late at night. Yer, some lucky it's late. If it wasn't this late, ya wouldn't be sleepin' in my shed."

"Okay, relax, I understand what yer sayin'. I knows a lot of fellas on the Shore that are just as touchy about hockey as you are."

"Ya sayin' I'm touchy?"

"No, Joe, I'm not. I appreciate ya givin' me a place to stay this late at night."

"The Leafs mightn't have won the Stanley Cup in fourteen years; I got a feelin' they're buildin' a team that will win it in the next couple of years. And Vaive is flyin' this season. A possible Hart Trophy candidate.

I'm goin' in to go to bed. I'll fill the wood stove. It should last all night—no smokin' in bed. If ya wants to have a smoke, get out of bed and have it. I wants no mattress catchin' fire. With the shed so close to the house."

"The missus cooks Sunday dinner. Jiggs' dinner with all the

fixin's. Even cooks turnip greens. She even makes a molasses duff. So ya goin' to hang around for a feed?"

"Well, if yer offerin'. Not goin' to turn down a feed like that."

Joe filled the stove before going into the house. Butch was asleep before the door shut.

"Butch, wake up!"

"Mornin', Joe. What time is it?"

"Ten-thirty."

"Holy shit, Joe, best nap I've had in a long time. I dunno if it was this soft mattress or the lovely heat from the woodstove."

"I was out here fillin' up the stove around seven, ya never stirred."

"I never heard ya, Joe."

"I didn't think ya did. I always sleep well when I stays out here. I thinks it's 'cause of the woodstove. The missus won't let me put a woodstove in the house. She's as nervous as a cat. Had a bad experience with fire when she was young."

"Joe, what time does yer woman serve dinner?"

"Around twelve. She's gone to Mass with the kids. I'm keepin' an eye on it. When she gets home from church, she makes the gravy. Her gravy is the best in the harbour. Hers is better than her mothers, her mother is the best cook in the harbour. She knows how to brown the onions just right."

"Joe, ya don't have to feed me. A place to get in out of the weather was all I needed."

"Don't worry about it—more than enough to go around. I gotta warn ya: for God's sake, don't say anythin' about weed or any type of drugs at dinner. The missus hears anythin' about drugs, she'll have the cops on me like flies on shit. Don't dare say anythin' about any drugs, ya hear me?"

"I won't, I promise. Does she know I'm here?"

"Yes, told her this mornin' when she got up."

"Do she mind ya havin' people stayin' in yer shed?"

"Now, Butch, I don't make it a habit of lettin' people stay in me shed, especially people I dunno. I only let ya stay 'cause yer Rory's buddy. I tell ya now, don't go makin' it a habit of comin' down the Shore smellin' around for young pussy and thinkin' yer stayin' here any night ya can't get a run home. I'm not runnin' a bloody youth hostel."

"I know, Joe. I do appreciate ya lettin' me stay here last night."

"Wanna beer for a straightener?"

"Sure, if ya got one to spare. Joe, what d'ya do for a livin'?"

"I fish for cod with an old guy down on the New Line; his name is John Mullowney. He's retirin' next year, so I'm takin' over his enterprise."

"Ye trap fish?"

"No, gill nets, Salmon nets, and we sets a few Lobster pots."

"That's a big undertakin'."

"Yes, I knows. It's that, or I'll have to go to work in the fish plant. I've been on the water since I was fourteen. I knows nothin' else but fishin', I knows it inside and out."

"Who's goin' to fish with ya when ya takes over the enterprise?"

"Me nephew, Greg Abbott. He has never been on the water; he wants to give it a try."

"How old is he?"

"He'll be seventeen by the time I takes it over."

"Where do ye sell yer fish?"

"At the Cape Pine Fisheries Plant here in Witless Bay."

"Good luck with it when ya gets at it."

"C'mon, Butch, let's go eat."

As soon as they sat, Beatrice asked Joe to say grace. Joe looked at Butch and said, "Sunday dinner is the only meal we say grace." All five bowed their heads in unison.

"Joe, where's Mullowney's stage?"

"On the other side of the harbour. On Gallows Cove Road, about a half-mile from Ragged Beach. Below where the nuns have their summer cottage."

"Takin' over this enterprise will not be a cheap venture?"

"Yer right! I'm givin' John a down payment, payin' it off with ten percent of my by-weekly catch. I could pay it off in as little as two or three years. If fish is scarce, it will take me as long as five years to pay it off."

When Butch was finished eating, he thanked Beatrice for the lovely meal and told the girls it was nice meeting them. Joe and Butch went to the shed for one last beer and draw.

"Joe, I'm headin' to the highway to hitch a run up the Shore."

"Okay, Butch. Nice meetin' ya."

"Same here, Joe. Thanks for yer hospitality."

"Tell Rory to drop in next time he's down the Shore."

"I will. See ya later."

CHAPTER SIX

Rory was sitting at his kitchen table, staring out at the ocean listening to classical music on CBC radio. Enjoying a cigarette when Butch strolled in. "Rory, ya'll never believe where I stayed last night." Butch sat on the opposite side of the table.

"In Witless Bay? Did ya go to Joe's?"

"Yup, I did."

"Was he pissed off?"

"No. Other than when I told 'im I was a Habs fan."

"I warned ya not to tell 'im that."

"Well, I didn't blurt it out. It came out in conversation." Butch reached for a cigarette in Rory's open pack on the table. Rory pushed it closer and passed him a match.

"How pissed did he get?"

"A little, I guess," said Butch, striking up. "Ya were right, he is fanatical about the Leafs. Even thinks they're goin' to win the cup sometime in the next few years. Listen to this one: he said Rick Vaive might get MVP this season. Some chance of 'im gettin' it over Gretzky." Butch threw the spent match down on the table. Rory picked it up and dropped it in the ashtray.

"Anyway, he let me stay in his shed for the night."

"Fine, fella, ain't he?"

"Yes, a dandy fella with an awesome shed. He got everythin' in it, TV, CB, and a police scanner. I had the best sleep in months there. He even gave me a few beer. His woman, Beatrice, fed me Sunday dinner, an awesome feed of Jiggs, 'fore I left to hitch home. Even had turnip greens and a molasses duff."

"Who picked ya up?"

"Three fellas from town goin' birdwatchin' at Cape Race Lighthouse, lookin' for a rare bird. The driver was a fella named Bryce McSomethin'. The fella in the passenger seat in front was named Len. When he got out to let me in the back of the Chevy Blazer, he must have been nearly seven feet tall, as tall as Kareem Abdul-Jabbar, man, he was tall. There was a fella Jack in the back. He never spoke at all; all he did was sleep and snore the whole way up the Shore. All they talked about was birds, birds I never heard of 'fore, ya'd swear they were talkin' about women. A fine bunch of fellas, though." Butch took a long draw and blew the smoke out slowly.

"What kind of rare bird?"

"I got no idea. They told me what it was, I don't remember. Somethin' from Florida or Texas, I dunno. Joe told me to tell ya to drop-in next time yer down the Shore for a beer."

"Did he say he wanted anythin'?"

"No, said for ya to drop in. Rory, did ya do any drivin' this mornin'?"

"Yup, ya won't believe this—the ol' man let me have his truck. Even let me go to Renews by meself. I couldn't believe it."

"I can't believe it either. He babies that truck like he babies his Newfoundland pony. She's standard?"

"Yes."

"I didn't know ya knew how to drive a standard."

"I couldn't when I left the yard. By the time I got back, I had the gear stick on the wheel pretty well mastered. Nothin' to it, when ya gets movin'. The hardest part is startin' off."

"Were ya nervous by yerself?"

"Nah. I'm sure I broke the speed limit."

"Yer ol' man don't go faster than forty in that truck. Probably was the fastest time it has ever gone since yer father bought it. Rory, why don't we go into the cabin for a few nights? Drink some rum, set a few snares."

"When d'ya wanna' go?"

"I figured we go tanight or tamorrow."

"I can't go tanight. I'll go tamorrow afternoon. I guess we'll walk in."

"Rory, I hates walkin'. Especially when it's six or seven miles."

"Well, Butch, I loves it. It's good exercise. I could walk to town if I had to. I gotta run now. We'll leave tamorrow around one o'clock."

"Okay. Where ya off to?"

"Have to go see a fella about a big sale of weed."

"Who?"

"Tell ya, tamorrow."

Rory jumped in with Brock, Butch walked down the road to home. The next day, Butch showed up at Rory's house at one o'clock. He walked in and yelled from the front hallway, "Rory, ya up?"

"Yes, b'y, up an hour or so." Rory appeared on the stairs, pulling his sweater straight.

"Ya ready to head to the cabin?"

"Hang on, I gotta do the dishes. The ol' man will go berserk if he comes home with the sink full of dishes. I'll only be ten minutes or so."

Butch pitched in and dried.

"Okay," said Rory, "Let's go."

They grabbed their knapsacks and headed out the door. They walked for a mile on the old train track that ran into the country behind Cappahayden. The sky was overcast, great weather for walking any distance. They took the path known locally as Slavery Path, which men of the community used to haul firewood and logs.

A little over two hours after they had left Rory's house, they arrived at the one-room cabin, more of a shack than a cabin; locals called it both. A man from Cappahayden had built it, using it for trapping beaver, mink, and muskrat, in the sixties and seventies. He had passed away, so no one owned the shack. The few who used it kept it in decent condition, although it hadn't been painted in a decade or more. Fifteen feet by twenty, with one small window, four bunks, an old cast-iron wood stove, a table and two chairs.

"Butch, I brought all the fixins for a Jiggs dinner. I'm thinkin' we'll have it tamorrow evenin' for supper. I'll put the salt beef in soak now."

"Sweet Jesus, no, Rory, ya'll wash it out, there'll be no taste of salt left in it. Put it in soak tamorrow mornin'!"

"Yer right, I'll put it in water in the mornin'. We'll have steak with it since there's no oven to do a roast or a chicken."

"Rory, this is the last fuckin' time I'm walkin' in here."

"Butch, get over it. A bit of exercise."

"Well, I'm not into exercisin'."

"I can tell, with the gut gettin' on ya."

"Go fuck yerself, yer not too small either."

"Thirty-inch waist. And yers is?"

"None of yer business. Give me a beer. I'm sweatin' like a fuckin' racehorse."

"The beer is warm."

"Do I look like I gives a fuck if it's warm? I wants somethin' wet."

"Here, drink away, my friend."

"Rory, ya goin' to set a few snares?"

"I might. I'm goin' to try and get the power saw goin' that's under the bunk. It looks like it wasn't goin' in a while. Goin' to drop some green wood to mix with the dry wood."

"Rory, there's enough wood here for a month."

"I know Butch, ya knows the rules: we have to replenish what we burn. If I cuts some now, I'll have less to cut 'fore we leave. Butch, I got somethin' I wants to discuss with ya later."

"What is it?"

"Tell ya later. So, try to stay a little straight."

"What do ya mean, stay straight?"

"Don't touch the Screech 'til after our chat."

"Can I have one drink?"

"Okay, one and no more."

"Rory, yer like me ol' man. Always givin' orders."

"Well, Butch, someone has to try and keep ya on the straight and narrow. I'm goin' out back to drop some juniper and black spruce. Might not limb 'em up, I'll get a head start by droppin' half a cord."

Forty-five minutes later, Rory walked into the cabin soaked in sweat. "Butch, give me a beer 'fore I passes out."

"I put it in the river to cool it. I'll go get ya one."

Butch was back in minutes with the half-cold beer. "Okay, Rory, spill yer guts. What d'ya wanna' talk to me about?"

"Well, Butch, I got an idea. Well, it's not an idea."

"What is it? It always takes ya fifteen or twenty minutes to tell somethin', I can say in two or three minutes."

"I'm thinkin' about goin' big, sellin' weed and other drugs."

"Aren't ya big already?"

"No, not really."

"Rory, yer sellin' four or five ounces of weed a week. Plus, an ounce or two of hash."

"Yes, Butch, but four or five bags a week is not big. I'm makin' less on hash."

"So, what's yer plan?"

"I'll need three or four fellas to cover the whole Shore, from the Goulds to Trepassey. One in Bay Bulls or Witless Bay, someone in the Cape Broyle area. Me and you can cover Ferryland to Cappahayden. Perry can cover off the whole area from Portugal Cove South to St. Shott's.

There's four nightclubs in Bay Bulls and Witless Bay, plus two pool halls in Witless Bay. Three fish plants between Bay Bulls and Tors Cove, that area is boomin'. Cape Broyle and Calvert are also boomin': three nightclubs and a hotel with a bar. There's a fish plant in Cape Broyle and one in Calvert. I don't have to tell ya about Trepassey. Ya knows how well Perry is doin' with his sales every week. The big challenge will be the Goulds. I gotta find someone I can trust, who will be careful all at the same time. I wants no heat from the cops. Butch, 'fore ya knows it, I'll own the Shore when it comes to drugs."

"How big are ya goin'?"

"Well, Butch, what I'm hearin' from a few of the b'ys on the Shore, if someone went at this full-time sellin' drugs, ya could easily sell anywhere from two to three pounds a week. And hash is startin' to take off. All I gotta do is give better counts than everyone else. In no time, I'll have a stranglehold on the market. When I do, I'll cut back on the counts. The reason I'm tellin' ya this is I wants ya to help me with it."

"So ya wants me to be yer partner?"

"No, Butch, not partners. I'll be runnin' the show. You can pick up the stuff any time I'm busy, either in the Goulds or town. Ya could weigh it out, bag it up into ounces. Deliver it and collect money for me."

"What will the pay be like?"

"Say if you and Brock runs to town to pick up a few pounds for me, I'll give ya half an ounce for every pound ya pick up. Then ya'll always have yer own supply to smoke."

"Can I sell it?"

"No, Butch, I'm the dealer. Okay, a small bit for pocket money."

"Rory, if ya pays me likes ya says, I'll never be able to smoke all the weed I'll be gettin' for my services."

"Butch, if I'm givin' more than ya can smoke, I guess I'll have to pay ya a bit of cash. But remember this: I'll have my own set of wheels in a few weeks, I'm hopin'. An expense that will have to come out of the dope money. Ya interested in helpin' me?"

"Let me think about it."

"Butch, what's there to think about?"

Butch looked doubtful, but he usually did as Rory requested. Rory sighed. "I'm goin' out to file the chain on the saw, Butch—be back in a few minutes."

Butch lay down on the bunk, he lit up a smoke. Free weed to smoke daily was a no-win offer.

Rory was patient filing the saw. Filing power saw chains was not an easy thing to do, not everyone can do it. The weather had changed, it was cooling off.

Butch was half asleep when he heard the door open and the tap of Rory's boots on the floor. He rolled over in the bunk and sat up. "Now, Rory, let's get back to yer idea of goin' big with the dope. If ya go to town late at night or in the early mornin' hours, how are ya goin' to supply yer man in each town?"

"Don't worry, Butch, I got that figured out. I figured I'd drop their weekly supply of dope off in a secluded spot. Say I'll bury it. And have 'em bury the money from the previous week's sales. I leave the dope; they leave the money. Like, say in the Goulds, we bury it at the bottom of Shoal Bay Road or down by the racetrack."

"Yes, but what if someone sees us buryin' it?"

"They won't. All this will be done in the dark. Say I stop for a piss at the bottom of Shoal Bay Road, stroll in the woods a couple of hundred feet. Drop the dope and grab the cash. Use the same area for three or four weeks. Then switch to the next area. Buryin' is liftin' a bit of sod or bog and pokin' it under there. Or even under a fairly flat rock."

"Sounds interestin' sounds very interestin'. Are ya goin' into the Credit Union on Friday to check on the car loan?"

"Yes, when I'm headin' back from town."

"Think they'll give it to ya?"

"I dunno. Time will tell."

"I hates walkin'."

"Suck it up, buttercup. We'll be home in less than an hour. We're much lighter than when we went in. All the booze and grub we lugged in was a fine weight."

"D'ya have Brock lined up to bring ya to town in the mornin'?"

"I mentioned it to 'im last Sunday. I can't see it bein' a problem, never is."

"Tell ya what, call the Credit Union and double-check if they have any news on the loan."

"I'll do that if I gets around to it."

CHAPTER SEVEN

"Good day, Fishermen's Credit Union. Maggie Harrigan speaking, how may I assist you today."

"May I speak with Lisa, please."

"One moment, please."

"Hello, Lisa speaking."

"Hello Miss Lisa, Rory O'Ryan callin'."

"Good day, Rory, please call me Lisa. Calling me miss makes me feel old."

"Rory, I have been going over the numbers on your car loan application. Unfortunately, your income does not meet the criteria for us to grant you a loan. It's difficult for lending institutions like ours to make loans to seasonal workers, which is unfortunate. If you can get someone to co-sign for you, it shouldn't be a problem."

"Well, Lisa, that's goin' to be a big problem. Everyone I knows either works in the fish plant or fishes for a livin'. Both are seasonal, as you know."

"Rory, I tell you what, I'll leave the application open for a few weeks. Which will give you some time to hopefully find a co-signer."

Just as Rory got off the phone, Brock hauled in at his house with Butch aboard. Rory walked out and got in.

"Butch, bad news on the car loan."

"What?"

"They wants a co-signer. Says my income does not fit the criteria for a loan. Bein' a seasonal worker also goes against me."

"Ya mean, we needs someone to sign the loan for us."

"No, for me."

"Whatever, Rory. Who can we ask?"

"I got no idea. Everyone I knows works seasonally. Who do we know with good credit or any credit at all for that matter? I'm not askin' me ol' man."

"I can't ask my ol' man to sign for it, Rory. He never had a loan for anythin' in his life. He says if ya can't pay for it with cash, ya don't need it. So, I guess our dream of havin' a set of wheels for cruisin' up and down the Shore and runnin' our little enterprise is not goin' to happen."

"Butch, I have an idea. I'll ask Lisa to let us both sign for the loan."

"Ya mean both of us will own it?"

"Yes and no."

"What do ya mean, yes and no?"

"Both of our names might end up on the loan. But I'll be takin' care of the car. She'll be with me most, if not all the time. Butch, it's we either try that, or we will never get a car. We won't save for one."

"Alright, b'y, I got no problem with it. Think she'll go for it?"

"I dunno. Two people workin' seasonally might have a better chance of gettin' a loan together. I'll call back and make an appointment for 10:30 next Friday."

"Ten thirty in the mornin'?"

"No, Butch, at night. How many businesses d'ya know are open at ten-thirty at night?"

"Okay, don't blow yer fuckin' top."

"Well, wake the fuck up. I got to explain almost everythin' I tells ya."

"Rory, I wish I had been born like you."

"What d'ya mean?"

"Yer fuckin' perfect. It must be a nice feelin'."

"Butch, shut up. I'm goin' home. You won't see me for a while; I'll be into the bag of books Father O'Deady gave me."

"Brock, bring me back to the house, please."

Brock pulled over in front of Butch's house, Butch got out. He watched the car go up the road, taking Rory home to his books.

He wasn't interested in selling dope. He had his own plans, but they weren't as solid yet as Rory's. Now that he was going into town a few times a month with Rory, his mind worked harder than ever. He had seen a few things that might be just what he needed if he could figure out the risks. Would it even be worth the hassle, though? Butch imagined him and Rory up in Toronto. Might never see his old man again, but so what.

Rory was a voracious reader at twelve. The first book he read was Hunter S. Thompson, Fear and Loathing in Las Vegas. He enjoyed reading; it took him to different parts of the world and introduced him to interesting, worldly characters—another way to further educate himself beyond schooling.

Eight days later, he walked into the pool hall in Renews. McCarthy's pool hall was beige outside, dark blue inside, with two bar box pool tables, four pinball machines, and a Pacman machine. Butch was there, naturally. No wonder Butch was good at pool. All he ever did was hang out at the pool hall, hustling teenagers for one and two-dollar bills.

"Rory, I didn't expect to see you taday. Weren't you readin'?"

"I was. Read five books in eight days."

"Anythin' interestin'?"

"Yes, but not to you."

"Why not?"

"Butch, yer not a reader, so tellin' ya what I read would be like water runnin' over a ducks back."

"Well, if ya told me the names of some of 'em, they might interest me."

"Butch, when the priest gave me the books, he said he didn't want them back. So, when I'm finished with 'em, ya can have the whole bag for a while. Not that ya'd read any."

Butch laid his cue against the wall. He turned to Rory, his face screwed up. "Well, I'll surprise the fuck out of ya. I'll read 'em, to prove a point, I can read and understand what I'm readin'."

"Yes, when pigs fly."

"Rory, ya know what?"

"What?"

"I never saw ya for seven or eight days. And ya know what? I never missed ya. Interested in a game of pool?"

"You said you never missed me?"

"I didn't."

"I am interested in a game of pool, but not with you."

"Why?"

"Ya beats me nine of every ten games we play."

Butch grinned. "I guess I'm better at somethin' than you are."

"Yes, Butch, I hates to admit it. If I played the amount of pool you play, I'd be good at it also."

"We play two bucks a game."

"No."

"C'mon, Rory, don't be so fuckin' tight."

"I'm not, I'm not goin' to throw away money so ya can prove a point."

"Rory, I tell ya what. We play a race to seven. I'll spot ya three games to start."

"Does that mean I'll be startin' with three wins even 'fore the balls are broke in the first game?"

"Yes."

"Okay, I'll play. Call shot, straight-eight. What're we playin' for?"

"How's ten bucks sound?"

"Fine with me."

"Wipe the fuckin' grin off yer face."

Butch beat Rory easily. As was normal.

"Rory, ya don't know how much fun it is to whip yer ass."

"Enjoy it. That will be the last time ya sucker me into losin' a ten spot."

"Wanna draw 'fore I goes home?"

"Sure."

"Got any papers?"

"Yup."

Butch rolled a small reefer, they went outside, behind the pool hall, to smoke up.

"Jesus, Rory, this weed is burnin' the throat out of me." Butch coughed and spit into a clump of sting nettles.

"Here, Butch, finish it, that's enough for me. I'm gone, see ya Friday mornin' around eight-thirty, nine. Brock is bringin' us down the Shore for our appointment at the Credit Union. I called and made it a few days ago. And Butch, for fuck sake, clean yerself up. Shave put on a clean shirt and a clean pair of jeans. And comb that mop of hair."

"Yes, 'cause yer always so clean."

"I'm a lot tidier than you."

"Fuck you, Rory, ya righteous bastard."

"All right, later."

CHAPTER EIGHT

Brock's car pulled up in front of Rory's house. Rory was sitting on the steps, having a smoke. The grass was still wet with morning dew. He threw the cigarette on the ground, got up and ground it out with the heel of his work boot. After shutting the car door, Rory sighed, he pushed his hair off his forehead with both hands.

"Glad ya picked me up 'fore Butch. I prefer the front seat. When Butch is in the front, all he does is tell ya what he's seein'. As if the people in the back seat are blind. He's like a recordin'. 'Look at that new house bein' built. Look at the ponies. Look at the arse on that piece of tail.' Look at that, look at this'. He drives me nuts."

Butch slid into the back seat. "Mornin', b'ys. Did ye' notice the old truck that went past? Looks like a 69 Fargo. First time I ever saw it. She came down the Shore. One of the McNeill's from Trepassey most likely owns it, I'm thinkin'."

Before they went into the Credit Union, Rory gave Butch a warning not to talk too much.

"Butch, listen to me and listen good. When we gets in the office with Lisa, don't open yer mouth unless she asks ya a question."

"What d'ya want me to do, sit and act like a dummy? Sure, I got an account there."

"So what? I knows you, ya gets on a rant about somethin' the poor girl will have not a clue what yer talkin' about. She's a townie, and 'em townies miss half of what we say 'cause of our accents and the fact we talks so fast. So please, let me do the talkin'."

"No sweat, big shot."

"Butch, I'm not a big shot. I'm tryin' to do this as smoothly as possible. The less talkin' by both of us, the better."

"Alright, b'y."

A half-hour later, they were back in the car.

"That went well, Rory."

"Yes, Butch, but why the fuck did ya tell her ya fell out with yer old boss at the plant in Aquaforte?"

"I dunno. I have this habit of tellin' the truth all the time. Some stuff comes out of my mouth even 'fore, I thinks."

"Well, Butch, at times like this, the truth is not a good thing. Anyway, somethin' positive, she's goin' to consider the loan, that's the main thing."

They stopped at Betty's Drive-in, at the top of Petty Harbour Road in Goulds for a feed, before going to the Hayloft.

Brock parked in front of The Hayloft, all three got out of the car.

"Okay, b'ys, go in and have a few games of pool and leave me alone with me, man."

"Sounds good, Rory. C'mon, Brock, I'll give ya a free lesson in pool."

A half-hour later, they were back in the car.

"Get in the back, Butch."

"No, Rory, I likes the front."

"In the back and shut up."

"Fuck you, Rory."

"Brock, take yer time goin' up the Shore. I got two pounds of weed and a half-pound of hash in the trunk."

"Rory, where we are goin' to stash all this dope?"

"In the loft of me ol' man's barn."

"Good idea. No one will go in his barn, 'cause all hands in Cappahayden are afraid of yer ol' man."

"Butch, why d'ya think I came up with the idea? It will do for now. But I gotta find a good spot or two in the next week or so. Can't leave it in the barn for too long. The ol' man finds it, he'll shoot me. I'm serious."

"Brock, can we make a run to Trepassey after supper? I needs a bit of practice drivin'. I only gotta week 'fore I goes for me road test for me license. And I wants to give Perry half of what I got taday."

"Can I go with ye?"

"Sure, Butch, but ya gotta keep quiet when I'm drivin'. People gabbin' will make me nervous, especially in the dark."

"Not a problem. I'll have a nap goin' up."

After supper, they headed south for Trepassey. They kept a slow pace on the barrens. Perry was handsome, one of the people who only shave once a week. Being a blonde helped.

"Hey, Perry."

"Hey, Rory, what are ya at up here on a Friday night?"

"Jump in. We'll go for a run around the harbour and have a chat."

"Sure."

"Perry, I gotta pound of weed and a quarter pound of hash. Ya interested in sellin' it?"

"Yes, sure—why not?"

"How long d'ya think it will take ya to sell it?"

"I'd say ten days, two weeks at the longest. Sales are takin' off in the past few weeks. My name is gettin' around that I always got gear."

"Good sounds great. Make yer counts a little bigger. I'm tryin' to take over the Shore with sales. Bigger counts, and we'll force the other pushers out eventually. Ya got me money from the last batch I gave ya?"

"Yes, but it's buried in the Cove. Had I known ya were comin' up tanight, I woulda gotten it taday for ya."

"No sweat. I'll dig it up on the way back down the Shore."

"No can do."

"Why?"

"I didn't bury it in the same spot. I bury it in a different spot every time. I buried it out on Cape Race Road."

"For fuck sakes, that means we'll have to bring ya back here after ya gets me money."

"I'll get Larry to drive me down."

"Hardly, Perry. He'll know where ya bury yer dope and money."

"Not to worry. Larry is my best friend since kindergarten. He's my Butch, sorry, meant to say, bitch."

Rory laughed. Butch was nobody's bitch, but most days, he was bitchy. Butch was listening to the conversation and not smiling.

"Hope he's not as hard on the head as Butch is," Rory said with a laugh. "Ya sure, ya can trust 'im?"

"Without a doubt. Trust 'im as much as I'd trust me ol' lady."

"Okay, fine. We'll go out Cape Race Road a couple of miles and wait for ye. Hurry up. There's stuff to do and people to see on a Friday night."

"Ya mean chicks to do."

"Whatever. See ya in a half hour or so."

The long road was gravel, between the bumping and the noise of the tires crushing in the loose surface. Rory thought about the lighthouse at the end of it and the lighthouse keeper in 1912, who was the last person to have contact with the sinking Titanic. He must have told that story for the rest of his life. Rory hoped he'd pick up a few good stories to tell his kids and grand-kids; so far, he had nothing, unless you counted women and sell-ing dope, and none of it was fit for kids.

Finally, Brock stopped the car, and the boys bones settled back down into their skin.

Ten minutes after stopping, Butch tapped Rory's shoulder. "Look, b'ys, headlights comin'!"

Rory turned to Brock. "Roll down yer window. It must be the b'ys. Who else would be out here this hour of the night on a Friday?"

"Could be anyone," said Brock. "There's several cabins at Long Beach and a few at the Drook."

Residents of Long Beach and the Drook were relocated in 1966 in one of Smallwood's resettlement programs.

A few minutes later, Larry hauled up alongside Brock's Cordoba. The occupants got out.

"Hey, Rory—here's yer money. I told ya I wouldn't be long gettin' it." Perry handed Rory a wad of bills. Rory counted it and put it in the trunk of Brock's car.

Larry turned to Brock. "Hey, likes yer wheels; what year is she? She a Cordoba or a Chrysler 300?"

"Cordoba, '78, 360 four-barrel."

"Cool, I knows she can't pull ass."

"No sweat to bury the needle on the barrens. She drinks it when I drives her hard."

"Don't they all."

"Ya have a nice set of wheels. Firebird or a Camaro?"

"Firebird,77, with a 400, four-barrel, five-speed."

Larry asked Brock if he had seen the grey 78 Dodge Magnum Wayne Mulcahy has in Bay Bulls. Brock said. "He had said he turned it in on a Trans Am."

"What year is the Trans Am?" asked Larry.

"An 80 or an 81, I believe, black with the scalded chicken on the bonnet."

Larry laughed. "First time I heard that!"

Rory slapped Perry's shoulder. "Hey, Perry, I'm goin' for me license next Friday. In Ferryland."

"Which cop is takin' ya out?"

"Campbell."

"I hear he's a nice fella."

"One of the nicer cops, ever stationed in Ferryland."

"I hear he doesn't fail many."

"I heard the same thing."

"Hear the nickname they put on 'im?"

"No, Rory, what is it?"

"Soupy."

"Where the fuck did they come up with that nickname?'

"Campbell's Soup."

"I'm on the hunt for a set of wheels."

"What's ya got in mind for a set of wheels?" asked Larry.

"Well, I'm a Mopar man, Dodge or Plymouth. There's a fella Maddicks in Bay Bulls with a '68 RT Charger for sale. With a 383 in it."

"What's he lookin' for it?"

"I wasn't talkin' to 'im yet. Someone told me at the Beehive last weekend he wants twenty-four hundred dollars for it. It might have been Paul Barr, the fella who owns the Beehive, who mentioned it when we were havin' a yarn."

"Many miles on it?"

"Barr said he heard there were 110,000 miles on it."

"Not bad, not a lot of miles for a 383. They're good for a couple of hundred thousand miles."

"I also heard there's a red '72 Barracuda for sale in Bay Bulls, with a 340 slapstick in it."

"Who owns it?"

"I heard a fella' Ryan owns it. One of the Ryan's who owns the funeral home. Rumour has it, he drives it like he stole it. Most likely has the shit torn out of it."

"He related to you?"

"Perry, how is he related to me? He's a Ryan, I'm an O'Ryan."

"I always gets confused with Ryan's and O'Ryan's on the Shore."

"They're two different tribes." Rory nodded at Perry and Larry. "Okay, b'ys, we're outta here. I'll be back up in ten or twelve days, two weeks at the latest. And like I told ya 'fore, don't go frontin' too much. Cash on the barrelhead. It shouldn't be a problem in Trepassey. If yer livin' in Trepassey and not workin', yer a lazy good for nothin'."

"I agree," said Perry. "Not too many walkin' the roads scratchin' their arses. I'll keep an eye out for a set of wheels for ya."

"Thanks, Perry, see ya later."

"A dark night," said Rory. "Could be a bad night for moose on the road. Or a herd of caribou crisscrossin' the highway on the barrens."

"Brock replied, "no sweat, I usually takes me time at night."

"How big is the caribou herd on the barrens, Rory?"

"Around ten thousand animals, Butch, accordin' to Wildlife."

"Rory, that's a lot of hooves."

"Yes, Butch, it is, forty thousand if ya use yer head."

"Brock, stick on 'Night Moves' I loves that tape."

"B'ys, ya wanna' go down the Shore for a run?"

Brock replied, "sure, why not? Nothin' else to do."

CHAPTER NINE

The boys cruised down the Shore. It was overcast and cool.

"Let's hit the Beehive first," said Brock. Rory replies, "I'd prefer to go to the Petrel; the Beehive always has an older bunch hangin' out there. Half the women there are widowed or divorced."

"Okay, we'll go to the Petrel, I agree, a better place for the young ones."

An hour later, they were at the Petrel.

"I was talkin' to Bill Gensom in the washroom. Said he might be interested in sellin' a few ounces of weed a week for me."

"I didn't know ya knew 'im, Rory."

"I didn't, Butch, 'til he approached me. Said he has seen me around. Someone told 'im I was into sellin' a bit of gear."

"He's quite the pool player, almost as good as me."

"Now, Butch, don't go braggin'."

"I knows 'im a little meself, from playin' pool with 'im. He seems to be a spot-on fella. Never, ever cheats and is a real gentleman at the table."

"I'm goin' to front 'im two ounces next week. If he sells it and has all my money, I may have 'im as one of my main sellers, get 'im to cover Bay Bulls to Tors Cove."

"So, Rory, all ya needs now is someone to cover Cape Broyle to Ferryland. And the Goulds."

"I got someone in mind for Cape Broyle. Jerry Mugford. He's a big boy and doesn't mind fightin'. No one is goin' to shaft 'im with money, and I doubt if anyone is goin' to try and move into his territory. I'm goin' to get Brock to dart me down to Harold

Hayden's tamorrow afternoon to try and find 'im. I'll start small with 'im, like Gensom. If he's trustworthy, I'll slowly increase what I gives 'im. I'll have the whole Shore covered, with me and you coverin' Aquaforte to Cappahayden."

"What about the Goulds?"

"I'll be honest, Butch, I'm a little nervous about the Goulds. There are already several pushers in that area, some from the city. I don't wanna' go steppin' on toes. And ya knows how the clique from the Goulds likes to fight. Somethin' I'm not goin' at. Not gettin' the shit kicked out of me over a bag of weed. Maybe over a piece of tail, but not drugs. Hopefully, down the road, I'll find someone I can trust. But in the meantime, I'm happy with how things are pannin' out."

The Petrel was dead. The band sucked.

"An hours enough of this, Butch. Brock, time to head south."

"My quarters are next on the pool table, Rory. After a few games, I'll be ready to leave."

Twenty minutes later, Rory said to Brock, "We headin' back up the Shore?"

"I'm ready when you are."

"Where the fuck did Butch disappear to?"

"Who knows. Out in the back seat of someone's car, bangin' some man's daughter or some ol' man's granddaughter."

"Well, if I don't find 'im in two minutes, he's on his own. He can find his own fuckin' way up the Shore. I bet he's with the chick he met here a few weeks ago. The pretty one with the long coal-black hair and big tits who moved up from the Goulds. If he is, he better hope she's worth it."

Rory and Brock were about to pull away when someone banged on the trunk of the car. Butch opened the door, got in the back, shoving the seat ahead, nearly knocking Rory into the dashboard.

"Butch, where the hell were ya?"

"No odds to ya."

"Waitin' around for ya, ya lagger."

"No, 'cause I knows no one ever had to wait on you."

"They may have, but it wasn't 'cause of some piece of ass."

"Oh, excuse me, Mister Perfect."

"Was it that chick from the Goulds?"

"Yup. B'ys, I gotta tell ye this. She's the sweetest smellin', tastiest chick I was ever with."

"Butch, they all smell like that at that age. Ya'd drink soup out of 'em now, ya wouldn't piss in 'em when they're forty."

"Brock, here's some money for gas, for drivin' me to Trepassey earlier. How about some afternoon we'll go for a run down the Shore? I'll need the last bit of practice 'fore I go for me license on Friday mornin'."

"Listen, Butch, I'm finishin' up the books the priest gave me. If ya don't see me around for a few days, ya knows where I'm at. Don't come lookin' for me to play pool, I will not be interested."

"Not a problem, Rory. Remember, I'm gettin' those books off ya when yer finished with'em. Don't lend 'em to someone else."

"I won't. I'll drop 'em off to ya when I'm finished with 'em. I'll tell ya now, though. Some are hard reads."

"Well, I'll pick through 'em and see what interests me."

"Brock, drop me off first."

"Rory, the fella that moved into the McGraw place, do ya ever see 'im around?"

"Not much."

"What about you, Butch?"

"Not much. Sees 'im in the yard with his animals every now and then."

"Why ya ask, Brock?"

"I dunno, he seems a bit strange to me. Never sees anyone over there. He associates with no one. I guess he's one of 'em type people who likes to be left alone."

Brock dropped the boys off. Butch was lost without Rory around. As much as he hated to admit it, Rory was like his right arm. Butch spent most of his time at the pool hall hustling teenagers. Butch loved hanging out with teenagers, and they seemed to enjoy his company. Occasionally he had a few beer with them. When he was planning on drinking with the teenagers late at night, he called it having a business meeting. Both he and the teenagers called it that. This was his way of hiding it from Rory. If Rory knew he was drinking with underage teenagers, he would flip on him. Rory worked hard at keeping Butch on the straight and narrow. Trying to keep him from ending up in a reform school or jail had been a full-time job since childhood.

Rory finally left his house on Wednesday afternoon. Butch was walking the road in front of his house.

"So, Butch, what've ya been up to?"

"Not much. Went over to Mickey Blacks one night to shoot some pool. The place was like a funeral home, hardly enough people there for a decent wake. Went down to Witless Bay one night with Lip Chidley and got hustled big time."

"Who beat ya?"

"I went to Lar Smith's first to see if I could make a few dollars. I played a fella named Jimi Dunphy from Bay Bulls, two out of three for ten bucks, lost two straight. I played another fella from Bay Bulls, Ronnie O'Driscoll, and lost another ten bucks. After two beatin's, I decided to try me luck at Kent's. I played a fella by the name of Don Murphy from Bear's Cove, he beat me three in a row for a twenty. Decided to try me luck again. I played a short fella, Kenny Tobin, nickname Crusher, he beat me ten to six, for another twenty. Turns out, he's the son of the man who owns Kent's, Tommy Tobin. I lost sixty bucks in total. Me worst day ever playin' pool."

"Butch, don't get too hung up on it. Ya'll have lots of days like that; ya can't be hot every night. C'mon, let's get Brock to drive us down to the club in Cape Broyle. I wants to find Mugford and have a chat with 'im about peddlin' a bit of gear for me."

The boys hitchhiked to the pool hall in Renews. Rory sat and watched Butch hustle the teenagers as they waited for Brock. McCarthy's pool hall was a teenage hangout. Poor Butch, he wasn't any mentally older than they were. Brock picked them up, they headed for Harold Hayden's in Cape Broyle. There was hardly anyone in the club, but it was a Wednesday evening. They played pool to pass the time and wait for Mugford to appear. Rory hoped he'd show up.

Mugford showed up an hour later. When Rory noticed him go into the washroom, he followed and introduced himself. It was a waste of time; Mugford knew his face from being in the club the last year or two. They chatted about what was involved in pushing a few ounces a week. Mugford said he'd sleep on it and get back to him.

Rory drove Brock's Cordoba back to Cappahayden for the practice; His road test for his license was on Friday. Before he got out of the car, he asked Brock if he could use his car for the test.

"Sure, why not?"

"What about goin' for a run tamorrow afternoon?"

"Sure thing, Rory."

CHAPTER TEN

Rory was reading a biography on Abraham Lincoln. He read for an hour before turning in.

The next day was beautiful, sunny, and warm. Brock picked Rory up at one o'clock.

"Let's make this a long run. Why don't we go down the Shore, cross the Witless Bay Line and head into town for a feed?"

"Sure, Brock. I'll even pay for it."

They stopped at Jose Maher's in Witless Bay; the yard was blocked with cars. Maher's was known for good grub, especially wings and chips. They continued and turned onto the Witless Bay Line. They took the best part of an hour to make it across the thirteen and a half miles of dirt road. The potholes were as wide as graves, some were almost as deep. Rory told Brock he was nervous about driving on the Trans-Canada Highway. Brock told him he'd have to get used to it, and if traffic was heavy, he'd take the wheel. It was a weekday in the afternoon, with not too many people on the move. Rory relaxed and got the Cordoba to the Avalon Mall parking lot in one piece. He wanted Chinese food; Brock wanted Kentucky Fried Chicken. They ate and got back in the car.

"Brock, I don't like the idea of drivin' in the city."

"Ya gotta learn to drive in the city eventually, so why not now? C'mon, we goes down to the waterfront, I'll show ya how to get there."

Brock loved boats; the bigger, the better. They parked on the apron and walked around, admiring the boats for an hour or more. They watched Portuguese fishermen of the White Fleet kick a soccer ball up and down the apron. What must it be like to cross the ocean and be away from your family for months, fishing the Grand Banks. And coming into St. John's for supplies, where no one spoke your language. The men looked happy; they were grinning as they sent the black-and-white ball flying along the pavement. Rory wondered if there was a bookstore downtown where he could buy a book about the White Fleet, which had been coming to Newfoundland for a good long time, when a sudden desire came over him, bigger than the desire for the book. It had something to do with the screaming gulls, the smell of the sea, and the lapping of water against the wharf. He wanted to ask a Portuguese if he could go aboard one of their ships; he wanted to feel it rock under his feet and see how they lived while at sea. And to hear the sailors speak their foreign words.

"Rory. We gotta leave now, get to a gas station."

They went to Wayne Williams Irving on the west end of Water St. for gas.

"Brock, d'ya s'pose we could go look for the fella Maddicks in Bay Bulls whose sellin' the Charger on the way back?"

"Sure, why not? I got nothin' else to do taday."

When they made it to Bay Bulls, Rory hauled into the Texaco gas bar at the Southern Discount Supermarket. He asked the gas bar attendant Jim Moakler, an older man, who had been pumping gas for decades for Jack Crane and now pumped it for Dave Walsh. Rory asked him if he knew where a fella Maddicks lived. Moakler gave him directions to Maddicks' house on Irish Town Road.

The house was easy to find, especially since there was a '68 Charger in the yard, yellow with a dark green vinyl roof. She looked like she was in good shape. Rory got out and walked up to the house, and knocked on the door. A middle-aged gent answered.

"Sir, can ya tell me who owns the Charger for sale parked in front of the garage?"

"I owns it. I'm Will Maddicks."

"Well, Mr. Maddicks, I'm Rory O'Ryan from Cappahayden.

I'm lookin' to buy a car; I'm interested in her. Can I have a look at her?"

Rory and the man walked to the car together. Brock got out of his car and joined them. The car looked good: no rust. Tires appeared to be good, lots of tread still on them. The green interior matched the vinyl roof. She had split seats in front with a console shift. When the man raised the bonnet, Rory could see it had a 383 in it. It was dry as a bone, with no oil anywhere. Which meant the car hadn't been driven hard.

"How much d'ya want for her, Mr. Maddicks?"

"I wants twenty-four hundred dollars for her."

"Sounds like a good price based on how she looks. Can ya take us for a run in her? I'd like to hear the engine, see if she rides smooth and what kind of pull she has."

"I can, b'ys."

A few minutes later, they were heading east towards Sts. Peter and Paul Catholic Church. Rory liked the console shift. Looked better than an automatic shift on the steering wheel. The engine sounded good—no pinging. She rode smoothly for a fourteen-year-old Chrysler product.

They went down the harbour, turned around at the bus stop in Bread and Cheese, the most easterly part of town on the north side. They went back up the harbour. Rory told Maddicks to gun her on top of Gatherall's Hill and keep the pedal to the floor on the Cliff. Maddicks gunned her the length of the Cliff. Rory liked the sound she made, not a ping.

They slowed, took a left by the Catholic Church, crossed the bridge on the Main River and went up Scott's Hill. Took a right at Goodwater, cruised down the highway, passed Ryan's Funeral Home and Southern Discount Supermarket and went back to the west end of Irish Town Road.

"Mr. Maddicks, does she have positive traction?"

"She does, as far as I know. I never ever burned her out to know, she is excellent in snow."

Rory told Maddicks he would know the next day if he would be approved for a car loan and asked if he could hold the car for a couple of days as he'd like to buy her. Maddicks said he would.

Going around Maggoty Cove Pond in Bay Bulls, Rory asked Brock if he could have a draw of weed.

"No way, Rory. No one is drivin' my car stoned or drunk."

Going thirty-five or forty minutes without a draw was no big deal, although he wanted one. Rory had his first draw of weed behind the old Baltimore High School one night at a sports banquet dance. It was a Saturday night, the night the high school burnt, May 28th, 1978. He always remembered his first draw. It happened on that night. For the first time in his life, he felt relaxed, like his skin was a good fit. Before the weed, he had a habit of drinking too much, waking up in weird places, and not knowing how he got there. After that first draw of weed, he slacked off on the booze and started selling marijuana and hash, which was one way of making sure he had a good supply of it to smoke every day.

That evening, Rory, Brock and Butch went for a run down the Shore.

"Rory, who were 'em people ya were wavin' to in Bay Bulls when we were drivin' around in the Charger?" asked Brock.

"I didn't know ya knew many in Bay Bulls."

"I knows more people on the Shore than ya thinks."

"Well, who were they?"

"The two older fellas by the war memorial? Mike Ryan, the shorter fella, he's the local undertaker. He built and was the first person to have a gas station on the end of the Witless Bay Line. He's the biggest Tory on the Shore. The other man, Ambrose Hearn, is a great storyteller. Best weddin' MC on the Shore. Both of 'em could talk the arse off a Newfoundland pony. A few years ago, Ambrose and Paddy O'Dea had a couple of heifers for beef; they bought 'em in the spring and were goin' to butcher 'em in the fall. They let 'em out to roam the harbour to fatten up. Before they did, they painted their initials on 'em with red and green paint. On both sides of the animals. Ya could see their initials a mile away, they stood out like billboards."

"Ya serious?"

"Yes, everyone gotta laugh out of it."

"The three fellas workin' on the punt by the greenhouse were Bobby Wakeham and his younger brothers, Joey and Chrissy, Joey is the redhead. Most likely doin' repairs on the boat for someone. They're great woodworkers. People say their father, Pad, could put an arse in a cat or a motor in the arse of a dog.

And the two fellas further in the road, sittin' on the saw-horse havin' a yarn were Mike Mulrooney the redhead fella and Randy Mulcahy. Randy's nickname is the Cat, 'cause he's as fast as a cat with his dukes. He do be on the ESSO oil truck with his cousins Jimmy and Brian Mulcahy. Jimmy is a good pool player. And everyone knows Brian Mulcahy, one of the best hockey players on the island, plays with the St. John's Caps in the Newfoundland Senior Hockey League. Howie Meeker said one time, Mulcahy had a two million dollar set of legs."

"How d'ya know all those people?" asked Butch.

"Butch, when ya plays pool all the time, yer playin' the same fellas over and over. That's all ye do, play pool, with little or no talk. All too wrapped up in yer heads about winnin'. Bars and taverns are a great place to socialize, meet people, learn a few things, and hear a few stories. Ya should take a break from the pool table."

"Not likely."

The three went into Hayden's for a beer on the way back up the Shore. Mugford was there, shooting pool. By the looks of it, it wasn't the first time he held a cue. Rory watched as Mugford broke the balls and ran the table against Butch. Butch was not impressed with losing. He was impressed with the two-piece cue Mugford shot with, the first two-piece cue he ever saw. Rory enjoyed watching good pool players, despite what he told Butch. Good pool players are a breed of their own, admired by many and despised by more.

"Hey, Mugford. Ya made up yer mind about sellin' some dope for me?"

"I s'pose I'll try it for a few weeks, to see if it's worth goin' at, see if there's any money in. If the heat gets on me, that's it. I don't want no trouble with the cops."

"Okay. I'll be back here tamorrow evenin' with two ounces of weed and a half-ounce of hash. If ya gets rid of it in a week, I'll give ya more the followin' Friday."

CHAPTER ELEVEN

On Friday, Brock drove the Cordoba from Cappahayden to Ferryland. He told Rory he didn't want Rory to make some small mistake and have it throw him off for his driving test. The weather was good, as Rory had hoped. He didn't want to do his road test in the rain. When they walked into the RCMP detachment, the young, cute female officer was standing at the counter doing paperwork. Rory glanced at her tits and thought of what Butch had said about tit-fucking her.

"Excuse me, miss, I gotta road test with Constable Campbell." What a pretty woman. Rory figured he could be a lesbian for a night, too.

Campbell walked up to the counter a few minutes later. He and Rory left the building.

"Get the fuck out of bed, Butch. In bed, this hour of the day."

"So, what if I'm in bed this hour of the day?"

"Good news passed me drivers test."

"Cool."

"C'mon, let's go for a run. Brock is with me."

They went as far as Admiral's Cove. Rory and Butch sipped a few beers and smoked a few reefers as they drove around. They grabbed another six-pack at John Coady's Golden Eagle gas bar in Cape Broyle and headed for home. They parked at Bear Cove Beach. Rory looked out at Horn Head Reef and thought of the men, women and children who perished when they were shipwrecked on it in a frigid winter sea in 1918. The SS Florizel had been on her way to New York from St. John's when she struck the reef in a blizzard. Close to a hundred people had died, two of them a rich man and his three-year-old daughter Betty Munn. Her grandfather, Sir Edgar Bowring, erected a Peter Pan statue in Bowring Park in St. John's in her memory. Rory figured he'd be lucky to get a headstone if anything happened to him.

"I still wants to go to Toronah someday, Rory."

"Ya never know, Butch, we might get to drive there now that I have me license."

"Rory, that would be a good idea, drivin'. I dunno if I wants to get up in one of 'em jets. I hears about 'em crashin' all the time on TV. So, drivin' sounds better to me. We should plan it out and do it next fall."

"Yes, we'll start plannin' and costin' it out. Gas, ferry and hotels."

"Forget the hotels, we can sleep in the car. What's on the go the weekend?"

"Butch, I'm not goin' far this weekend. When I gets a set of wheels, it will cut into me readin' time. I won't be on the go this weekend."

"Fine with me, Rory. I'm almost broke. I don't get me pogey 'til Wednesday or Thursday. I might hang out at the pool hall and hustle a few bucks."

"Butch yer a poster child for a great Mark Twain quote. Twain said, show me a good pool player, and I'll show you a man with a misspent youth."

"And who the fuck is Mark Twain?'

"An American writer who died seventy-odd years ago, he was a billiards enthusiast. Time ya grew up. Takin' money from the poor teenagers."

"Well, Rory, if I don't take it, they'll only waste it. Better in my pocket than bein' pissed up against the back of the pool hall."

"I hope yer not sellin' 'em anythin'. That's all I wants goin' around, me and you are sellin' drugs to teenagers."

"Rory, I don't sell anythin' to teenagers. There's a young fella I sells it to, he sells it to the teenagers. I can't control that."

"I guess ya can't, don't be seen sellin' to anyone who resells it. Sell it to 'em alone when no one is around."

"I'll try, Rory, I can't guarantee anythin'."

"Ya got much stuff left to sell the weekend?"

"I got half of what ya gave me from the last batch."

"Okay, good. Might see ya the weekend."

Brock dropped Rory off first.

On Monday, Rory was on the phone with the Credit Union. His old man had finally gotten a phone put in. No more running to his grandmothers in Port Kirwan to make calls and to check to see if anyone left a message for him. Lisa had good news for him. The Credit Union would lend Rory and Butch the money. A co-shared loan: both would be responsible for it. They could come in and sign for it on Thursday. Rory called Maddicks immediately. The man still had the car; said yes, he could hold it for him until Thursday. He said the car would most likely pass an inspection. Rory hauled on his boots and headed to Butch's. When Rory walked into Butch's. Butch was asleep on the daybed in the kitchen.

"Butch get up, we got the loan."

Butch was ecstatic when he heard this. The next day, when the two were at the pool hall, Rory was trying to figure out how he would convince Butch the car had to go in his name. Butch was too careless, too irresponsible. A case when he got on the beer, more of a case if he was drinking and smoking pot. How was he going to break this to Butch? He figured if he got him into the country, in the shack for a few days, and waited for the booze and weed to run out, he could convince him the car was going in his name, or he was having nothing to do with it.

"Butch, what about it, we go into the shack for a few days?"

"Yes, nothin' else to do."

"Okay, we'll leave tamorrow mornin' around nine. Dress warm; temperature is s'posed to drop overnight and stay there tamorrow."

"Nine? Why so early?"

"Well, it's givin' out for snow in the afternoon. I figures an early start; we'd beat the weather 'fore it sets in."

"Alright, b'y. What are we goin' to bring with us to drink?"

"I gotta bottle of Golden Weddin' Whisky. I'll bring a chunk of hash; we can blast it. I believe there's a set of knives at the shack for blastin' hash. I'll bring another set just in case. We'll meet at nine, at the mouth of the river. Now Butch, don't sleep in. I wants to get in 'fore the snow starts. Get the fire goin', stretch out and relax."

"Okay, I'll be there. I for gotta tell ya, there's lots of mushrooms on the go. What ya say we swap some weed or hash for a few grams of 'em? Boil 'em up, make some tea, a bit of a different stone."

"Forget it, Butch. I had an awful trip on 'em last fall, swore I'd never do 'em again."

"All right, I can take 'em or leave 'em.

"Who has the mushrooms, and where did they pick 'em?"

"The b'ys from Calvert have 'em. They picked 'em on Ricky Walsh's farm in Bay Bulls."

"Butch, did ya hear the story about Ernie Smith havin' a bad trip on the shrooms last weekend?"

"No, I never heard."

"Ernie went home, wasted out of his mind. Threatin' to harm 'imself. His sister spent three or four hours talkin' 'im down. When she finally had 'im asleep in bed, she went to bed thinkin' he was okay. When she got up in the mornin', Ernie was gone. Left a note sayin' he was goin' to jump off the bridge in Cappahayden."

"Butch, laughed, jump off the bridge? Sure, there's no bridge in Cappahayden."

"Exactly, that'll tell ya how fucked up ya can get on the shrooms."

"I heard there's bennies on the go down the Shore. They looks like little pink houses. Ya interested in tryin' 'em?'

"No, I'll pass."

"I also heard there's some St. Pierre booze on the go, fairly cheap. Ya interested?"

"I'll pass on that, too. St. Pierre booze, ya don't know what yer drinkin', could be a Frenchman's piss."

CHAPTER TWELVE

The boys met at the mouth of the river at nine o'clock. Rory was there before Butch, as usual. Rory was a stickler for being on time. Butch was always late in his life, one of his womanly traits. The last two years he was in high school, he showed up on time, maybe ten or fifteen occasions. Not that he showed up that often. It would be a comfortable walk to the shack. The temperature was hovering around forty degrees, there was a light breeze at their back.

"Rory, did ya watch "Gilligan's Island" last night?"

"Butch, I don't watch "Gilligan's Island." It's a stupid show."

"I loves it, it's me favourite show."

"Go figure. Ya know, he reminds me of you."

"Quit laughin' and go fuck yerself, arsehole cunt!"

"Gilligan might be yer new nickname."

"Ya fuckin' better not! I won't hang around with ya no more."

"Ya promise?"

"Rory, my other favourite show is The Walton's. I lives for Sunday nights for it to c'mon. Always wanted a family like what they had. They were always so happy and content. I often wonder how me life may have turned out if I had to have a brother or a sister."

"That's TV. Not many families like that."

"I guess not. Did ya bring the whiskey and the hash? Knives, ginger ale and ice?"

"I did, I did, I did."

Their knapsacks were half full. Rory had two large saltfish and a few salted vins with him. He loved saltfish but preferred vins. He would have loved to have drawn butter with both. But forgot to bring flour to make drawn butter, so it would be melted butter with lots of pepper for the topping.

There was always lots of grub left in the shack. Anyone who used it had a habit of bringing more than they could eat, if someone got lost hunting rabbits, partridge, moose or caribou. Caribou came as far north as Cappahayden and occasionally as far north as Renews. You could get storm-bound in the shack and have enough to eat for a week or more. It might not be the best grub in the world, but grub, all the same, could get you out of a bad situation.

They walked to the cabin faster than they usually did, trying to race the bad weather forecast. They crossed two ponds, Freshwater Pond and American Pond; the cabin sits at the bottom of Clark's Pond. Butch always found the walk too long. Whatever time of year it was, he complained non-stop the whole way. His feet hurt him. His back was aching. His knapsack was too heavy, even when it was almost empty on the way out.

When they arrived at the cabin, Rory asked Butch to put on a couple of cans of tomato soup for lunch while he downed some spruce and juniper trees for firewood before the snow set in. And by the look of it, it wasn't far away. The sky was grey and low, and the silence was the calm before the storm. Twenty minutes later, when the power saw stopped buzzing, Butch made a roar. "Grubs ready!"

There was no tomato soup, so they had chicken soup with stale crackers, courtesy of the shack cupboards.

"Rory, what're yer plans for this afternoon?"

"Goin' back out at the wood after I haves a smoke or two. 'fore the snow starts. I brought a book with me. I'm goin' to get into it."

"What's the name of it?"

"Labrador by Choice. About a trapper from Labrador in the fifties and sixties. Tells his whole life on the trapline. I had a quick breeze through it. Looks like my type of book."

"Ya didn't happen to bring another one with ya?"

"I did. It's at the bottom of me knapsack. I haven't read it yet. Figured ya might be interested in it. It's about the thoroughbred racehorse industry in Kentucky. The state of Kentucky is known for havin' the most winnin' thoroughbred horses in the eastern US for the past one hundred years. I'm lookin' forward to readin' it. Ya might like it, havin' grown up with horses and ponies all our lives. Butch, I can't believe ya don't read."

"I've tried a few times, but I can't get into it."

"Know what's wrong with ya?"

"What?"

"Ya haven't found a topic ya likes. That's the problem with most people. They haven't found the right topic. When ya find it, ya'll know."

"How will I know?"

"Ya'll know 'cause ya won't be able to put down the book yer readin'."

"What d'ya mean, Rory?"

"Well, ya'll start a book and read non-stop 'til it's finished."

"Yer off yer head. Me read a book without stoppin'. I don't think so, not in this lifetime."

"Ya will. Ya'll read and read and only stop for food and a scattered smoke."

"Some chance of that happenin'. It will take me a month to read that book on horses."

"Wait and see. I bet ya'll say to me in a week or less, ya have it read."

"I can't see that happenin'."

"Bet ya a dozen beer."

"Rory, only thing I bet on is pool when I knows I'll have a ninety percent chance of winnin' ever 'fore the balls are broken."

"Some cocky about pool, aren't ya?"

"That's it when yer good yer good."

"Yer good on the Shore. Wait till ya start playin' the big b'ys from town. The Furlong twins, Randy and Robin, from down east. Randy won the all-Newfoundland 8-ball tournament last year. Wait till ya cross paths with 'em. They'll give ya a lesson in how to chalk a pool cue. And there are others, just as good, Rick Kavanagh and Ernie Layman."

"Yeah, we'll see. I might not beat 'em. I'll give 'em a run for their money."

"Butch, yer not good enough to chalk their cues."

"Yeah, we'll see. Hope yer with me when I cross paths with 'em. And remember, Rory, 'em fellas are older than me. When I gets their age, I'll be that much better."

The weather set in. It snowed heavily and blew a gale for two days and two nights. At the end of those two days and nights, they were out of hash and whiskey. So, Rory decided it was time to discuss the car. Trying to explain and convince Butch about anything was like trying to pull teeth with a pair of scissors.

He waited until supper was finished with the dishes done. Both were stretched out on their bunks, enjoying the heat from the woodstove. Listening to VOCM's top ten on the transistor radio, the wind was howling and shaking the shack. He started the conversation by explaining to Butch how the car had to go in one person's name. He told Butch about registering a vehicle, how insurance worked, and how expensive it was. How it had to be paid every month. He told him the car was going in his name, or there would be no car.

"But why, Rory? Why can't it go in my name?"

"I'm more responsible than you."

Deep down, Butch knew what Rory was saying was right, but agreeing to it was another thing altogether. He argued just for the sake of arguing.

"All right, Rory. But I gets to have the car every now and then when I gets me license."

Rory agreed, just to keep the peace. He knew letting Butch take the car by himself would never be a good idea. God knows what he'd do with it. Driving around with underage teenagers drinkin', and God knows what else. He liked to think, Butch might get some sense, it was wishful thinking. Even though Butch was going on twenty, he hadn't progressed intellectually past fifteen.

They stayed in the shack for another night, even though they were out of booze and hash and had only sixteen cigarettes left between them. They bunked down, got out their books, Rory read non-stop late into the night. Butch would read three or four pages, put down the book and talk. Rory spent a good deal of his time telling Butch to shut up, he was tryin' to read.

Overnight the bad weather had subsided. It was a beautiful morning, every tree laden down with fresh snow. Rory was looking forward to a peaceful hike. As soon as they started walking, Butch nagged him about the car.

"Drop it, Butch. What we agreed to last night is what's goin' to happen, end of story. Yer wastin' yer breath."

They took a fair bit longer to get home due to all the fresh snow underfoot and a light headwind. Rory took a bath when he got home. Butch had told him he was getting right into bed when he got home, sweat and all. Butch was a dirtbag. No one would argue with that.

Rory called Brock when he arrived home from the cabin, he asked him to drop over later. He wanted to speak to Brock about registering and insuring the car. After Rory's bath and nap, Brock showed up.

"Come in, wanna' beer?"

"No thanks, I already had two. I don't wanna' push it. What's up?"

"I'm wonderin' about how to go about gettin' the car registered and insured. I knows a little about it, but I wants ya to walk me through it."

"There's nothin' to it. Pay for the car, get the bill of sale, get the car inspected. Drop her back to Maddicks house, 'til ya get her insured and registered. Go to town; first, ya gotta get her insured, ya'll need the insurance slip to get her registered. Go to the Vikin' Buildin' on Crosbie Road for the registration papers. Then you got everythin' ya need."

"Would ya be able to take me and Butch to town to get all it cleared up?" Rory couldn't go to town without taking Butch. Technically, Butch owned half the car; if he left him out of the decision-making, it would piss him off to no end.

"No problem."

Rory browsed a magazine while they waited for their appointment with Lisa. Butch sized up everyone coming in or going out of the Credit Union, especially the women. A few minutes later, a tall dark haired girl beckoned to the boys, saying Lisa was ready to see them. They were both a little nervous as they walked to her office, even though they had been approved for the loan.

"Good morning, young men. I guess both of you are excited, getting a loan for your first car."

Butch said, "yes, very excited." In more ways than one, his eyes brushing her cleavage.

Lisa gathered the papers and laid them on the desk.

"Okay, gentlemen: I need both of you to sign in five different places on these documents. Butch, you sign below Rory's signature."

Rory glanced at Butch. Butch was not happy about his signature going under his.

"Lisa, could we get the money in cash? The owner of the car wants to be paid cash."

"No problem." She rose and left the office. When she returned, she had twenty-four hundred in twenty-dollar bills. She slowly counted the money on the desk, a hundred and twenty twenties. It was the most money Rory had ever seen at once, although he had collected his fair share of cash selling dope. Mostly in two, five and ten-dollar bills. Butch was gawking at the paper money. As if he'd never seen so much as a one-dollar bill in his life.

CHAPTER THIRTEEN

Maddicks walked out of the sawmill covered in sawdust from head to toe. The Maddicks family owned and operated a sawmill since 1964. "How are ye taday, young men?"

"Good. We have yer money for the car. I gotta go to town now and get her licensed and insured. We'll be back to pick her up."

"Well, I won't keep ya waitin'. I got the bill of sale already wrote up." He pulled the bill of sale from his jacket and showed it to Rory.

"Mr. Maddicks, I don't s'pose ya'd consider writin' in a lesser amount? So, I don't have to pay so much taxes."

"No, me son, I always does everythin' above board."

"That's understandable," Rory said. He counted out the twenty-four hundred dollars in twenties on top of the bonnet of the Charger. Mr. Maddicks handed him the bill of sale. Rory grinned; the deal was done. The boys finally had their own set of wheels. The Southern Shore would never be the same.

"Thank ya, Mr. Maddicks. We're goin' to Schinagl's in Big Pond to get her inspected, we'd like to bring her back here, we're darting into town to get insurance and get her registered. If it's okay with ya."

"I don't see no problem with that. Young man, 'fore ya go, there's a box full of 8 track tapes in the trunk, ya can keep 'em. A few John Prine, a few Cash, some Kristofferson and a few Harry Hibbs and Dick Nolan. Keep 'em and enjoy 'em."

When they got in the car, Butch said, "There won't be no fuckin' Harry Hibbs or Dick Nolan playin' in my car. Rory, the first thing we needs for the car is a CB."

Franz Schinagl was in the yard working on a VW Beetle when they pulled in. As they got out of the car, the wind was blowing off the pond. Rory walked over to Schinagl and tapped him on the shoulder.

"Mr. Schinagl, excuse me, can ya do an inspection on my car right away if ya don't mind?"

"Yes, I can do that." Rory tried not to smile. The man's accent reminded him of Schultz on "Hogan's Heroes."

After Schinagl inspected the car, he asked Rory who he bought it from.

"Will Maddicks in Bay Bulls."

"She's a fine car. The Maddicks men take good care of their vehicles. They've had some nice cars over the years. No need to put her on the ramp. Here's the slip. Eight dollars is the charge."

Rory paid the eight bucks and returned the car to Maddicks yard, and headed for the city. In the Goulds, they were forced to come to a crawl. Fifty or sixty Holstein dairy cows were on the main road north of Bidgood's, being driven to pasture.

"Fuckin' bovines. What a time to be on the road!"

"Rory, what's a bovine?"

"A fuckin' cow, Butch."

Several hours later, after they got insurance and had the car registered, Rory said, "Let's celebrate with a big dirty feed. I'll pay. I heard the Pink Poodle on Topsail Road has wicked steaks."

Butch said, "I'm starved."

"What about ya, Brock, where d'ya wanna' go?"

"I heard the same thing about the Pink Poodles grub."

"The Pink Poodle it is."

When the boys arrived, they ordered a beer to sip on as they waited for their steaks.

Butch took a long swig of his beer, belched, and looked at Rory. "There's a group of hikers plannin' on buildin' a hikin' trail on the Shore from Fort Amherst to Cape Race."

"What?" said Rory. "Who told ya that, Butch?" Rory was usually the first one to get local news and gossip on the Shore. It was strange for Butch to have one upon him.

"I was at Mike Hayden's Hotel on Saturday afternoon. A group of people walked in with bog up to their knees. I got talkin' to 'em; they told me they were hikers from MUN. Said they were cuttin' a hikin' trail along the coast on the old traditional footpaths, said they're hopin' to get government fundin' someday down the road to go at it on a big scale. Said they've been hikin' alongside the ocean for years, said it needs some widenin', and a few make shift crossin's to navigate the rivers. They said hiking was one of the fastest-growing outdoor activities.

Did ye know that there's a sea geyser between Bay Bulls and the Goulds that sprays water a hundred feet or more in the air. It's called the Spout. The b'ys from Bay Bulls were talkin' about it at the Beehive one night. I'd love to see it."

"What's a sea geyser? Some old fella?" asked Brock.

Butch rolled his eyes. "A crack in the rocks on the water's edge where a freshwater stream runs in, and when the current from the ocean hits it, up she goes. Rory, did ya know the first road—cowpath, I guess ya could call it, that connected all of the Southern Shore from St. John's to Renews was in 1840, with all rivers bridged?"

"Who told ya that, Butch?" Rory found it hard to believe, Butch knew anything outside pool, women, dope, and booze.

"My father said his grandfather told it to 'im when he was ten or eleven years old. Me father's grandfather was always tellin' stories about the old days. I wish me ol' man had written it all down 'fore Great-grandfather passed away. One of 'em hikers had a small pair of binoculars hangin' around his neck. I asked 'im what they were for, and he said birdwatchin'. Takes all kinds to make the world go round, and ya know what, they're all here. They were a strange mix of people. Some had accents I never heard 'fore. Not that I have heard a lot of foreign accents in my day, only townie ones and buddy we met taday who owns the garage in Big Pond."

Rory asked Butch if the hikers had a name picked for the trail. Butch said, "they had a few picked but couldn't decide on which one they were going with." Said, "he'd tell 'em on the way up the Shore."

Rory said, "Okay, B'ys, I sees our grub comin'." Rory envied Butch because of the chat he had with the hikers. He wished he had been there. He would have gotten a lot more information out of the hikers.

CHAPTER FOURTEEN

Butch was getting antsy about learning to drive. Rory never offered to teach him; he was getting fed up. One Saturday afternoon after they'd left Riverside Lounge in Bay Bulls, known locally as Anthony's O'Brien's. Butch had won another 8-ball pool tournament. He had a few beer in him and was in the mood to pick a fight, he popped the question. "Rory, isn't it about time ya taught me to drive?"

"I was waitin' for ya to start on that."

"Ya were, were ya? We got this car almost a month, and ya never once offered to teach me to drive."

"Butch, it's like this: if I try to teach ya to drive, we won't be friends by the time ya knows how to drive. So, I'm suggestin' ya ask Brock to teach ya. Use our car. Brock is easy goin', as ya know. You and me, we'd be like a married couple. We'll be fell out 'fore we got out of Cappahayden."

"Rory, that's a good idea. You ask 'im. You and 'im are closer than me and 'im. There's times I wonders if he thinks I'm nuts."

"Why, Butch—any idea?"

"Fuck off, Rory."

"Not a problem, I'll ask 'im next time I sees 'im. I haven't seen 'im around in a while. It must be the new chick he has on the go. Someone said she's from Tors Cove."

"He went far enough away for a piece of ass."

"Good one talkin'. Didn't ya get stuck in Witless Bay a while ago 'cause of a piece of ass?"

"Yes, I did. But it was only for a piece of tail. I didn't start goin' steady with her or anythin'."

"Butch. It doesn't matter where they're from when ya falls

in love. Love has no mileage. It's like the passage of time and tide, ya can't control it."

"What's on the go for tanight?"

"Nothin', I'm stayin' home. I might start a book."

"Why are ya stayin' home?"

"Well, with so much dope on the go, I'm keepin' a low profile."

"Ya serious?

"Yes. Ya knows the RCMP will eventually hear about me supplyin' the Shore with drugs if they don't already know. Ya knows there's a snitch in every community. Stayin' home and not bein' seen cruisin' around on the weekends might keep the heat off me."

"Rory, yer off yer head. Life is passin' ya by."

"No, not at all, Butch. I'm not like you. All ya wants is partyin', drinkin', smokin' dope, non-stop, and bangin' skanks. Ya'd screw a Cape Shore sheep if ya had the right rubber boots on."

"Sure, that's what life is about."

"No, Butch, there's more to life than partyin' 24/7."

"I'll tell ya what when I gets me license, I'll be havin' the car on the weekends for cruisin'."

"We'll see."

"There's no 'we'll see.' Remember, I makes half the payments every month."

"Butch, this car will do us for years if we takes care of it and keeps the mileage down. She won't melt, parked in the driveway. She's not an ice cube."

"Rory, we bought it to drive."

"We did, but it's mostly for us to use to distribute drugs. We play our cards right; in two or three years, we'll both have brand new wheels."

Butch grinned. If his plan worked out, he'd be having a new set of wheels sooner than two or three years.

"What are ya smilin' about?"

"Nothin', b'y."

Rory knew when Butch had an evil side on-grin, he was up to something. Most likely, something no good. Stund as Butch was, he was a player. He might not be book smart, but on the street, he was keen. If he saw or heard something that interested him, it went in his head and stayed there.

Rory had to figure out who he would get to sell drugs for him in the Goulds. He'd heard there was a fella from Kilbride who was peddling weed but trying to get him to sell for Rory was not a good idea. Breaching a pushers' area could get you a good shit-knocking.

He needed a person living in the middle of the Goulds. Someone who could drive or even walk to the three clubs and move around, not hanging out in the same club. If a pusher was in the same club, running in and out twenty or thirty times day and night, the heat would be on them. Rory decided a day or two hanging out at the three clubs in the Goulds was in order.

But how was he going to do this without having Butch with him? Looking for someone to sell dope was a challenge. Having someone with you who would hustle half of the club while doing business would make it even more challenging. Every time the starting motor turned over on the Charger Butch was glued to the passenger seat.

There might be one way to get rid of Butch: tell him he had to go into town to the hospital for tests. Butch would never hang out in town all day by himself. He wouldn't go to a strange club or beer tavern alone in town, as much as he loved to hustle pool. Butch was a little paranoid when he hustled people, afraid he might get jumped and beat to a snot with a pool cue for taking their money so easily. He would get lost in a shopping mall in two minutes. Poor fella had no sense of direction.

CHAPTER FIFTEEN

On the run to Trepassey, Butch started about the car.

"Can I drive?"

"No, and for two reasons, Butch. It's rainin', and we already had this conversation about ya learnin' how to drive. I said I'll ask Brock to teach ya."

"Well, why don't ya?"

"Butch, Rome wasn't built in a day."

"Rome . . . where's Rome?"

"In fuckin' Italy."

"What has someplace in Italy gotta do with me learnin' how to drive?"

"Butch, ya stupid prick, it's a comparison. Meanin' there's no rush for ya to get yer license."

"Why isn't there a rush?"

"Butch, we wanted a car. We got it. One of us needed their license to drive so we wouldn't have to depend on Brock all the time. So, we're on easy street."

"Easy street, easy for you to say, ya got yer license and has the car all the time."

"Butch, ya'll have yers in a few months. Relax, I knows ya owns half the car. When ya gets yer license, I'll let ya have her every now and then."

"Like the fuck. I'll be havin' her half the time. If not, ya'll be makin' the full payments. Rory, I might not be as smart as you, but I'm smart enough to know half car payments equals half the time with the car."

"Butch, let's end this conversation now. We're wastin' our

voices on nothin'. When ya gets yer license, we'll have a serious conversation about this car."

"Okay. In the meantime, ask Brock about teachin' me to drive."

"Good day, ma'am, is Perry up?"

"Yes, up and gone. He worked last night at the plant. Got up, showered, said he was goin' to the club for a beer."

"Did he say which club?"

"No idea, son. There's three; I'm sure he's in one of 'em. If ya finds 'im, tell 'im I said he better not come home half drunk. He got work tanight."

"Yes, ma'am, I'll tell 'im if and when I finds 'im."

Rory drove around looking for Larry's car, maybe Perry was cruising around with him. He and Butch went to Transatlantic Lounge, Perry wasn't there. Next, they tried Harbourview. The parking lot was full of cars. Rory was curious, what was on the go, soon as they walked in the door, his question was answered: a mixed-dart tournament was on the go. Sixty or seventy people were shooting darts, two people playing pool, a man and a woman. The woman was a fine shooter, much sharper than her opponent. Rory looked at Butch, who was almost drooling. He knew Butch wanted to shoot a game or two with her; she was a hot piece of gear, legs on her like a racehorse. As much as Butch loved playing pool, he enjoyed it ten times more when playing it with women. Butch would let them win most times, so he could get on their good side and charm the jeans off them. It always amazed Rory how Butch could hook the women. A dirtbag most of the time with an IQ on the lower end of the scale, sure, he could charm the habit of a nun in ten minutes—quicker if the nun was drinking.

Rory spoke before Butch did: "Forget it, we're not stayin'. I needs to get ahold of Perry; I'm not wastin' a run across the barrens to watch you play pool with some chick so ya can charm her. C'mon, we're headin' to Outer Limits."

There were three cars in the yard at Outer Limits; one of them was Larry's.

"Hey, b'ys . . . how the fuck are ye?"

Perry was hanging off the bar, obviously loaded drunk. Rory cursed under his breath. He didn't like to be the center of attention, especially when it involved the local drug dealer. If people noticed him talking to Perry, they'd soon enough put it together, this fella who's not from Trepassey must be into the dope also. Or Perry's supplier.

Rory went to the bar and put his arm around Perry. Whispered in his ear, "Settle down, don't be so loud." He knew Perry was a scrapper, he felt him tense. Then Perry relaxed. He realized that starting a racket with his supplier would mean the end of his dope supply in a hurry.

"Sorry about that, Rory."

"No harm, no foul, my friend. What the fuck are ya on the beer for taday?"

"Well, how do I explain this? First, I had one, then I had two, I said the third won't hurt me. And now I'm tryin' to look at ya without seein' four or five Rory's. I'd say I'm after havin' nine or ten or more, who knows and who fuckin' cares."

Rory hustled Perry to the far end of the bar, which was clear of people.

"Perry, you on the beer in the middle of the day is not a good idea."

"Why not?"

"Well, for one thing, ya got work tanight."

"I agree, I won't argue with ya."

"Well, why are ya on the beer?"

"Well, I guess I'll tell ya. The chick I was goin' out with for the last six months went to town last weekend for her sisters' stagette party in one of the George Street bars. One of me buddies saw her leave the bar with a fella after the lights came on. He told me last night on our three o'clock lunch break at the plant."

"Sorry to hear. Ya'll survive; we all do. I came up to talk about rampin' up my supply, but yer in no state to talk business. I'll drop back up in a few days. I got nothin' on me now, when I comes back up, I'll have yer regular supply, maybe more. Listen, a little advice: go home, have a nap. Ya knows how lucky ya are to have a decent payin' job in yer hometown."

"I dunno about work tanight."

"There are more women in Trepassey than her, Perry."

"Yes, I knows, but I thought she was the one."

"Don't we all think the one we're bangin' at the moment is the one? And 'fore I goes, I sees ya in a state like this again; our relationship will be over."

"Relax, Rory. First time I was drunk in a year or more."

"I hope yer not bullshittin' me."

The boys drove Perry from the club to his house on the Lower Coast.

"Rory, thanks for the run home. Rory, I thinks the world of ya."

"Perry, go in the house and go to bed. Yer drunk. I gotta be back down the Shore to meet someone."

They watched as Perry staggered into his house. "Jesus, Rory, he can hardly walk."

"Butch, he's loaded."

"I never took 'im to be someone who drinks like that."

"I never either. His girlfriend cheated on 'im downtown last weekend. He's takin' it hard."

"Sure, Rory, I thought he was goin' to start cryin' on yer shoulder at the bar. He sensible enough to have sellin' for ya?"

"That's what I'm wonderin' now. I'm goin' to keep a closer eye on 'im."

"Who ya meetin' down the Shore?"

"No one."

"Ya told Perry ya had to go 'cause ya were meetin' someone down the Shore."

"I told 'im that to get rid of 'im. He's drunk, and I didn't wanna' listen to 'im. I can't stand listenin' to drunk people, especially when I'm sober."

"What a friend ya are."

"Butch, I hates drunks, especially ones who don't shut up when they're drunk."

"What's the plan for tanight?"

"I gotta few books to browse. Might decide on readin' one of 'em."

"Rory, think ya'd ever write a book?"

"And exactly what would I write a book about?"

"I dunno."

"I dunno, either."

"Well, I figures anyone who has read as many books as you should be able to write one."

"Reading books don't make ya a writer. Dale Earnhardt races cars. He don't build 'em, does he?"

CHAPTER SIXTEEN

Rory watched his neighbour, Gerald Goffman, trying to round up his animals, a Newfoundland pony with a foal, three cows, two with calves. Good thing his pasture was only three or four acres. "Need any help?"

"No, thanks, I'll get these stupid animals in eventually."

Rory puffed on a cigarette, he kept watching Gerald. He wasn't having much luck. When the animals were almost corralled a number of times, one would take off across the field. Rory was on his second cigarette by the time all seven animals were in the barn.

Gerald made his way over to the fence and leaned on it. He was huffing and puffing like a freight train, so out of breath he could hardly talk.

"Gerald, ya gotta give up smokin' the pipe."

"I don't think so, Rory. It's the only thing that keeps me sane."

"Try a draw of weed, might relax ya."

"The last time I smoked weed was at Woodstock."

"You were at Woodstock? Not many people in Newfoundland can say that." Although Gerald and Rory were neighbours, they had never had a real conversation. Rory suddenly thought a real conversation might be possible with Gerald.

"You're the first person in Cappahayden I've told that to."

"Can I ask ya a question? And I don't mean to be nosy."

"Sure."

"Whatever provoked ya to move from St. John's to Cappahayden at yer age?"

"I'll tell you. I always wanted to have a small farm, a hobby farm, I was tired of living in the city. Last spring, a friend of mine who's a bit of a nature photographer and a birdwatcher wanted to do a run around the Southern Shore, the whole loop from Bay Bulls right around to St. Mary's Bay and back to the Trans-Canada Highway, he asked if I wanted to go with him. I said yes, sure, why not, a day away from the hustle and bustle of city living. As we drove, I kept an eye out for old rundown properties, preferably saltboxes, with a barn or a small stable. Something small and cheap that needed a little work. My friend decided to stop in Cappahayden to take some pictures and look for European birds that blow across the Atlantic in the spring. Cappahayden is one of the best spots on the Avalon for European golden plovers; they usually find one here every few years. My friend was taking photographs and looking for birds. I decided to have a look around. I wasn't out of the car five minutes when I came across this old spot tucked in behind all these mature maple and birch trees. It had a for-sale sign on it. As soon as I saw it, I loved it. It had everything I was looking for. So, a few weeks later, I bought it from the old woman who owned it. She told me her husband had passed away in '75, said she'd stayed there for a year after her husband passed, but she couldn't keep the property up on her own. I guess you must have known her and her husband well."

"I was thirteen or fourteen when Skipper McGraw passed away. I never liked 'im, and he never liked me. We started off our relationship on the wrong foot. His crabapples and plums were the tastiest and juiciest this side of Cape Broyle. Every year, late summer, his trees would get raided. And who always got the blame, me and Butch. I don't mind takin' the blame for anythin' I do or did. But I don't like to be blamed for somethin' I didn't do. So, every summer, when he blamed me for stealin' the fruit, I let his goats and sheep out of the yard. He finally put a chain and lock on his gate, not 'fore I let 'em out three or four times. He'd be days 'fore he'd get the Billy goat back in the yard. As for the ol' woman, ya never saw her. Ya might see her out in the yard a half dozen times in the summer. She'd never speak to anyone, hardly look in yer direction. I believe the ol' man was stern and ruled the roost."

"Why don't you hop over the fence and come in for a drink of Scotch. Do you like Scotch?"

"I have never tried it. I'm not much of a drinker. When I do have a few, it's usually Screech. Most of the big drinkers on the Shore drink Screech. Jimmy Boland, who owns and runs the Seaview Tavern in Bay Bulls, most people calls it the Swamp, the older crowd call it the long rubber club, Jimmy told me a few months ago, he goes through twenty to twenty-five bottles of Screech a week."

"Scotch is an acquired taste. My father and his friends from college drank Scotch, so once I was old enough to drink, that was my choice. It's good once you get used to it."

"Gerald, tell ya what—I gotta dart in the house, I'll pop back in a half-hour."

Rory went home, made a potted meat and bologna sandwich and gulped it down. There wasn't enough of either to make a decent sandwich, so he made do with what he had. It wasn't the first time he paired up different types of meat to make a sandwich. He rolled a half pack of cigarettes and figured he'd need a few smokes if he would be drinking. He grabbed a chunk of hash. He figured he'd be having a draw; he might even convince Gerald to stuff a little in his pipe. Rory climbed over the tall fence; Gerald kept a chain and padlock on the gate, like old man McGraw. When Rory spotted the padlock, he hoped Gerald wouldn't be a prick like McGraw. Honest people don't put locks on anything unless they're dishonest themselves. But Gerald was different. Tall with a Jesus Christ beard, he rarely, if ever, wore jeans, and the pants he wore were always four or five inches too short. Always had sandals on, even in the worst weather. He wore coloured ponchos.

Rory wasn't one for talking too much or asking too many questions. He was inquisitive by nature and had spent no time in the company of people he didn't know. He figured it would be interesting to pick his neighbour's brain to see what made him tick.

It was his first time entering the house; he knocked on the rough wooden porch door.

"The doors are open; come in."

Rory pressed the latch, pulled out the storm door and pushed the second wooden door in. The first thing to hit him was the heat and a homely smell he could not place. It must have been eighty degrees. The house was small and cozy. The kitchen walls were a deep green colour, an acorn wood stove heated the saltbox. The stove was crackling and snapping with burning wood.

"Welcome, my friend, grab a chair. Not the one against the wall, though. I have to sit with my back to the wall. It's a phobia I've had since I was a teenager." Gerald opened a cupboard door and took out a bottle of Johnny Walker Black, with three or four drinks gone out of it.

"Now, Rory, you drink Scotch either on the rocks or with water. No throwing Pepsi or coke into it. People who drink Scotch want to enjoy the unadulterated taste of it. I drink mine with a little water and plenty of ice. Since you haven't had it before, you should mix it with water, half and half. Drink it slowly; Scotch is a drink to savour, not gulp down like other liquors."

Rory was looking forward to trying this new alcohol. He wasn't much of a liquor drinker anymore. He might as well let his hair down for once in a long time. He wasn't in public; he was close to home. Sure, what could happen besides a fall over the fence on his way back home. He put a couple of ounces of Scotch in his glass with equal water. The first sip was good, smooth. Different, not bad. It tasted different than Screech. Went good with a cigarette.

"Gerald, you said ya were at Woodstock. That must have been somethin'."

"Yes, Woodstock, what a weekend. I only wish I could remember more of it. I do remember seeing some of the bands. Arlo Guthrie played on the first night, Friday; The Who, Jefferson Airplane and Janis Joplin played the second day. Jimi Hendrix was the last one to play on Sunday night. The weather was terrible, I was in good company."

"Why do ya have trouble rememberin' it?"

"Well, Rory, it's like this—if you did fifteen or twenty hits of acid over a four-day weekend, would you remember it?"

"Probably not. I haven't done acid; I'm hopin' to stay away from it. I have had a few good trips on the shrooms and a bad trip as well. Heard too many stories about fellas havin' bad trips. From what they tell me, you can do ten or twenty hits, and everythin' is fine. Then all of a sudden, ya'll have this bad trip. Bawlin' non-stop for hours, thinkin' about jumpin' off a bridge or the steeple of a church. An occasional draw of weed or hash is good enough for me. What other drugs have ya done?"

"There's not much I haven't done, Rory. Acid, MDA, peyote, amphetamines, cocaine. Magic mushrooms. As you said, they're a bit like acid: a peaceful stone until you have one bad trip, like a bad acid trip. If I had my time back, I wouldn't have touched any of them. Nothing wrong with a draw of weed or hash, or even hash oil. When you get into chemicals, you're asking for trouble. Especially coke. It's so addictive you'd sell yer mother for a snort."

"So, Gerald, ya from St. John's?"

"I'm originally from Toronto. My father came here to teach at Memorial when I was a kid."

"Did ya go to Memorial?"

"Yes, I have a BA in political science, with a minor in philosophy. What about you, did you do anything after high school?"

"No, I haven't done anythin' yet. I plan on doin' a trade or goin' to university someday down the road. Ya don't mind if I smoke a joint?"

"No, I don't mind."

"It's hash. I prefer a draw of hash over weed. Weed gives me the munchies like ya wouldn't believe. I'd eat a dog's back leg if I found it in the fridge with a weed draw in me. Why don't ya mix a little of it in with yer baccy when ya refill yer pipe?"

"Many years since I smoked a draw of anything. I'm afraid I might like it."

"Not a problem. I always have a bag of weed or a chunk of hash around. If ya ever wants a little, I'll give it to ya for cost."

"Rory, I tell you what, I'll make up my mind after another drink or two. Would you like another drink?"

"Sure, after I get this joint rolled and smoked. The first one went down smooth enough. I kind of likes it."

"It takes most people a while to develop a taste for Scotch. But when they do, they won't drink anything else. I won't, that's for sure. Not that I drink much anymore. Back in the late sixties and early seventies, drugs and drinking were part of the culture. I'm in my late thirties now, and as you age, hangovers get more unpleasant."

"So, what did ya do with yer degree?"

"Not much. I travelled around Canada, working in bars and at any other unskilled work I could pick up. Backpacked around Europe for a bit. Later, I did a stint with the provincial government, writing reports and some consulting work, and so on. Now I freelance. I once contemplated becoming an Anglican priest."

"Ya must have been on the shrooms." Gerald laughed and poured both another drink.

"A priest? I can't imagine life without a woman."

"Anglican priests marry, Rory. It's only Roman Catholic priests who can't. It's a bad rule, in many ways."

"I thinks they're all either queers or faggots. Not that I got anythin' against queers or faggots."

"I had a friend at university who went to Brother Rice. He said the Christian Brothers who educated him were a bunch of cruel cold-hearted sadistic bastards. He said they'd strap you for the smallest things, like a stain on your shirt. You got two or three lashes, and it might be the only shirt you owned. He was from a poor family with an old washing machine that didn't work well. I didn't believe him at first because his upbringing was so different from mine."

"Is yer mother from Toronah too?"

"No, she's from a little town in northern Quebec. She's part Cree. She met my father at the University of Toronto. She works for the federal government."

"So, what are ya doin' out here?"

"I love this place, love the smell of the salt air. I love to go to Bear Cove Beach and meditate for hours. I enjoy searching for mushrooms."

"Ya eats wild mushrooms?"

"Yes, my parents were into it. Taught me which ones were edible and which ones were toxic."

"Gerald, I've attempted to drop over to have a chat a few times."

"Same with me. I see your father has a few animals also."

"Yes, he has a Newfoundland pony with a foal, two cows with calves. Milks 'em till they dry up, then he butchers 'em. Not every year, he has one to butcher, but most years. He has a half dozen Rhode Island Reds as well. So, we have fresh eggs every day."

Rory took a sip of his drink, "do ya read much, Gerald?"

"I got me nose in a book most of the time. I just finished a book on Stalin. Do you know who Stalin was?"

"Yes, he led Russia from 1922 to his death in 1952. I read a book about 'im a few years ago."

"I'm reading a biography of Napoleon at the moment; would you like me to lend it to you after I finish it?"

"Yes. Gerald, where do ya get yer books from?"

"Well, I get most of them from secondhand bookstores. I

also go to a public library in town. What about you?"

"I usually bum 'em off the old folks around here. The last batch I got from the priest Father John O'Deady in Renews. He gave me a pillow sack full. Must have been fifty-five books in it. He told me to keep 'em."

"What kind of books are they?"

"Most are books of history. There's one on Cuba after the revolution in '59. One on the Vatican, one of the wealthiest organizations in the world. One on the American civil war."

"Sounds good."

"Me buddy, Butch Hynes, is plannin' on readin' a few of 'em too. He's the fella that's always with me, big fella. We're always together. We just bought the '68 Charger together; ya have may seen it in me yard."

"Bought a car together? I didn't know you drove."

"I didn't, up 'til a few weeks ago. Got me license from the RCMP in Ferryland."

"What about your friend? Does he have his license?"

"Butch doesn't have his license yet."

"I see a white Cordoba coming and going at your house all hours of the day and night."

"That's Brock White's car, our buddy. He taught me how to drive. I'm hopin' he's goin' to teach Butch."

"Why don't you teach him?"

"Well, Gerald, it's like this. If I try and teach 'im, it will be the end of our friendship."

"You serious?"

"Yes, poor old Butch is special, a slow learner. The poor fella only has a grade seven education. But he's as sharp as a lance. I guess ya could say he's street smart. Been on his own since he was ten or twelve. No family other than his ol' man. I gotta soft spot for 'im. He's one of the best pool players on the Shore. Makes a minimum of ten to twenty bucks a night playin' pool. Spends day and night over at McCarthy's pool hall in Renews, hustlin' teenagers. He must be after winnin' seven or eight tournaments on the Shore in the past two years. Woulda won more tournaments only for his age. We've been sneakin' in and out of clubs this past two years, but now we're legal."

"I guess you and your friend are on unemployment insurance this time of the year—your father told me you work in the fish plant. Will you be going back to the plant in the spring?"

"Yup, we're on the pogey. I'd give up working in the plant in a heartbeat if there was anythin' else to do that paid as well. Filletin' fish eight, ten, twelve hours a day gets pretty monotonous. Butch feels the same way. He's been on the skinnin' machine for the last six summers. Fourteen when they took 'im on. Fastest skinner on the Shore. When Butch gets his rhythm goin', he's like a machine. Head down, a fillet on the belt every second or two. It's a pleasure to watch 'im."

"Would you like another drink?"

"Okay, a small one. Startin' to get a buzz on the go. Don't mind if I light up another joint?"

"No, I don't mind."

"Gerald, here's a little chunk. Stuff it in yer pipe. I guarantee ya, it's good hash, black Moroccan."

"I'll have a small draw. I'm sure everyone around here thinks I'm a pothead already. A townie pothead and maybe gay. A strange man, living by himself on the old McGraw property. I happen to like my own company."

"I never thought ya were strange. I figured ya were someone who wanted to be left alone and keep to 'imself. I can picture livin' like you someday when I gets old. Somewhere other than Cappahayden, though."

"Why?"

"People in this town are too fuckin' nosy for my likin'."

"They don't seem to be nosy about me. I haven't had anyone one bit interested in me, as far as I can tell. Everyone says hello as they pass by if I'm in the yard. Met a few men on Bear Cove Beach last summer. They were collecting seaweed for their vegetable gardens. They told me if I ever needed to borrow anything, wrenches or tools, for instance, to drop by their place. Friendly men." Gerald put the hash in his pipe, lit it and coughed. "Holy shit, Rory, this hash is some hard on the throat."

"No, it's pretty smooth, compared to some stuff I've smoked over the years. Gerald, I soon gotta go. I dunno if I'm more drunk or more stoned." The men chatted for twenty minutes. "Gerald, it was finally nice to get to actually meet ya."

"You too, Rory. Pop by again for another drink or two of Scotch. I've got some books you may be interested in. Have you ever read Hemingway?"

"No. Isn't he English?"

"No, he was an American writer, wrote some great novels."

"I have never read a novel—pack of lies, someone's imagination gone wild. I only read non-fiction. But yes, I'll drop back again. Good night take care. Thanks for my first drink of Scotch."

"Thanks for the draw of hash."

Rory staggered across the yard, climbed slowly over the fence, wondering if Gerald was queer, living alone, reading novels. Although he never got that feeling of him. He appeared to be a good fella, generous with his booze.

CHAPTER SEVENTEEN

"Where were ya to this mornin'?"

"Why ya askin', Butch?"

"Well, I got up around one o'clock, and our car wasn't in Cappahayden. Where were ya?"

"Well, Butch, one o'clock in the afternoon is not mornin' in my books."

"Fuck off, dickhead, ya knows what I meant."

"I had a doctor's appointment in Ferryland."

"Why—ya sick or somethin'?"

"I was up all night and the night 'fore with a massive headache. I called Dr. Morry's clinic this mornin' and told the receptionist what was on the go. She told me to come down immediately."

"So, what did the doc have to say?"

"Dr. Morry's sendin' me to St. Clare's tamorrow for tests."

"Jesus, Rory, this sounds serious. Don't ya go and pop off on me. I'll feel guilty ridin' around in our car, with you up on Boot Hill."

"Ya wish. I'm not goin' anywhere. Doc says it's probably nothin', but he's not takin' any chances. I'll be leavin' here at seven in the mornin'. Doc said I could be there most of the day. Ya wanna' come with me for a run?"

"Rory, what am I goin' to do in town all day with you at the hospital? I wants to get a tattoo at Black Rose Tattoo Parlour."

"I dunno, I figured I'd ask. Cause if I didn't, I'd have to listen to ya for the rest of the week. When did ya get the idea of a tattoo?"

"Been thinkin' about it for a while."

"What kind of tattoo are ya gettin'?'

"An anchor, five or six inches long on me forearm."

"No worries, we'll get to town in the next few weeks for ya to get a tattoo."

"I'll see ya when ya gets back. Good luck, I hope it's nothin' serious."

Rory was up before seven. He had to be out of the driveway well before noon in the rare chance Butch got up early. When he made it to the city, he ate breakfast at Newfoundland Hotel, an eight-story building, which welcomed guests in 1926. He had never been in a hotel before. The meal was okay, pricey for bacon and eggs. Two men in uniform sat at the table next to him; pilots, he realized, after listening to their conversation. They would be spending the night in Nashville, Tennessee. Rory wondered how long it would be before he spent the night somewhere other than his childhood bed in Cappahayden.

Before he left, he asked the waitress what the new building being built next door was. She said it was the new Newfoundland Hotel, due to open in December. After Rory left the hotel, he drove to Signal Hill. When he reached the parking lot, there was only one other car there. It had an Ontario license plate; Rory wondered why someone from Ontario would be doing on Signal Hill this early in the morning. He figured it must be a tourist. He had heard people were coming to Newfoundland to see whales and puffins. And why would they come to this rock out in the middle of nowhere to see whales and birds? Something we've eaten since John Cabot landed here in 1497. If they had the money to waste on whales and puffins, it was theirs to spend.

Rory pulled out a pair of binoculars Gerald had given him the day before from under the front seat. Said he found two identical pairs, the old lady had left in the house, and perhaps Rory might find a use for them. He told Rory if he spotted a flamingo on his way down the Shore one day, to let him know, so he could call his birdwatching friend. Rory had laughed politely, thinking the whole time, it might not be a bad idea for a drug dealer to have binoculars in the car—you never know when they would come in handy?

Rory got out and sat on the cement retaining wall. He scanned the ocean, which stretched from where he sat all the way to Ireland. There were two boats, both past the mouth of the harbour. One was a deep-sea fishing trawler: you could see the trawl doors hanging off the stern. The other one was orange in colour, most likely a supply boat for the offshore oil industry.

Rory turned his binoculars to the city. He was amazed at how big it was and how far back it went. Too big to live in, okay to visit occasionally. He stood and went back to the car. Time to head to the Goulds to find someone to sell a little dope for him.

When Rory arrived at the Soundbone, there were only two cars in the parking lot. He figured he'd go in anyway, would meet no one sitting in his car.

A middle-aged woman with red hair was going around the club, cleaning tables with a wet rag, dumping the contents of ashtrays into a large tomato juice can. A young man was filling the beer coolers.

"I'd like a Coke in a large glass with ice, please."

The bartender smiled at him. "Not many fellas ask for a pop in this bar." Rory smiled back. He was in the Goulds to find a pusher, not to drink. A large coloured TV was mounted on a shelf in the corner behind the bar. Rory watched a rerun of the final game of the world series, Los Angeles Dodgers winning against the New York Yankees, winning the title four games to two. Rory thought, wouldn't it be nice to have cable TV to watch reruns. After the game ended, Rory headed to the Sou' Wester. The bartender was about to say something when Rory ordered a Coke, Rory cut him off with, "I heard it 'fore." He made his way to the pool table, placed two quarters on it. The best way to start conversations with the locals was over a game of pool. Rory watched a fella he knew beat three chaps. Then someone else beat him. Rory asked the winner his name before he flipped a quarter to see who would break.

"Angus Boyle, from the harbour."

"Ya mean Petty Harbour?"

Rory wanted to make sure he was on the right track with names and hometowns. He could have been from Harbour Grace or Harbour Breton for all he knew. He knew Boyle was a common name in Petty Harbour.

Boyle won the break and the game. "Boyle, do ya wanna' draw of weed?"

"Sure."

"In here or outside?"

"In here. The cops are in and out of the parkin' lot a half dozen times day and night, so we smoke up in here."

"The bartender won't say anythin'?"

"No, he's cool. He has a scattered draw with us when there's no one else in the club."

"Ya, sure he's cool?"

"Yes, don't be so fuckin' nervous."

They went into the bathroom; Rory passed a bag of weed to Boyle. "Here, you roll."

"Nice draw, pretty smooth on the throat. You got any to sell?"

"Sure, how much ya interested in?"

"I dunno, maybe a bag, say an ounce."

"I got some in the car. Let's go for a run."

As they drove through the Goulds, Boyle asked Rory how much he wanted for a bag of weed.

"I'm sellin' an ounce for a hundred and five bucks."

"Is it the stuff we smoked?"

"Sure is—here, stick yer nose in this." Rory opened the glove box; he took out a bag of weed.

"Aw, what a beautiful smell! You sell weed up the Shore?"

"Yes, weed and hash, been at it a while now."

"How's business?"

"Good, really good. I'm lookin' for someone from around this area to sell a little for me."

"You serious?"

"Yes, been lookin' for a few weeks now."

"Where are you getting the hash? I haven't had a draw of hash in months. It's hard to get."

"I gotta good supplier. Think ya'd be interested in sellin' a few bags and a chunk of hash a week for me?"

"Never ever thought about selling drugs, I guess if the price is right, I'm game."

"Well, if yer interested, I can supply ya with a few ounces on Friday. And a quarter ounce of hash."

"Sounds good to me."

"I'll pop into The Hayloft, say around three or four on Friday."

"Let me think about it for a few days. I'll tell ya what, if I'm at The Hayloft when you pop in on Friday, that means I'm interested."

"Boyle, what do ya work at?"

"Nothin' now, on the pogey. I fish with me old man, me brother and me uncle. We set three cod traps every year."

"Let's get a few things straight 'fore we start business, I'll front ya a few bags a week and a little hash. Ya have my money every Friday afternoon. And if ya do, I'll increase my supply. We're goin' to start out small."

"Sounds good to me. I never did get yer name."

"Rory O'Ryan. I'm from Cappahayden."

A few hours later, Rory cruised back up the Shore, confident he had a pusher for the Goulds. Now he had the whole Shore covered. Perry in Trepassey, Mugford in Cape Broyle, Genson in Bay Bulls and with any luck, Boyle covering the Goulds and Petty Harbour. It was only a matter of time before he drove the small pushers aside. All he had to do for the first month or two was make sure his boys were giving better counts than the other pushers. And to keep a steady supply of hash going. When he got home, Butch was waiting for him.

"Rory, how'd ya make out at St. Clare's?"

"Good—had all the tests done. The specialist said he's not worried, told me a small percentage of the population has headaches for no known reason. He said they might go away, or I could have 'em for the rest of me life."

"Maybe yer not smokin' enough weed."

Rory chuckled. "Probably smokin' too much."

"Jesus, Rory, that's all ya wants, headaches every day. Yer as contrary as a woman, ya'll be worse if ya gets headaches all the time."

"Butch, yer the woman in this relationship!"

"Fuck off! I never had a headache in me life."

"Butch, ya needs a fully functionin' brain to get headaches."

"Go fuck yerself!"

"Now, Butch, don't go leavin' in a bad mood."

"Fuck off, ya arsehole."

"I was goin' to tell ya I found a fella in the Goulds, interested in sellin' some gear for me."

"I thought ya went to the hospital?"

"I popped into the Sou' Wester for a few beer on the way back up the Shore. Figured a few beer might ease me headache. Met a fella Boyle, from Petty Harbour. He said he might be interested in sellin' a bit of gear, said he'd have his mind made up by Friday. I'll warn ya now, he's an excellent pool player."

"So what? Ya tryin' to scare me?"

"No, just tellin' ya."

"I'll see how good he is when I gets 'im on the table."

CHAPTER EIGHTEEN

Rory picked Butch up after supper, they headed for Cape Broyle. It was a dark night; he took his time. When the boys hauled into the San Juan Lounge, Brock's car was there.

"Now, Rory hit Brock up about me drivin' lessons."

"Okay, I will."

Rory went to the table where Brock was sitting with his new chick from Tors Cove.

"Brock, I needs a favour."

"What is it?"

"Butch wants to get his license, and I'm not teachin' 'im."

"Sure, no problem. Here's the deal—someone other than me pays for the gas that's burned."

"No problem. Between me and Butch, we'll cover it. Ya can use the Charger if ya wants."

"Nah, I'll use my car."

Butch walked over as Brock was about to leave with his missus. "Well, Butch, Brock says he'll teach ya how to drive. And Butch, ya don't pay for gas on the first lesson he won't take ya on yer second lesson."

"Sure, not a problem."

"Drop down to the cop shop tamorrow and get a date to go for yer license."

"Rory, I can't drive yet."

"Yes, we know. But it might take three or four weeks or longer to get an appointment for a road test. Ask for Campbell. He was good to deal with when I got mine. And he most likely knows we're buddies."

"Okay, the first time Brock takes me out for a run, I'll drop in. I hope the hot blonde is on shift. I'd like to get a close-up look at her tits."

"I'm headin' home. Ya comin'?"

"No, I'm on a roll. With a chick at the pool table."

The next time Rory saw Butch, Butch informed him, he had a road test in two weeks.

"Good to hear. I'm headin' to the Goulds on Friday to pick up my supply. And to give my new man his first supply, that's if he's made up his mind. Then I gotta find Gensom and Mugford. Saturday, I'll be goin' to Trepassey to give Perry his supply. Ya comin' with me?"

"No, I'll be doin' a bit of drivin' with Brock. He said I may take a little longer to learn than you. He can't get over how nervous I am."

"What makes ya nervous?"

"Well, if I knew, I wouldn't be nervous, would I?"

"Butch, there's fuck all to it. I hope yer not stoned when yer tryin' to learn."

"Hardly, Brock would go out of his mind if he knew I had a draw 'fore goin' drivin'."

When Rory finished business with his dealer outside The Hayloft on Friday, he put two pounds of weed in his trunk, went inside the club, looking for Boyle. When he walked in, Boyle was playing pool. When the game was over, Rory gave him a nod, they headed to the can. Rory checked the stalls to make sure they were empty.

"What about it, ya' interested in sellin' a little gear for me?"

"Sure, why not? I told ya if I was here taday, I would be interested. I spends half a day every day in a club or bar, so I may as well make a few bucks while I'm at it."

"Okay, this is how we're goin' to be doin' this. I fronts ya on a Friday; the followin' Friday, ya pays me the full amount of the front. And if ya do, I gives ya another front. If ya don't got all me money every Friday, ya don't get anythin' more."

"Yup."

"Okay, here's two ounces. Next Friday, ya owe me two hundred and ten bucks. Understand? Oh, and give decent counts!"

"Okay."

"You play the game. Both of us can make some big money in this area."

Rory saw Gensom when he entered the Swamp. They did their business in the washroom, and he was back on the road in ten minutes. Taking his time going up the Shore. He had to be extra careful in Bay Bulls and Witless Bay. Holyrood RCMP cruised these communities, even though it wasn't their jurisdiction. Once he got past Mobile, he could relax a little. There was no sign of Mugford at Hayden's in Cape Broyle. Rory made a quick run to the hotel to see if he was there, no sign of him. He cruised around the harbour he found Mugford jogging on Beaver Pond Road. Mugford jumped in, Rory gave him a run home, they conducted their business.

Rory was relieved when he got home. The Friday afternoon dope run always stressed him out. He had twenty bags of weed left, he was hoping Perry would take fifteen bags. He'd keep five bags for himself and Butch.

Rory arrived in Trepassey at 3:30 the following afternoon. When he hauled into the driveway at Perry's house, Perry was sitting on the doorstep, having a smoke, looking grim. Perry got up, strolled over to the car, and got in.

"Perry, what's with the long face?"

"The girlfriend."

"Oh, for fuck sake, Perry, don't tell me yer still poutin' over her."

"I gotta admit it, I'm heartbroken."

"Perry, get over it, ya foolish bastard. There's a thousand chicks on the Shore waitin' to get pounded, and yer two weeks goin' around like a zombie over one of 'em. Get ahold of yerself. I'm sure she's not frettin' over you."

"I can't. It's so fuckin' hard."

"Ya'll be all right this time next year." Rory laughed. "Anyways, I got fifteen ounces. Ya want 'em?"

"Yes. I'm out of gear since Thursday night."

"Listen, my supplier wants me to start takin' a larger supply. Five or ten pounds, rather than shaggin' around with a pound or two every week."

"Seriously?"

"Yes, but there's two problems. One, gettin' it up the Shore without gettin' busted? And two, where would I store it?"

"Well, I could store it for ya."

"Where?"

"Bury it out on Cape Race Road. No one ever touched my stash since I put it there. And like I told ya 'fore, there's never anyone out there."

"Sounds like the perfect spot."

"Only the lighthouse keepers are ever on the move on that road on a regular basis. Stroll into the woods five or six hundred feet and bury it behind some tuckamores."

"Sure, tuckamores are all that's out there. A fully-grown vertical tree on Cape Race Road is rare."

"How much will ya'll want stored up here?"

"I dunno. Could be five or ten pounds or more."

"Ya serious?"

"Yes. Like I said, my supplier, is gettin' bigger into it. He doesn't wanna' be havin' to meet me once a week with a pound or two of weed and hash. He told me he just as soon give me the mother load and collect once a month. So, when I gets a big supply, I'll need a safe and secure place to stash it."

"Leave it to me. Next time yer up, I'll have a spot scoped out for it. Might use the same spot."

"Sounds good."

They drove around, did their business, and went back to Perry's.

"Perry, I got to head back down the Shore now. I'll try to get back up next weekend. Yer on days next week at the plant?"

"Yes, ya'll only get me on Sunday. Or after supper durin' the week."

"Okay, I might see ya next Sunday. And give yerself a shake over the ex. In the long haul, she'll only be a number. Women, they're all only a number. Lots of numbers yet left to bang."

"See ya later, Rory."

As Rory cruised down the Shore, he gave serious thought to Perry's suggestion to bury a big supply on Cape Race Road. A desolate and isolated spot. He needed a second spot to stash his supply, somewhere in the Goulds, the lower end of the Goulds around The Hayloft. Too many subdivisions going up on the other end and anywhere around a farm was out of the question. Farmers watched their fields like hawks. The only time farmers left you alone on their property was in the fall, when they figured you were picking mushrooms. He'd look for a spot-on Shoal Bay Road, down past the last house.

Butch pranced into Rory's house around eight, looking for a run to Tinkers Lounge in Tors Cove. On the way down the Shore, Rory filled him in on his idea of stashing drugs on Cape Race Road and maybe Shoal Bay Road in the Goulds. Butch couldn't understand why Rory had to bury the drugs. Rory had to explain it to him a second time. Most stuff had to be explained to Butch a second and sometimes a third time before he got it.

Butch agreed with him. He always let Rory make the hard decisions most times. But with the car, it was different. Rory's decisions on the car involved his money. Butch would not hold his tongue when his money was being spent on the car. Shit would hit the fan in two weeks when Butch got his license. Rory dreaded the thought of it, he had to suck it up. He knew there'd be no car without both signatures.

Rory dropped Butch at Tinkers.

"Are ya comin' in for a beer, Rory?"

"Not likely, with twinkle toes Brian Finn playin'. And Butch, wrap it if ya find a chick."

"Wrap what?"

"Yer fuckin' pinky finger, ya stupid prick. Yer fuckin' dick . . .

wear a rubber."

"Rory, where the fuck am I gettin' a safe this hour of the night?"

"I got no idea. But with all the chicks ya bang, I wouldn't leave home without 'em."

"Condoms, I might have used 'em a handful of times in me life. Besides, most women like the raw meat!"

"Well, ya should be usin' 'em all the time. The fuckin' thing is goin' to fall off ya if ya don't change yer habits. We could have little Butches runnin' around the Shore in fifteen years!"

Butch laughed.

"Rory, I'm not changin' a fuckin' thing. I'm here for a good time, not a long time. Ya wouldn't happen to have a buddy in Tors Cove?"

"Why?"

"In case I can't get a run home."

"Sorry, don't know many in Tors Cove. I'm sure there are people here tanight from up the Shore. It's pay week at the fish plant in Trepassey, sure to be a couple of carloads of fellas here from Trepassey. If ya sees anybody walkin' away from the bar with a tray of beer, guaranteed they're from Trepassey. They don't mess around when it comes to drinkin'. Get out. I'm goin' home to finish a book I started last night."

"Okay, see ya tamorrow.

"Sure, if some old fella doesn't kick the shit out of ya for bangin' his daughter."

CHAPTER NINETEEN

Rory saw Butch on the shoulder of the road, hauled in and picked him up. Butch had a smile on his face, you couldn't wipe off with a baseball bat.

"I guess ya passed the road test."

"I did. Campbell said I was a decent driver. He told me not to be so heavy with the right foot. We gotta celebrate. Let's go to the Goulds or town for a feed."

"Now or later?"

"Now. And I wants to drive."

Rory opened the driver's side door. If he didn't let Butch drive, he would never hear the end of it. Within minutes of Butch driving, Rory told him not to be driving with both feet. Butch told Rory to go fuck himself, called him a prick for correcting him. Said," I asked you to teach me to drive, and ya wouldn't; now that I knows how to drive, ya wants to tell me what to do. That boat sailed, so fuck off!"

The boys went to Spring Gardens, a Chinese Restaurant on Water Street, west of Woolworth's Department Store. After they ate, they headed to the Eager Beaver to have a look at the strippers. Rory knew Butch would be like a child on Christmas morning, seeing he was a male whore. Rory watched Butch like a hawk. With a few beer in him, he was reckless enough to grope the strippers. The bouncers at the Beaver were some of the toughest in the city. Rory finally got Butch out of the Beaver, three parts drunk, in one piece. They headed for home.

Friday rolled around, Rory and Butch headed to The Hayloft for a meeting with his dealer. His dealer was sitting in his burgundy '78 Volare with a T-bar roof. Rory got in; Butch strutted inside to hustle anyone who could hold a cue.

The dealer had two and a half pounds of weed plus four ounces of hash. He told Rory he'd be out of the province for the next ten or twelve days, and when he saw him in two weeks, he would be giving him five or ten pounds. Enough to do him for a month or more.

"Ya don't mind frontin' me that much?"

"I've been dealing with you for a while now, and I trust you. You're one of the best people to front too."

Rory liked the compliment. He felt even better about getting enough weed and hash for a month instead of having to drive to the Goulds every Friday. Rory put the drugs in the trunk, went inside to get his sidekick, who was hustling the young female bartender. Not actually hustling, he never took money from women. Playing them was reward enough for Butch. Butch was staring more at her cleavage than at the balls on the table. What a starn she had on her; her jeans were as tight as they could be. If she farted, she'd rip the arse out of them.

The boys left The Hayloft and headed for the Soundbone, where Boyle spent most of his time, doing the same as Butch did most days, hustling pool. Butch told Rory he wanted to see how good a shooter Boyle was; Rory told him there was no time to stay put. This made Butch sulk like a child, he stayed in the car. Rory found Boyle; he gave him his cut of the drugs.

"Next stop, the Swamp in Bay Bulls," Rory said when he got back in the car. Butch was still sulking, Rory didn't mind—at least he didn't have to listen to him go on about everything and nothing on the way to Bay Bulls.

When Rory entered the Swamp, Gensom was sitting by the door, chatting with an old fisherman with a black stocking cap that looked like a dried-out sod. It looked like it hadn't been washed in years. The Swamp was always half full of fishermen, who could get tangly occasionally, especially on the day each spring when cod trap berths were drawn next door at the parish hall. The RCMP were usually called to the Swamp that day to break up a fight or two.

Rory was finished with Gensom in under ten minutes. The boys stopped at the two drinking holes in Cape Broyle, there was no sign of Mugford. Rory wasn't worried; he figured he'd see Mugford over the weekend.

The next day, the boys hit the road for Trepassey. Butch was tickled pink, he was driving. Rory warned him to take his time. It was snowing a little, enough to make the road greasy.

When they walked into Outer Limits, Perry was playing Pac-Man. Rory motioned him into the can, where they conducted their business. Rory explained that his dealer was going out of town, so he gave Perry enough for two weeks.

"Perry, have ya scoped out a spot-on Cape Race Road where we can bury some gear?"

"I was out there a few days ago. I may have found a decent spot. About two miles out on the left, there's a fairly big mound with many tuckamores around it. All we gotta do is leave a grubber and shovel for buryin' 'em and diggin' 'em up."

"Sounds good. I'll check out the spot next time I'm up."

The winter passed slowly, mild with little snow, on the morning of February 15, 1982. Rory barged into Butch's house, telling him to get up and turn on the TV. A semi-submersible oil rig, the Ocean Ranger, had capsized overnight and sunk in a fierce storm off the coast of Newfoundland, with the loss of eighty-four men. Of the eighty-four men onboard twenty- two bodies were recovered. Amongst the crew were fifty-six Newfoundlanders.

"Butch, I often thought about goin' to work offshore, I guess that's not goin' to happen now."

"Sure, Rory, any job on the water in the North Atlantic is dangerous. How many men have been lost overboard on the draggers goin' out of Trepassey?"

"A few."

A few months later, in April, Rory asked Butch if he was going to the Goulds with him the following day for his drug pick-up.

"Sure, if I can drive."

"Okay, but only on the way out."

Rory went to his old man's stable before they left for the Goulds and got a grubber. His supplier was giving him bigger and bigger quantities every month. He had the Shore covered as the main supplier of drugs. He had been putting off burying drugs and cash. He figured it was time to bury it. So, finding a location somewhere in the Goulds was his goal today. On the way to the Goulds, two moose crossed the road as they passed Courtney's Farm, slightly north of Middle Pond Hollow. Luckily, they were going at a decent speed to avoid a collision with the animals. When they arrived at The Hayloft, Butch got out; Rory told him he'd be back in ten or fifteen minutes. Rory made his way to Mary Brown's, across the road from Betty's Drive-in. Two minutes later, his dealer, Simon Littlejohn, hauled up alongside the Charger. Littlejohn was originally from Nova Scotia. A former motorcycle member of the 13th tribe in Halifax, he was covered in tattoos from his belt line to his neck. He looked like a rough and tough fellow, not someone to mess with. He handed Rory a black gym bag through the window. Rory was thrown off.

"Okay, Rory, here's the deal. There's fifteen pounds of weed and a pound of Afghani hash. I'm going out of the province for six to eight weeks."

"For what?"

"Long story haven't got time to get into it. That should keep you goin' while I'm away."

"What's the price on this amount?"

"Since you're takin' so much in one lump. The price for the weed is ninety bucks an ounce. The hash is one hundred an ounce."

Rory handed over a large wad of cash.

"You have scales?"

"Yes."

"Well, weigh it when you get a chance. I guarantee you there's an ounce in every bag. The hash is two eight-ounce blocks. It's real soft, be careful handling it. I got to run. Take care."

The dealer hauled out of the parking lot and went left, heading towards town.

Butch stood at the bar; he went over in his head how his big plan would go. He needed to do a dry run first. He had to factor in the traffic on the main road.

When Rory went into the club to get Butch, he was standing at the bar with his back to the two pool games going on. He must have something on his mind or be upset about something. Whenever Butch had something going on in his head, he got reserved.

"What the fuck is on the go, Butch?"

"Why?"

"You standin' at the bar with pool goin' on behind yer back. There's somethin' up."

"No."

"Now, Butch, ya knows who yer talkin' to. I've known you since we were nose pickers. I knows ya better than ya knows yerself. Ya goin' to tell me?"

"Nothin' on the go. I didn't sleep well last night. Kind of strung out."

"Okay, I'll leave it at that. Butch, I knows there's somethin' up. When these beers are gone, we're goin' to the bottom of Shoal Bay Road."

"For what?"

Rory leaned into Butch. "My man gave me fifteen pounds of weed and a pound of hash."

"So, what're ya doin' on Shoal Bay Road?"

"I'm goin' to bury some of it."

"Ya serious?"

"Yes, I'll bury three pounds of weed and half the hash and give my three men a half-pound of weed each and give Perry ten pounds and half the hash to bury."

"Why are ya givin' Perry so much?"

"For a number of reasons. Having a stash in Trepassey is safer than goin' to and from a stash in the Goulds. A lot less heat in Trepassey than there is in the Goulds."

"Ya trust Perry enough to give 'im that much?"

"Yes, why not? He hasn't messed me around since we hooked up."

"I guess yer right. He does seem to be an up-and-up fella."

As they passed the last houses on Shoal Bay Road, Butch told Rory he had to take a crap.

"Butch, we just left the club."

"I can't help it; a cramp just came over me."

"Okay, no sweat. I'll get the grubber, the garbage bag and the gear out of the trunk, I'll go a few hundred feet down the road, I'll bury it on the left side of the road. Take the car and go somewhere for a crap. Remember what's in the trunk. Take yer fuckin' time! Pass me the orange hunters' tape in the glove compartment."

Rory went five or six hundred feet down the road and into the woods on the left. He eyed a large birch tree, the only one among hundreds of mature coniferous trees. Underneath the birch tree sat a flat rock, measuring roughly eighteen inches in diameter, two inches thick. Rory moved it aside and dug. Digging for ten minutes until he reached a depth he figured was deep enough. He wrapped the drugs in an industrial-grade clear garbage bag, buried it under a foot of soil. He threw the excess soil into the woods and put the rock back in place.

He cut off twelve six-inch strips of flagging tape with his pocketknife. He tied two pieces close together on the birch tree, walked down the road towards the ocean, tying a piece of tape on a tree every sixty or seventy feet. Which would confuse people. If he tied tape only on the tree his weed was buried under, someone could figure out the tree was marked for a reason and poke around. People would think they were left here from the fall or winter by putting tape on multiple trees where people had marked their rabbit snares.

He walked back to where he buried the stash, went into the

woods on the other side of the road. Found a small gully with a foot of water in it and placed the grubber in it. He'd need it when he came back to get some of his stash.

While Rory was busy working up a sweat, Butch went to Bidgood's Plaza, pulled into the parking lot in front of Elizabeth Drugs, next to Scotiabank. He went into the drugstore, bought a can of Diet Coke and returned to the car. He figured he took four to five minutes to get out of the car, casually walk into the drug store, buy the soda, and get back to the car. He wished he had a watch to time himself.

When he passed The Hayloft, he figured he was four and a half minutes from Bidgood's. He mentally kept timing himself until he was at the bottom of Shoal Bay Road. It was about ten minutes since he'd left Bidgood's. Note to self, approximately fifteen minutes for a trial run.

Butch parked, got out and walked down the washed-out road. He noticed the orange flagging tape on the trees, but there was no sign of Rory.

"Rory, where the fuck are ya?"

Rory ran out of the woods with his jeans half hanging off him. "Keep yer voice down!"

"What are ya at?"

"Havin' a crap, if ya must know, could ya shout any louder? That's all I needs is for people to see us here. They'll figure there's somethin' on the go."

"Why?"

"Butch, do we look like hunters? No. And ya don't hunt anythin' in Newfoundland in the spring of the year. It's too early to pick berries. We ain't hikers. You screamin' yer head off like a retard, people will know we're up to no good."

"What's with all the tape?"

"I'll tell ya on the way up the Shore."

As they drove around Big Pond, Rory tried to explain to Butch why he put tape on ten or twelve trees. Butch figured if you marked your hiding spot, everything would be okay.

"Butch, someone would figure it out. They're not all like you."

"Anyway, are ya goin' to drop some gear to Gensom and Mugford on the way up the Shore?"

"No, they got enough. I'm goin' straight to Trepassey to see Perry. I wants all this buried as soon as possible. I'm not goin' drivin' around with it in the car. And there's no way I'm stashin' all of it in the ol' man's barn. I'll get ahold of Perry and bury most of it on Cape Race Road. Are ya comin' with me?"

"Nah, drop me at McCarthy's."

When Rory got home, he called Perry. Rory made his fastest run ever to Trepassey, fueled by his nervousness about having so much gear aboard. Driving fast on the barrens was not a problem; it was rare to see an RCMP cruiser on the barrens. He found Perry at Harbour View. Rory ordered two beers, he strolled over to the pool table, Perry was shooting a game. He gave him a beer and said in a low voice, "We needs to go for a run after yer finished shootin' pool."

Twenty minutes later, they left the club, Rory told Perry how much he had gotten from his supplier, and he was giving him ten pounds of weed and a quarter pound of hash.

"Rory, what am I goin' to do with that much?"

"Perry, I had no other choice than to take it. My dealer is goin' out of town for six to eight weeks."

"Okay, I'll take it. We're goin' to have to go out on Cape Race Road right now and bury it." The boys made their way to the highway and headed for the Cove. Darkness was upon them as they drove out the dirt road. They had driven about two miles when they crested a small hill; Perry motioned to Rory to slow down and haul over on the shoulder.

They got out, Rory took his flashlight, he got a second grubber he had bought, and a shovel out of the trunk.

"Why aren't ya takin' the drugs, Rory?"

"I wants to check out the spot first, if it looks good, we'll dig a hole. I'll come back for the drugs."

They went a short distance over the barrens. Perry found the spot he had scoped out; Rory agreed the spot looked good. They took turns digging for ten minutes; Rory told Perry he was going back to the car for the drugs. When Rory got back, Perry was sitting beside a large hole, breathing heavily.

"Sweet divine Jesus, Perry, what are ya diggin'?"

"Rory, we're buryin' ten pounds, not ten ounces."

Before Rory wrapped the black gym bag in industrial plastic bags, he unzipped it and handed Perry eight bags. When they finished burying the gear, Perry put a piece of moss over the tamped down soil.

"Perry, I'm goin' to put a piece of orange flaggin' tape on a few of the tuckamores closest to the spot."

"Why?"

"To make sure you or I can find it when we comes lookin' for it."

"There's no need for tape, I knows this area like the back of me hand. Been huntin' partridge out here since I was young."

"Yes, but I dunno it."

They walked a couple of hundred feet away from the stash, hid the grubber and shovel among some tuckamores.

On the drive back to Trepassey, Rory told Perry to make one trip a week to the stash. Any more than once a week will only bring attention to what he was up to. He told Perry to bury the cash he collects every week.

"Won't it get damp?"

"Do ya got an old round or square tin cans, they put fruit cakes in at Christmas?"

"I'm sure there's a few at the house. Me mother bakes fruit and cherry cakes every Christmas."

"Well, put the money in one. Wrap it in a plastic bag 'fore ya put it in the tin can. Also, wrap the can in a plastic bag. When we dug the hole, the soil was reasonably dry. Perry, make sure ya tells no one about where our stash is."

"Well, Larry will know. He's the only way I'll get back and forth to it."

"Okay, but no one else. I might not be back here for two or three weeks. Be careful with both the drugs and the money. If anyone wants an ounce, sell it to 'em. We don't gotta worry about dimes anymore with the amount we got."

"What's an ounce worth?"

"An ounce is one twenty, one twenty-five.

"Sounds good."

"And if ya gets busted, ya don't tell the cops who yer supplier is. Drug dealers have the same motto as the mafia. 'Omerta,' a strict code of silence."

"I'd hardly rat ya out."

"That's what I wants to hear, be careful. If ya needs me, call the house, don't mention drugs on the phone. I'll know if ya calls, which means ya wants to see me. Ask if I'm sellin' me car, say someone told ya I might be. I'll know to dart up to see ya. Ya never know who might be listenin'."

"Okay. It all sounds good."

CHAPTER TWENTY

The following Thursday, Rory and Butch went to town to get a feed and grab a few bags of weed from the Shoal Bay Road stash on the way back. The boys parked on the waterfront, they went to the Captain's Cabin at Bowring's for fish and chips with dressing and gravy. After they ate, they walked around downtown.

Going back through the Goulds, Rory hung a left and headed down Shoal Bay Road.

"How long are ya goin' to be, Rory?"

"Fifteen, twenty minutes. Why ya askin'?"

"I gotta pain in the guts and needs to have a dump."

"Go in the woods and have a crap."

"Like the fuck. If I'm shittin', it will be on a toilet, not crouched down with ants tryin' to climb up me arsehole or bite me balls."

"Yer so delicate."

"Shag off. I'm dartin' to The Hayloft. I won't be long."

"Ya better not be too long. I'm not waitin' all day on ya."

"I won't be long, I promise."

Butch looked in the rear-view mirror and watched Rory head down the road. Butch passed The Hayloft and headed north through the Goulds.

As he got closer to Bidgood's Plaza, his hands started to sweat. This is it, go through with his big plan today or not at all. He had the note for the teller, which said: "I got a gun, fill this bag, or I will use it." The bag was a white pillowcase. He had a black wig, fake mustache, sunglasses, a baseball cap, and a pair of black leather gloves. The items Butch was using for his disguise, someone had left at his house from mummering at Christmas. He pictured himself walking up to the teller, passing her his hand-printed note.

This was the plan, which he had been going over and over in his head for some time. And now he was only minutes from executing it. He was shaking like a leaf, and he wasn't even in the parking lot. Not a good sign, being this nervous. As he pulled into the parking lot, he made sure his car had access to the exit lane going up the center of it. He parked a fair distance from the bank, leaned back and gave the rear seat a jerk from the bottom, which loosened it from the frame. The seat fell forward; Butch leaned back and pulled the pillowcase holding the gear he needed into the front seat. Wiping sweat from his brow with his sleeve, he put on his disguise. He left the keys in the ignition, with the driver's window down. As he walked to the door of the bank, he kept saying to himself, "I can do this . . . I can do this."

When Butch got inside the bank, there was no line-up. Three tellers sat at their windows. Two customers were being served. Butch went straight to the free teller, whose head was down over the money she was counting. The fine blonde hair on her fringe bounced with each upward flick of her thumb as she counted the money.

Butch leaned on the counter, shoving the note in the tellers face. She jolted and leaned back, startled. Then, as though recalling her training, she slowly raised her hand, taking the note. He could feel her breath and see the effort she was making to keep cool. She raised her eyes and scanned his face; she scooped up the paper currency she had been counting and dropped it into the pillowcase. Butch couldn't see her raise her right leg, so her knee hit the alarm button mounted on the side of the drawer. It would alert the police a robbery was in progress.

Butch was trembling; the tellers calmness unnerved him. She meticulously scooped up fives, tens, twenties, fifties and hundred-dollar bills from a second drawer below the first; she laid each bundle in the pillowcase. Butch tried to make eye contact, she looked only at the till and the pillowcase.

Sweat roll down his forehead and temples. The hands-on the

clock behind the counter had only moved a minute or two, but it seemed like an hour. He sensed a teller to the right was looking at them. Did the man she was serving notice what was going on? He hoped not.

The teller pushed the pillowcase forward. He took it, turned and walked to the door, fighting the urge not to run. When he was outside, fresh air hit his face, it was relieving. The hard part was over. All he had to do now was keep his cool and drive out of the parking lot in a routine and sensible fashion.

When he got in the car, he removed his disguise; he caught sight of his face in the rear-view mirror, it was shining with sweat. He wiped it with his sleeve, started the car, put it in drive and made his way out of the parking lot. Luckily, there were no cars in front of him. He put on his indicator and turned left. So far, so good.

As he passed Keith Drive, a Royal Canadian Mounted Police cruiser with its lights and siren on pulled onto the street heading toward Bidgood's Plaza. Sweat suddenly trickled down his armpits, his mind raced. How could the cops be on to the robbery so fast? He tried to keep the speed limit; his foot was itching to step hard on the gas pedal. As he went over Ryan's Bridge, he met another RCMP cruiser. By this time, Butch was ready to piss himself. He watched the cruiser pulling further away from him in the rear-view mirror. Then suddenly, its brake lights came on and stayed on. Something was up. The cruiser hit the shoulder, did a U-turn and started travelling in his direction. It had to mean; someone had flagged his car to the cops.

He pressed the pedal to the floor and prayed out loud. "Hail, Mary, full of fuckin' grace." He knew the Charger was fast; he knew cop cars had plenty of horsepower under the hood too. Butch had never driven fast before; He gunned the 383 engine and continued to pray, taking the turn onto Shoal Bay Road almost on two wheels. He could hear the siren behind him. He was sure he could get to the end of the road before the police got him, but what was he going to do when he got there?

Butch came to a screeching halt on the gravel road, raising dust into the air. He jumped out of the car and ran. The sound of the siren was getting louder with every step he took. He knew Rory was roughly five or six hundred feet down the road from where they usually parked the car. Rory was standing in the middle of the road.

"Run, Rory, run!"

"Run?"

"The police are chasin' me."

"Why?"

Butch tried to reply, he couldn't speak. He had never been in good physical shape, and being a heavy smoker didn't help his running any.

Rory could hear the siren, he figured he should run. He figured Butch had been caught with a little weed on him and had made a run for it. Or maybe they had tried to pull him over for speeding. Butch was stupid enough to try to outrun the cops over a speeding ticket.

Rory caught up with Butch about a quarter-mile along the road, the two slowed down. They could still hear sirens; the sound got fainter the further away they went down Shoal Bay Road.

"Butch, what's on the go?"

"Ya don't wanna' know."

"I do wanna' know, and I wants to know now."

"Let's go a little farther, and I'll tell ya."

CHAPTER TWENTY-ONE

They ran beside each other for four or five minutes. Rory was getting more and more pissed. Here he was, running away from the police and not knowing why. What had Butch done now? He couldn't hear the siren any longer, he hauled on Butch's arm and motioned towards the woods. They went in a little through the trees, both sat on a fallen tree to catch their breath.

"Okay, Butch, spit it out."

"Rory, yer goin' to kill me."

"Why, Butch, why am I goin' to kill ya? Fuckin' tell me, or I will kill ya."

"I robbed the bank."

"Ya what?"

"I robbed the bank up at Bidgood's."

"What?"

"I did an armed robbery at the bank up to Bidgood's."

"You stupid, cocksucker. Ya robbed a bank?"

"Yes."

"Why?"

"I dunno. I wanted lots of money. I have been plannin' it for a while."

"Ya wanted lots of money, but ya didn't need it! I gotta mind to beat ya to death with a limb off one of these spruce trees. Fuck, fuck, fuck, ya stupid cocksuckin' fuckin' bastard. Ya got me involved with a fuckin' armed bank robbery. Not only that, but the cops will get me stash."

"Why?"

"Well, when I heard the commotion, I went out to the road

to see what was on the go. I left the weed and hash spread out on one of the plastic bags. The cops will get it."

"How?"

"Well, Butch, it's not rocket science. There'll be more than one police dog on Shoal Bay Road in the next half hour lookin' for ya. And police dogs can smell weed in a farmers field on old Bay Bulls Road from Shoal Bay Road. And once they runs the plates on the car and finds it's registered in my name, they'll have dogs at me ol' man's house and barn, sometime taday or tamorrow. There's three pounds stashed in the beams in the barn. And I'm with ya. So, I'll end up bein' an accessory to arm robbery."

"How will ya, Rory?"

"When they catch ya, which they will taday, tamorrow, next week, whenever, my prints will be all over the plastic bags the drugs are in. They won't even need to do a fingerprint analysis on the hash. The hash is soft, me fingerprints will jump out at 'em like a picture on a postcard. Just as well, I had me name carved into it."

"Rory, what're we goin' to do?"

"You tell me, Butch, yer the idiot who got us in this fuckin' mess."

"I'm sorry. I panicked."

"Fuck off, Butch, sorry gotta thousand different meanings. Ya should've had a better plan than to bring the cops to where I had me stash. Not only are you and most likely me gettin' charged with armed robbery and drug traffickin', but now I owe my supplier for drugs, I never gotta sell 'cause of yer stupidity."

"Butch, where's the money ya stole from the bank?"

"I left it in the car. I forgot it; I was so flustered with the cops chasin' me."

"Butch, tell me ya never used a gun."

"No, I said in the note I had one."

Rory let his head drop to his chest. "That's the same as if ya did have a gun. Threatenin' ya've a weapon is considered armed robbery. Butch, yer dense!"

"Okay, Rory, yer the smart one. What are we goin' to do?"

"Butch, ya got me addled, this is beyond stupid. Albert Einstein 'imself couldn't think of a way to fix it. The first thin' is, we gotta keep movin'. Those dogs will be on us like a beagle on a rabbit in no time if we don't keep movin'. Let's jog."

Twenty minutes after they jogged, they reached the ocean. There was a walking path going in both directions along the coast. They headed south toward Bay Bulls. Within ten minutes, they came to Queens River.

"Stop, Butch. Look at the river, sure that's a gift."

"What, Rory?"

"I read a crime story one time about two prisoners who escaped prison. They walked a ways in a river, so the bloodhounds couldn't follow their scent."

Butch said he wasn't fussy about getting wet. Rory waded out into the cold water and told Butch to get in the river behind him. Butch complained. Rory let out an awful roar.

"Move now, or I'll drag ya into this river by the head of yer hair and drown ya! Move now!"

Butch complied.

They had walked roughly five hundred feet up the river before getting out on the other side. The river was roughly two and a half feet deep; it was bitter cold. Rory wished he had taken off his sneakers. Their sneakers kept them safe from cutting their feet on the sharp-edged rocks in the river. Both were soaked up to the crotch of their jeans.

"I wants to take off me jeans and squeeze the water out of 'em, Rory."

"I'm not babysittin' ya. I got ten pounds of weed and a chunk of hash buried on Cape Race Road. I gotta get to it 'fore we turns ourselves into the cops. It's bad enough losin' what I had on Shoal Bay Road. When Perry hears about the armed robbery and hears we're on the run, he'll put two and two together. He'll be thinkin' I'm comin' for what's stashed on Cape Race Road. We're not gettin' bail after we turns ourselves in, not with a charge of armed robbery against us."

Rory's mind was racing full tilt. If he didn't get to the stash sooner rather than later, he would never get it or its worth. Armed robbery carried a lengthy sentence in Canada. Even if he got away with the armed robbery, he would be charged with a drug offence, most likely trafficking. They were guaranteed a federal sentence of at least two years plus a day for the armed robbery and maybe another two years served consecutively for the drugs. Rory trusted Perry, but there was no way Perry would hang on to ten pounds of weed and the hash until he was released from prison. And he wouldn't be hanging on to the money he would get from selling it either.

Rory was getting colder by the minute. At least there wasn't any underbrush to make walking even harder on them. Strange to have such a clear path out this way. Then it hit him; he remembered Butch's story about the hikers.

"Hurry the fuck up, Butch!"

Butch caught up with Rory, cursing under his breath. "Remember the people ya met at Mike's Hotel?"

"Which people?"

"The fuckin' hikers."

"Yeah, I remembers 'em."

"Well, we're walkin' on the trail they're cuttin'."

Butch looked down at the ground. "Jesus, Rory, we are! How'd ya figure that out?"

"Well, they said they were hopin' to build a hikin' trail from Fort Amherst to Cape Race. This is it."

"Rory, yer some smart."

"No, Butch, I use the brain the good Lord gave me."

"So, this is it, the trail they told me about."

"I remembers ya tellin' me and Brock at the Pink Poodle, they had cut the trail into the place they called the Spout."

"Yes, I did hear about a sea geyser called the Spout on the trail between Shoal Bay Road and Bay Bulls. I don't remember if it was the hikers who mentioned it."

"Well, I guess we're goin' to see the Spout either 'fore dark or early in the mornin'."

"Ya serious, Rory?"

"Well, yes, unless ya wants to walk back up Shoal Bay Road and turn yerself in. I'm not. I gotta get to Portugal Cove South and get what's buried there. If I don't get it in a hurry, it will be moved and sold, and I'll never see a cent for it. I'll also have my supplier houndin' me for years 'til I have 'im paid back."

"Didn't you say ya could trust Perry?"

"Yes, I did. I'm sure either taday, tamorrow or the day after, 'im along everyone else on the Shore will know we're on the run due to yer stupidity. He'll know we'll get caught eventually. He'll know he won't see me for a few years. So, he'll sell all me drugs and party with the money. Sure, why wouldn't he? I'd probably do the same thing if the boot was on the other foot. He'll be like everyone else, thinkin' we're both goin' to a federal prison for years."

"Rory, I'm startin' to get cold."

"I hope ya freeze to death, ya dense bastard. Whatever got in yer head to rob a bank?"

"Well, it's like this, Rory. The pogey don't cut it, and I smokes more of the weed ya gives me than I sells. I wants a few luxuries in life."

"Like what?"

"Well, one, we coulda' went to Toronah."

"Yer tellin' me, ya had to rob a bank to go to Toronah."

"Not only Toronah. I wants me own car."

"Sure, that woulda happened. When we had ours paid off, I'm sure one of us woulda bought the other out. And the other person could have bought 'emselves a car."

"Yes, Rory, yer right. But I didn't wanna' wait that long."

"Well, do ya know how long it will be 'fore ya can get a car now? Anywhere from two to five years."

"Why?"

"I'm not one hundred percent sure. I believe armed robbery in Canada is a federal sentence of at least two years plus a day. That's the least we'll get. Don't forget the weed and hash that's most likely in the cops' hands as we speak. We're also gettin' charged with that. And after doin' an armed robbery, we'll get no break on the drugs. We can kiss the Charger goodbye. Cops auction off cars they've impounded. They can't keep 'em forever. I believe they hold 'em for a year 'fore auctionin' 'em off. So, we'll have no car, and we will have to pay the bank loan back when we are released. If not, we'll both have bad credit for the rest of our lives. Not that good credit will be the biggest issue. We'll be pegged for life as armed robbers. Whichever way ya spin it, Butch, you and I are goin' to a federal penitentiary up on the mainland for a few years. What were ya thinkin'? Didn't ya know a fella robbed the same bank back in the summer of 1980? Got twenty-eight hundred dollars."

"Ya serious?"

"Yes, it was on August 26th, to be exact.

"They catch 'im?"

"The RCMP caught 'im a few days later. I believe he gotta away with it. They never had enough evidence to charge 'im. He fired three shots from a twenty-two rifle durin' the robbery, two shots inside and one outside that struck a window frame."

"Who told ya that?"

"I remembers readin' it in The Evening Telegram, or I saw it on the news."

"Had I known, I might have picked a different spot to rob."

"Butch, wherever ya robbed, ya were gettin' caught. It's not as easy as the movies makes it out to be. Ya never hear tell of smart people robbin' banks."

"Rory, I thought the Royal Newfoundland Constabulary took over policin' in the Goulds from the RCMP."

"The RNC takes over the first of May next year."

"How'd ya know that?"

"I'll repeat it for the hundredth time, The Evening Telegram."

"Rory, when I started runnin', I was half scared they might start shootin' at me. Explain to me what the plan is from here? What're we goin' to do? How are we gettin' to Cape Race?"

"Well, Butch, technically, it's only you on the run. I don't believe the police saw me. Anyone who knows us knows we're always together. I'm sure the police are headin' to my house as we speak since the car is registered in my name. And someone was baggin' up weed while the robbery was in progress. It won't take 'em long to put it together. I was the person baggin' the weed. Or I did the robbery, and you were baggin' the weed. They won't know 'til we're in custody. They may have the fingerprint analysis back 'fore we're in custody. If they do, it won't be hard to figure out which one of us was handlin' the drugs."

"Rory, I'll ask again, what's the plan on gettin' to Cape Race?"

"Walk!"

"Walk? Rory, it will take weeks."

"However long it takes, it has to be done. We can't hitch-hike."

"Why can't we?"

"Cause the first person who picks us up is most likely goin' to squeal on us. Butch, ya have to remember, both our faces will be all over the news by tamorrow, evenin' on both channels. And most likely in The Evening Telegram and the Daily News. The Shore will be crawlin' with cops. There'll be more cops on the Shore than in the city. There'll be roadblocks everywhere, all over the Shore."

"So, yer serious about walkin'?"

"Yes."

"Okay, we could steal a car in Bay Bulls or Witless Bay. Sure, everyone leaves their keys in the ignition."

"Everyone on the Shore will know we're on the run. There won't be a set of keys left in an ignition in any vehicle on the Shore 'til we're in custody. And I don't have time to go checkin' every unlocked car in Bay Bulls, Witless Bay or any other community."

"So, we're walkin' to Cape Race? Great idea, Rory. We might get lost and never be found."

"The Shore wouldn't be that lucky. We wouldn't be here standin' on this trail in the middle of nowhere soakin' wet and freezin' our balls off only for you. And remember, runnin' away from the problem only makes the sentence longer. The quicker we can get to the stash and turn ourselves in, the better."

"Rory, I'm sorry. I'll admit it, I dunno what I was thinkin' to get ya involved. It never went like I expected."

"Butch, it never does. Life is not like what ya see in a movie or what ya read in a book. There are consequences for yer actions. Ya can't undo what ya've done. Ya must have known all tellers have alarms under their counters to set off in the case of an armed robbery."

"I guess I knows now. I never thought of it 'fore."

"So, ya goin' to walk with me to Cape Race?"

"I guess. I got no other choice. I'm not turnin' meself in without you."

"Okay, here's the plan. I'll explain it to ya as we walk. It's gettin' cold standin' here."

As they walked, Butch kept taking deep breaths and letting them out in shaky sighs, which irritated Rory.

"Butch, we'll walk between each community durin' the day. When it gets dark, we'll duck into a community or two and try to find somethin' to eat. If we don't get food, we won't make much headway. Don't forget, I got a few buddies along the Shore. If I can find 'em, I'm sure they'll help us out. But I got to give it some serious consideration. There might be a big reward for any information leadin' to our arrest. So, findin' someone to drive us might be out of the question."

"Rory, I'm sorry for gettin' ya into this mess."

"Okay, Butch, stop sayin' it. That's all we can do now. We gotta deal with it and try to stick to a plan. We'll walk for a few hours and find a sheltered spot to lay down for the night."

"Rory, what about these wet jeans and sneakers?"

"We'll light a fire and hang 'em to dry when we finds a spot."

They walked three or four miles. Listening to the sea pound the rocks below the trail. Before it got dark, they moved back from the shoreline a fair distance and took shelter in a stand of birch trees. Rory knew if a passing boat spotted a fire this time of the year on the coast, they would know something was up. They gathered up dry wood and started a fire, keeping it small. They had been careful not to get their lighters wet in the river.

Rory figured the police had a helicopter out searching for them, even though it was dark. It could be looking for this fire, thinking they might have lit one for warmth. He cursed under his breath and spit. He had to make it to Cape Race. If he didn't, he would be years paying off his debt to his supplier. And his supplier might even charge him more than the price of the drugs if he had to wait years to be paid back.

They dried their jeans and their sneakers as best they could. Rory used his pocketknife to make a small lean-to with spruce boughs. Around eight, with their clothes half-dried, they crawled into the lean-to and lay down on boughs. Rory knew it would be a long cold night. He couldn't get to sleep. The ground was like cement, even with branches as a makeshift bed, and it was damp. Spring weather in Newfoundland was not camping weather, especially without proper camping equipment.

Rory contemplated the situation. He was determined to keep his cool. Taking his frustrations and anger out on Butch would change nothing, wouldn't make the trip any shorter or easier. Bad company was better than no company, and he might need Butch to help him get to the stash. Cape Race was a long way away.

CHAPTER TWENTY-TWO

Rory woke before Butch; he hadn't slept much. It was pitch black; he was shivering with the cold and hungry. The temperature must have been below fifty during the night. Heavy fog had rolled in overnight. It was slowly burning off; it was a typical mauzy May morning in Newfoundland.

Rory was in a spin, he was thinking he had heard a helicopter overnight, or maybe he dreamt it. He walked out to the edge of the bank and pissed into the Atlantic Ocean, wondering if he was pissing his life away. He stared at the ocean, thinking to himself, he'd always known it was only a matter of time before Butch got him in serious trouble. Well, the serious trouble was at hand and had to be dealt with.

He sat on a flat boulder, lit up a smoke, listening to the cold North Atlantic Ocean wash in over the rocks a hundred feet below, wondering how many people had walked along this trail in the past century or two. It was well beaten, most likely from people hunting sea ducks and rabbits over the years. The path had been there long before the hikers ever started working on it.

Rory knew there was only a fifty-fifty chance his stash of drugs would be there if they managed the trek. Walking from slightly north of Bay Bulls to Portugal Cove South would not be an easy task. How accurate was Butch's information on the hikers opening a trail along the coast? He knew a train had run from St. John's to Trepassey from 1913 to 1932; maybe they could find the old tracks and walk them. Perhaps they should keep to the headlands. If that didn't work, they would have no other choice but to walk the highway at night.

As Rory stared out at the ocean, he seriously contemplated turning around and walking straight to Petty Harbour by bypassing Shoal Bay Road and staying on the coast until he reached Petty Harbour. Finding Angus Boyle, Angus fished; he would most likely have access to a boat. Angus might be able to take them to Portugal Cove South. But, no, the police would most likely have the Canadian Coast Guard stopping and checking every boat that moved, heading south from St. John's and beyond. He didn't know where Angus lived or if any boats in Petty Harbour were in the water yet. The salmon fishery might be underway, usually a few weeks or a month before cod traps were set. He didn't know if Angus fished for salmon. The bottom line was he didn't know Angus well enough to know if he could trust him. Walking was their only option.

Rory was getting cold. He went back to the lean-to, put his foot in through the side, and kicked Butch in the arse, and told him to get up.

Rory wanted to be in Bay Bulls before dark. He figured when they made it to Bay Bulls, they might be able to find something to eat. It had been twenty hours since they had eaten at the Captain's Cabin at Bowring's. He was hungry. He figured Butch must be gut-foundered as well. There would be salt cod in fishing stages and sheds in Bay Bulls, dried in the fall and stored for the winter. Finding a pot wouldn't be hard. All he had to do was find a skiff. All trap skiff crews cooked up a fish stew in the morning on the way back from hauling their cod traps. The cooking gear would still be in their boats.

When Butch got up off the boughs, he had a long face and started to complain. Rory told him to shut it.

"What're we goin' to do, Rory?"

"I said, I'm walkin' to Cape Race."

"Ya serious? All the way to Cape Race—sure that's impossible!"

"Butch, it's not impossible. A fella by the name of William

Cormack walked across the southern part of Newfoundland in the fall of 1822. And in 1925, Smallwood walked eight hundred miles on the west coast of the island signin' up pulp and paper workers. When he finished that, he walked the railway lines, signing up railwaymen to a federation of labour. So, us walkin' to Cape Race is not impossible. Everythin' always seems impossible 'til it's done—either yer with me, or yer not. Remember bein' on the run is the easy part. Doin' time is the hard part."

Butch stayed quiet. "Let's start walkin'." Forty-five minutes later, as they approached the Spout, Rory said to Butch, "remember ya said ya'd love to see the Spout...well, there it is."

They passed the sea geyser known as the Spout; Butch said he wanted to check it out.

"Forget it, Butch. We're not hikers; we've wanted men on the run. And whose fault is it? If we goes down the rocks to look at it, I might stick yer head in it."

They passed the sea geyser and kept walking.

"Rory, did ya hear wolves last night? I heard wolves, I'm sure of it.".

"There are no wolves in Newfoundland. They were eradicated in the thirties."

"Well, if they weren't wolves, they must have been coyotes."

"There are no coyotes in Newfoundland either. It was all in yer head, Butch—ya were dreamin'."

"How do ya know about the wolves and the coyotes?"

"I learned it in elementary school."

"Rory, yer some smart!"

"No. I paid attention when I was in school. Butch, did ya hear a helicopter durin' the night? I thought I heard one."

"I never heard no helicopter. Guess that was yer dream." Butch chuckled.

Three hours later, they passed two sea-stacks as they made their way towards the lighthouse at Bull Head. Passing through the resettled community of Freshwater, which was abandoned during the first world war, fieldstone foundations and rock walls were still visible. They crossed the small river in Freshwater without getting wet.

When they reached the lighthouse, they pried the heavy unlocked iron door open and made their way up the stairs to the revolving light. Rory was winded by the time they reached the landing. Both were in bad physical shape, having done nothing but drink beer, smoke cigarettes and weed all winter. It was dusk. They could see the beacon of a lighthouse to the south. Which was the lighthouse at Ferryland Head.

"How many lighthouses are there on the Shore, Rory?"

"Well, Butch, there's this one, Ferryland Head Lighthouse. There's a light and foghorn at Bear Cove Point in Renews, Cape Race Lighthouse on Cape Race Road in Portugal Cove South, Powles Head Lighthouse on the north side of Trepassey. And there's Cape Pine Lighthouse close to St. Shott's, fifteen miles south of Trepassey."

"Can we spend the night here?"

"No, Butch, we gotta be on the south side of Bay Bulls 'fore mornin'."

Walking in the dark was much slower than daylight, especially on paths with rocks and wet spots. Rocks looked like puddles of water, and water looked like rocks. Rory was aiming for Bread and Cheese. After a couple of hours of hard, wet slogging in the dark, they reached several large fields called Packs Hills in Gunridge. Gunridge was resettled in the mid-50s. With most residents moving to Bread and Cheese.

"Butch, we won't be walkin' the trail at night again if we don't have to, we will if we gotta. We could've broken a leg or sprained somethin' walkin' in here from the lighthouse, had we, we'd be finished."

"What's that fence for, Rory?"

Rory veered off to the left to have a look. When he reached the fence, he could see several old white headstones.

"It's a cemetery, Butch, most likely Protestant."

Butch took off like a bat out of hell. Butch feared anything that had to do with death. He had never gone to a wake in his life. When Rory reached the pavement, Butch was sitting on the side of the road waiting for him. Rory looked at his watch: it was eleven o'clock.

"Why did ya run, Butch?"

"Ya knows why I ran. I hates the dead."

Rory laughed. "It's the livin' we gotta worry about, not the dead. Butch, we're goin' to be passin' at least a half dozen cemeteries 'fore we get to Cape Race."

"If we don't see 'em, don't tell me about 'em."

They walked up the harbour. Rory told Butch he was checking the stages on the Cliff, hoping to find some saltfish and a pot and a kettle they could take with them. As they walked through Crockwell's Turn and headed for Blacks Hollow, Rory was tempted to tell Butch a few of the folklore stories he had heard about Mrs. Queen Maloney telling of the fairies taking people from Blacks Hollow a century ago. He knew if he did, he'd be all night looking for Butch.

"Rory, if there are lights on at Brian Smiths' place, can I see if he's up? He always tells me to drop in whenever I'm down the Shore. And besides, he might have a draw."

"No, Butch, we can't let anyone see us. Who knows, he might rat us out. A draw is the last thing on my mind."

"Rory, last time I was into Brian's, he said he was gettin' an old 68 Harley Davidson Electra Glide. I'd like to see it."

"Butch, ya'll see it when ya gets out of prison, that's if he still has it. Now shut up and walk."

"Okay, can we drop in and see if Billy Moakler is still up, he might have an extra draw or two to give us."

"Not likely, hardly wakin' Alex Moakler up this hour of the night for a draw. He's one old fella I wouldn't want to piss off, a war veteran with arms on 'im like tree trunks. Now shut up and walk!"

They continued walking at a steady pace, passing the Boom Defense on their left. They passed Alley Road; Alley Road was called Pepper Alley; it was the start of the footpath into St. John's before the advent of roads. They continued over the bridge on Stanley's River and put a push on for Gatherall's Hill. There was not a pole light anywhere except for an occasional one in a private driveway.

They reached the wooden steps going from the Cliff down to the four stages, which sat peacefully in the harbour. They had made good time on the pavement; no cars had passed them. They stepped over the guardrail and went down the wooden steps leading to the stages.

"What's the octagon-shaped thing moored off the stages, Rory?"

"A cod fish farm. It's moved since the last time I saw it. It was further east from where it is now. It's almost perfectly over where the Sapphire went down."

"What are ya talkin' about?"

"The HMS Sapphire was a British ship back in 1696. She was set ablaze by her captain. The French were chasin' her; he didn't want 'em to take her for a prize. A feed of fresh cod would be nice. If we had a little boat or a canoe, we could catch fifteen or twenty pounds to take with us."

"Rory, I'm not gettin' in a little boat and certainly not in a canoe on the ocean. I'm nervous when the bathtub is over-filled."

When they reached the first stage, it was not locked. It had a strong scent of brine and tar. The smell of brine meant there was salt present, which told Rory there was most likely saltfish in the stage. The scent of tar told Rory there was most likely tar present; he could use it to make a torch if he could find a rag. Rory lit his lighter and found an old wooden barrel with wooden hoops, which looked like it pre-dated Confederation. Removing the head, it was half full of rags covered in heavy tar. He made a primitive torch, rolling one of the rags on a stick he found hanging from the wooden beams. He lit the rag; it illuminated the stage. There were a half dozen barrels, one of them had a cotton cloth and a piece of plywood over its top. Rory figured it was most likely the one with the salted cod. He lifted the plywood, and as he suspected, the barrel was three parts full of large split salted codfish. Now all they needed was a pot to boil it in. He told Butch to stay put, he made his way to the second stage.

There was a trap skiff in it. Rory grabbed the gunwale and hauled himself into the boat. Sure enough, in the cuddy, he found a black cast-iron pot, a small flat-bottomed tin kettle with a long narrow bib on it, two brown one-gallon molasses jugs, two plastic mugs and enough splits for two or three boil-ups. He rooted around and found five small potatoes, a little spongy; beggars couldn't be choosers.

Further searching turned up two large onions, a well-filed Dexter boning knife, a few plastic spoons. They had everything they needed for a boil-up. He checked the other stages. They were padlocked; he contemplated breaking the locks. There was no need as they had everything they would need for the journey.

He made his way back to the first stage; with all he had found. Rory told Butch about what he had found. "Butch, we got enough food and gear to get us down the Shore."

"Fuckin' excellent, Rory!"

"There's a spring across the road from the fish plant, on the right-hand side of the road as ya head towards the Catholic Church, in Cutty's Bottom. We'll fill the molasses jugs and have a boil up in an hour or two. I'm fuckin' starvin', I'm sure ya are too."

They made their way back up the steep steps. Carrying what they had found in two brin bags, that they also found. The spring was only a short walk from the top of the Cliff. People working at Bay Bulls Sea Products used this spring daily.

As they stepped off the pavement, they could hear water running. Rory walked towards the sound of the running water. He lit his lighter and saw a black one-inch plastic pipe sticking out of the bank.

"Butch, keep yer eyes open for cars comin' or goin'." Rory squatted down and filled the two one-gallon jugs.

"Where we goin' to boil up, Rory?"

"On the other side of the harbour."

"Jesus, Rory, sure that's another hours walk."

"Well, Butch, it's like this: we can't be in Bay Bulls come daylight."

"Sure, why don't we get in one of the old army barracks in the cove for the rest of the night and stay there 'til dark tamorrow."

"Good idea, but where are we goin' to boil up? We lights a fire in one of those dried-out barracks; it will go up like a bonfire on New Year's Eve. I think it would get the attention of the cops. One of 'em barracks starts to burn; there'll be more cops in Bay Bulls than in the RCMP academy in Regina. The cops are expectin' and waitin' for us to screw up and bring attention to ourselves. But we're smarter than that. The first time they'll see us is when we turn ourselves in. We have to be between Bay Bulls and Witless Bay by daylight. The way I'm thinkin' is if we can get past a community each night, we should be on Cape Race Road in less than two weeks."

"Rory, how many miles is it from town to Portugal Cove South?"

"I got no idea; I'm guessin' sixty or sixty-five miles or more."

"You serious?"

"Yes, Butch. And whose fault is all this? Not mine! Listen, we can do this. Here, carry the bag with the water and pot; it's heavier than the other bag. Yer much bigger and stronger than me."

"I s'pose I will."

"I s'pose ya will, carry it—and shut up!"

"Rory, I got an idea. Let's go up Irish Town Road and break into the Molson's beer truck I've seen parked there. I'd love a few beer."

"Fuck, no, Pat O'Driscoll is the distributor for Molson's on the Shore. Hell of a fine fella, not robbin' anythin' from 'im."

"A beer would be nice!"

"Butch, we have more to worry about than beer!"

"Ok, another idea, let's go in the church. They're never locked and see what we can find."

"Butch, you tell me what the fuck is in a church that is goin' to help us?'

"Ok, yer the boss."

They passed the cannon gates that lead to Sts. Peter and Paul Catholic Church. A prominent landmark in the community. They crossed the Main River by the Parish Hall and turned left onto the Lower Road. They passed the War Memorial erected in memory of Jack Frampton, a member of the Newfoundland Regiment, who was killed during the July Drive of 1916 at Beaumont-Hamel. They walked to the bottom of Quays Road in a little over an hour. They passed the last house, which had a star-shaped roof. At the end of the road, they went into the woods. They came across an old one-room green cabin with three tear-drop windows in the door.

Rory said, "let's have a look at it." He tried the door; it was locked; he picked up a rock and smashed out one of the windows. Cleaned the glass from the edges, carefully reached in, turned the knob and entered. He lit his lighter; a Coleman lantern was on the table. He shook it; it had fuel in it. He turned up the wick; it lit on the first try. The lit lantern showed him two bunks with homemade quilts on them, an old franklin black cast-iron wood stove, which had plenty of dry wood along with some green wood stacked up behind it. There was even an armful of dry splits for starting a fire.

Rory told Butch to come in and light the stove while he got the fish, potatoes and onions ready for cooking. When the stove heated up, Rory put the pot of fish on to boil. Rory had a look around. There were twenty cans of food in a cupboard above the sink, everything from meatballs and gravy to corned beef hash.

"Butch, when we leave, all these cans of grub are goin' with us. There's a tin cookin' pot here; it's lighter than the iron pot; we'll leave the iron pot and take the tin one with us. There's also a box of Tetley, my favorite tea and a can opener. Me Aunt Hannah drinks Red Rose Orange Pekoe. I hates it—belly wash. There's a full bag of sugar here too."

When the fish was ready, they ate it from white china plates.

"Rory, there's some bones in this fish."

"It's split cod; yer goin' to come across bones; do ya want me to pick out the bones for ya, like me daddy useta do for me when I was little?"

Butch sensed the sarcasm. He put his head down and ate in silence.

After their meal, they removed their wet mud-caked jeans and hung them above the stove to dry along with their wet sneakers. The cabin was hot as a furnace, even with the missing window in the door. They opened the door ajar to let the cool air in.

"Butch, ya ate a fine feed of fish. Pretty good for a fella who said he wasn't struck on eatin' salted cod fish."

"Rory. Sure, I never had a mouthful of anythin' in thirty-six hours. I'd have eaten the leg of this table if the feed had taken any longer to cook."

"I believe ya woulda', too. Now we gotta worry about where we're goin' to get cigarettes. We only got twelve left between us."

"Are we stayin' here for the night?"

"Yes. Not goin' to pass up this heat and a bed with a mattress after sleepin' on the ground last night, with a cold North Atlantic wind blowin' in on us. We'll leave around eight tamorrow night and go see me buddy Joe Walker."

"Ya serious?"

"Why?"

"Ya trust 'im?"

"That's what I do. Joe will not only have a few beer, but he'll also have some smokes to spare. He always has a tub or two of baccy sittin' on the table in the shed."

"I hates rollies. I guess they're better than nothin'. What about Joe's woman?"

"She doesn't know what goes on in his shed. We could stay there for a week; she wouldn't even know we were there."

"Okay, I guess, if ya trust 'im. I'll have to trust 'im."

"We can't stay there, though. Someone tells the cops me and

Joe are buddies they'll most likely be keepin' an eye on his place expectin' us to show up there. Or they might question 'im about us if they haven't already.

"Butch, I'm a little worried about runnin' into the bunch cuttin' the trail."

"Why?"

"Well, ya knows 'em university types, they all lives on the right side of the law. One of 'em sees us; we're fucked. They most likely have a satellite phone or an emergency radio with 'em every time they goes out cuttin' on the trail in case someone gets injured. They'd rat us out in minutes. I guess we'll have to keep an eye out for 'em."

Butch went out to relieve himself in his underwear and t-shirt before turning in. He came back wiggling like a Labrador dog. "Rory, is that the light from the lighthouse I'm seein'?" "Yes, the same lighthouse we were in hours ago."

Rory laughed, "We're almost opposite it on the other side of the harbour. Butch, did ya know a German submarine surrendered at the end of the second world war and was towed into Bay Bulls."

"No, I never heard that story before."

"A week or so after the war ended, it surfaced off Cape Race and was brought into Bay Bulls by a Canadian Navy vessel. I believe it was numbered U-190."

"Never heard of it."

"The periscope from it is in a private club for commissioned officers in downtown St. John's. Called the Crow's Nest."

"What's a periscope?'

"It's like a telescope; ya raise it from the middle of the submarine. When the sub is almost to the surface, ya can see if there are any vessels within a few miles."

"Another question, what's the name of the big hill on the other side of the harbour?'

"Locals call it the Ridge. The proper geographical name of it is John Clay's hill. Someone told me it's eight hundred and fifty feet high, and the hill behind us is twelve o'clock hill."

"I'm callin' it a day."

Rory balled up rags he found under the sink and stuffed them in the small window frame in the door before turning in. He lay awake listening to the sea, pounding the coastline a few hundred feet or more below them. Butch fell asleep as soon as his head hit the pillow; he was snoring like a bull moose with his mouth open. Rory dozed comfortably, sliding down the edge of a dream about cops driving around smoking giant spliffs while looking for them.

CHAPTER TWENTY-THREE

The boys slept solid. Rory woke around seven, a little nervous about the cabin being so close to the community. He boiled the kettle, he found a washed-out hardcover green book with a dank, musky smell; the Political History of Newfoundland, 1832-1864 by Gertrude E. Gunn. Rory had forty pages read by the time Butch woke at noon. He contemplated taking the book with him, but the weight of it made him decide against it. When Butch woke, Rory had another feed of saltfish boiling, along with two cans of beans heating on the stove.

"Why we havin' fish again?"

"Well, Butch, saltfish is bulky to carry. The more we eat, the less we gotta carry."

"I guess ya have a point. Rory, why didn't ya look for Gensom last night?"

"I dunno where he lives. I only know 'im from the bars and clubs. Never got too friendly with 'im on a personal basis. Just a fella sellin' drugs for me."

The boys ate. "Butch, I'm goin' to lie down for a bit. Keep yer eyes glued on the window towards Bay Bulls. Throw somethin' on for supper—a few pieces of saltfish and two cans of meatballs and gravy."

As soon as Rory was asleep, Butch found a pen; he removed a large picture with former Premier Joey Smallwood on it and printed on the wall behind it, "BH and ROR were here May 1982." He didn't know what day of the month it was; he wasn't good with dates. He replaced the picture so Rory wouldn't see what he'd written.

Butch was bored. He took the sharp boning knife and Rory's

pocketknife from the table, went outside behind the cabin and found a large knotty spruce tree. He spent forty-five minutes carving, BH/ROR May82. Rory would be more upset with the initials in the tree than on the wall. He hoped Rory wouldn't go behind the cabin for a piss or a crap before they left.

Rory woke around five. "What did ya do while I was asleep, Butch?"

"Nothin'. I was bored out of me mind."

"How'd ya get all the turpentine on ya?"

"I was tryin' to break off a few snotty var branches for firewood."

"Go get the butter and clean up yer hands. Yer a state! There's butter in one of the cupboards. Is supper ready?"

Butch replied, "yes."

They ate and shared one of their last smokes. A few hours later, Rory said, "Butch, time to start gearin' up to leave here."

Rory put all the canned food in the brin bag with the thin pot and kettle. He let the fire burn out. It is bad luck to douse a fire in a wood stove in Newfoundland, and they didn't need any more bad luck.

They headed south towards Witless Bay. It was cold out. Colder than the previous night. They came to a wide path and walked along it for a few hundred feet.

"Butch, this ain't the hikin' trail they're cuttin'. It's too wide and well-travelled. I believe it's the old train track."

"Yer right—the hikers I spoke to at Mike's Hotel said they sometimes hike on the old Southern Shore train track. Look how wide it is and how level it is. Too bad the train is not still runnin'. We could hitch a ride on it like hobos."

"Butch, if this is it, it will cross Deans Road and pass close to the powerhouse, at the head of Lower Pond. If we keep walkin' past the powerhouse, we should come out somewhere close to Birchy Hill. We'll figure it out as we go."

"How do ya know that," asked Butch. "There's a road in Witless Bay called the track; it goes from the south side to the north side, it has to be a part of the old train track system."

A beagle suddenly appeared before them. Butch crouched down and ran his hand over the dogs head.

"Look, Rory, he gotta name tag. His names Hunter, good boy, good boy, Hunter. Hey, Rory, can we take 'im with us?"

"No. We got enough to worry about without havin' to take care of a dog. And, Butch, what would we feed 'im?"

"We could share the fish and canned food."

"Not likely. This food has to last us."

"Rory, I'll give 'im half of my share of the food."

"Yes, 'cause ya looks like a fella who would share a meal."

"Rory, yer some hard to get along with."

"Shut up, Butch, and walk."

The Beagle went left down the road.

"Butch, let's walk up the road towards the Southern Shore Highway. I'm pretty sure the road leadin' to the powerhouse is fairly close."

They hadn't been walking long before they saw a dirt road branching off to the left. Rory figured it led to the powerhouse. Sure enough, they soon saw the lights in the yard of the powerhouse. They could hear the roar of the turbines. The yard was lit up like a hockey arena.

Rory looked at Butch, put his finger to his lips, signalling to be quiet; there might be an overnight watchman. They walked quickly past the powerhouse, climbed a bank on the other side of it and turned left. Ten minutes later, coming to a paved road. There were two houses, one on the left and one on the right. Both houses had fishing boats covered in tarpaulins in their yards. In another fifteen minutes, they reached Birchy Hill.

"Rory, this is the road I used to walk that girl home from the swimmin' pool after we left the Petrel. Cutie, with the long coal-black hair, with the big tits, moved here from the Goulds. The night I stayed at Joe's."

"Right ya are. We'll be in Joe's shed havin' a beer and enjoyin' a few smokes and heat in no time."

CHAPTER TWENTY-FOUR

As they got close to Joe's house, they could see the light in the shed and see Joe moving around behind a small window. It looked to Rory; Joe was on his CB radio.

"Butch, go over behind the other shed and stay out of sight. I don't want Joe to freak out with two people at his shed door this hour of the night."

Rory walked to the shed, gently turned the doorknob, pulled the door open and entered. Joe's eyes lit up, about to say something; Rory put a finger to his lips. Joe told the old fella from Bay Bulls that he was talking to on the CB, he had to go. He hung the mic on the radio, turned it off, turned, and folded Rory into his arms.

Joe was smiling from ear to ear.

"Jesus Rory, I can't believe yer in me shed. Where the fuck did ya come from?

"Long story Joe, me buddy Butch is with me. Ya knows 'im?"

"Yes, stayed here one-night last fall. Where's he at?"

"He's hidin' behind the other shed."

"Well, go get 'im. Don't raise yer voice—the old lady will have her mug in the window if she hears anythin'."

Rory went and got Butch.

"Good to see ya again, young fella." Joe and Butch shook hands.

"Anyone else around?"

"No. I'm out here since supper, I haven't seen a soul. So, b'ys, where did ye come from?"

"I guess ya knows what's on the go."

"Jesus, yes, Rory. If I didn't know what's on the go, I'd have to be brain dead or actually real fuckin' dead. Yer pictures have been on both news CBC and NTV the last two nights."

Rory asked, "where did they get pictures of us?"

"High-school yearbook pictures, by the look of 'em. Ya looked kind of young, Butch."

"Butch only had his picture taken for the two years he did grade seven, Joe."

"B'ys, I guess ya'd like a beer?"

"Sure, if ya gotta couple to spare. We've been eatin' saltfish all day, and we're as thirsty as a Job's Cove whore on Sunday marnin'."

"A smoke would be nice too, Joe."

"Go ahead and roll a few, Butch; all the gear is on the table. B'ys, I got one question: I'm more interested in who owned the weed and hash the cops found on Shoal Bay Road than I am about the bank robbery."

"Fuck! I told ya, didn't I Butch? I knew 'em police dogs would find it." Rory made a sound halfway between a groan and a yelp. "Ah, Jesus, Joe—what else have ya heard? What's bein' said on yer police scanner?"

"Don't be talkin'—me scanner conked out on me last month. Been meanin' to get out to Radio Shack in the Village Mall to get another one. I wish I'd had one the past few days; I knows it's not hummin' with chatter about the two of ye.

The news is reportin', someone drivin' a yellow 1968 RT Charger with a green vinyl roof registered in the name of Rory O'Ryan from Cappahayden did an armed robbery on Thursday afternoon at Scotiabank at Bidgood's Plaza in the Goulds. They said a car chase involvin' an RCMP cruiser, which ended when the driver jumped out of the car and ran down the end of Shoal Bay Road. Said police dogs were brought in to look for the suspect. They lost the scent when they came to a river."

"Rory, I never doubted it wouldn't work. I didn't wanna' get wet."

"What are ye talkin' about, b'ys?"

Rory told Joe what they'd done when they came to Queens

River.

"B'ys, I gotta ask—how'd ye get here from the Goulds?"

"That's another story, Joe. What else the cops sayin'?"

"Their sayin', they're pretty sure there are two people involved. It's bein' reported that on the way back up Shoal Bay Road, dogs picked up a second scent and found the drugs."

"Ya got yesterday's and taday's newspapers?"

"No, sorry, I don't. I lit the fire with what newspaper were here when I came out after supper."

"I woulda loved to read about us."

"Had I known ye were droppin' in for a visit, I woulda' kept 'em," Joe said with a grin.

"What else are they sayin'?"

Joe's face became serious. "It's not good, not good at all. Cops raided yer ol' man's house and barn with a dog yesterday afternoon. I guess they were lookin' for drugs. They even showed it on the news last night."

"Damn, the ol' man will kill me when I gets out of prison. Did they find any drugs at me ol' man's place?"

"They never said. The gossip I'm hearin', mostly on the CB. There has been roadblocks all over the Shore since Thursday night. Roadblocks in the Goulds, one by La Manche Park. And, apparently, one by the turn-off to St. Shott's. The story is they're lookin' in everyone's trunk and checkin' the backs of pick-ups. Askin' everyone for IDs, passengers too."

"Why would they have a roadblock up by St. Shott's?"

"Well, Butch, what I'm hearin' is they're thinkin' ye may try to get back to Cappahayden usin' the Trans-Canada Highway through St. Mary's Bay. B'ys, I'm tellin' ye, yer fucked. Yer not only fucked, yer completely fucked!"

"Thanks, Joe." Rory scowled at him.

"Rory, I'm only statin' a fact. Ye got nowhere to go. I'm half expectin' the Mounties here any time at all. People knows me, and you are buddies."

"I was thinkin' the same thing. I was half afraid to come

here, thinkin' yer place might be under surveillance."

"I'll be honest with ye. The cops did go down the road last night. And passed up this afternoon. I don't see two cop cars in the run of a year on Birchy Hill. Apparently, the Shore is crawlin' with 'em. Another thing, I've seen three different helicopters since this started. Two went south this mornin', and I saw one goin' north yesterday evenin'. They're also sayin' on the news, if ye are seen, yer not to be approached, ye may be armed and dangerous."

Rory laughed. "Me and Butch dangerous, what a joke."

"B'ys, I'm goin' to give ye' some advice. Why don't ye turn yerselves in?"

"Joe, we can't turn ourselves in yet. I gotta get back up the Shore. Butch won't turn 'imself in without me turnin' meself in at the same time."

"Why do ya need to get back up the Shore?"

"Joe, I can't say why."

"So, what're ye goin' to do tanight? Yer welcome to stay here. If the cops finds ye, I'll say I forgot to lock the door, and ye crept in."

"Joe, thanks for the offer. It would be too risky to stay here; I don't want ya involved. But thanks again. I'm goin' to ask for a favour. If ya say no, I'll understand. Can ya give us a run to Moble in a couple of hours?"

"Sure, but don't ya think it would be careless to get in my truck with all the cops on the go?"

"Joe, I got that figured out. We won't go in yer truck. We'll go on yer three-wheeler."

"Why the three-wheeler?"

"For two reasons. One, the cops won't haul it in like a car or truck. Second, we'll leave the headlight off, even if we meets the cops, 'fore they notice there's a three-wheeler on the shoulder of the road, we'll be gone in the woods like gazelles. By the time they get dogs to track us, we'll be miles away. Might find another river to throw 'em off our scent again."

"Why ye goin' to Moble?"

"Like I said, we gotta get back up the Shore. One community, one day at a time."

"Ye walkin' to Cappahayden?"

"Yes and no. We're gettin' there in many different ways. Can ya bring us to Moble?"

"Jesus, yes, Rory. I wouldn't say no to ya any time, especially not now with the conundrum yer in. Where exactly do ya wanna' go?"

"Joe, could get us as far as the turn-off goin' down into Burnt Cove? It's a fair distance beyond Moble, but it'll help us a lot more in the long run."

"Yes, it is a fair distance beyond Moble, not a problem. A bit of a long run on the shoulder of the road for a three-wheeler. If ye wants to go that far, I'll bring ye. Sure, fuck it, I'll drive ye to Cappahayden if ye wants! But if we meets any cops beyond Moble, that'll be as far as I'll go."

"Not a problem. I needs another favour, though— can ya spare us a couple of packs of smokes?"

"Sure. Only thing is, ye gotta roll 'em yerselves. I'm terrible at rollin', with me big ol' Sasquatch hands. I'm sure Butch could roll a couple of packs in a half hour or so."

"Butch, ya hear Joe? Get rollin!"

"Joe, we got some grub we needs to take with us."

"Not a problem. I'll muster ye up some grub, get ye' a couple of loaves of homemade bread. It's frozen. I got a large Maple Leaf bologna, uncut. I can get some canned grub in the pantry when the old lady is gone to bed. I'll get ye a few rolls of bum wad; I'm sure ya'll need it."

"Thanks, Joe; much appreciated."

"Where did ye find the grub, ye have? I'm sure ye never went in to see Dave Walsh at the Southern Discount in Bay Bulls."

"A long story, Joe."

"I'm sure it is. There'll be many long stories 'fore ye gets yer day in front of a judge."

"Yer a real Job's comforter, Joe."

"The only thing is, with three people on the three-wheeler, we'll have to take our time. I'm curious—what's the plan? Ye can't stay on the run forever."

"The plan is to turn ourselves in, in ten or twelve days. Please don't tell that to anyone."

"Rory, I never saw ye tanight or any time in the last couple of months. Another question, b'ys—why'd ye rob the bank?"

"It was Butch who robbed the bank. I was on Shoal Bay Road, baggin' up some weed and hash from a stash I had there. When I heard the siren, I walked out of the woods onto the road to see what all the commotion was; I sees Butch runnin' towards me like a cheetah, he tells me to run. I guess instinct kicked in, so I ran. That's why I'm here with dried mud up to me balls. If I never ran and went back into the woods and buried me stash, I wouldn't be here now. I'm hopin' a good lawyer will get us out of this mess down the road."

"Rory, there's no such thing as a good lawyer. Ya'll learn that as ya gets older. Lawyers, most of 'em, are more crooked than the criminals they represent. They're all alike, they have a license to steal."

"Joe, I don't mean a lawyer that's a good man—I mean a lawyer who's good at his trade. Not the same thing."

"I s'pose, Rory. Okay, b'ys, here's the plan. Ye walk down Birchy Hill. I'll push the three-wheeler down the road a fair distance. If I starts it this hour of the night, the missus will know there's somethin' up. I never drives her in the nighttime."

"Sounds good, Joe,"

"Say we leave in another hour. B'ys, I for gotta ask ye if ye wants a draw of weed?"

"I'll pass," said Rory."

Butch was delighted, being offered a draw. "Awesome, Joe, I haven't had a draw in a few days."

Joe rolled a couple of thick joints. Rory turned on the CB radio and listened to the chatter while the boys smoked joint after joint. Rory was eyeing Butch through the smoke; he was pissed, smoking weed and drinking beer like it was a regular Saturday night as if there was nothing wrong.

Rory always knew Butch would do something stupid someday, but he never thought it would be this serious, and he would be in it up to his neck as well. Three fellas on the CB were having a grand old yarn about the two lads on the lam.

"Joe, who's these fellas chattin'?"

"They're all from Bay Bulls—an old fella Pat Glynn, a fisherman who lives on the north side of the harbour, John Deagen who also fishes, he's from the Alley Road and Dave Maddicks from Irishtown. The three of 'em are on there every night; they chats for hours, could be about anythin'. I enjoys listenin' to 'em yarnin'. There's nights I'd pay admission to listen to 'em. Ya don't know what they'll be discussin' on any given night. And the fella Glynn, wait 'til he starts with his smokers' cough. He can go non-stop coughin' for two or three minutes with the mic keyed on, priceless entertainment. Ya couldn't buy it."

Rory wondered if the Maddicks fella was related to the fella in Irishtown they bought the Charger from.

Joe said, "he heard the Deagen fella say he was up to the supermarket after supper, and there were eight RCMP vehicles in the yard, six marked cruisers and two grey ghost cars."

Was it even a good idea to go anywhere on the three-wheeler? Rory knew they had to take a chance. They couldn't stay at Joe's for the night. Getting a run to the turn-off going down into Burnt Cove would be a great help. They'd be bypassing Mobile and Tors Cove. Getting beyond these communities on wheels would mean fewer miles walking in the woods.

"Joe, I needs another favour. Have ya got two old pairs of rubber boots nothin' fancy, gully jumpers will do and two old sets of oil clothes, two jackets warmer than these jean jackets?"

"I do, Rory, down in the stage in Gallows Cove. We'll get 'em on the way along."

"We needs two pairs of woollen socks or vamps if ya' got any to spare."

"I'll get 'em when I goes in to get the grub for ye."

Butch was half asleep on the couch when Joe got back with

the gear. Rory wanted to flip on him for the state he was in, but not in Joe's shed.

"Joe, we'll start walkin'. If ya don't pick us up 'fore we gets to the track, we'll go down the road below the track; I believe it's called the New Line. We'll wait at the bottom, where it meets the road that goes down through the harbour."

"Sounds good, Rory. Grab the bag of grub, lay it by the shed as ye pass it. I'll strap it on the front rack with bungee cords. I'll be along in fifteen or twenty minutes."

CHAPTER TWENTY-FIVE

The boys left the shed and headed down Birchy Hill.

"Butch, ya enjoyed yer visit with Joe?"

"I gotta say, I did. Joe's a spot-on fella."

"Life's a fuckin' ride for ya."

"What? What do ya mean, Rory?"

"Smokin' weed like they're not growin' anymore. Wake the fuck up. We're on the run; every cop on the Avalon Peninsula is lookin' for us. And you with not a fuckin' worry in the world. Stoned out of yer head like a zombie. If we don't fall out 'fore we makes it to Cape Race, it will be a miracle. When we gets off the bike, don't tell Joe we're usin' the trail to get us down the Shore."

"Didn't ya say we could trust 'im?"

"I did say that, but he could get drunk and have a slip of the tongue."

They had a good pace going, making their way down Birchy Hill, they hung a right at the New Line. Before they reached the bottom, they could hear Joe's three-wheeler coming in their direction. They kept well in on the shoulder. Rory was always cautious; he had to be extra careful tonight, with Joe half-drunk and wired from smoking weed. It was pitch black out, and Joe wasn't using the headlight.

When Joe reached them, he stopped and told them to get on the rear rack and face backwards. After they were settled, they drove up the road a few hundred feet, crossed a beach and made their way to the shoulder of the highway. They took a left onto the road known locally as the Boozy Bottom. Joe gunned the old Honda three-wheeler going as fast as he could, going down

Gallows Cove Road. He slowed as he reached the turn-off to the stage.

When they reached the stage, Joe killed the engine and got off the bike; he turned on his flashlight, walked to the stage door. He unlocked the padlock and went in. He returned carrying two sets of oilskins along with two black flannel jackets.

"Here ya go, Butch, you take the green set. They're big enough for you, fits me. And the yellows for you, Rory."

"Joe, I'd be like a beacon on a lighthouse with 'em on. Or someone would think I was poachin' moose in the spring. Have ya gotta green pair?"

"I believe I do. Hang on, I'll go and get 'em." The boys took off their jean jackets, tossed them in the stage, and hauled on the flannel jackets. Both fit perfectly. When Joe returned, he had a set of green oilskins, two pairs of black hip rubbers cut off below the knee, two pairs of old orange rubber gloves and a brin bag to put everything in.

"Joe, ya knows ya might not get yer gear back."

"Don't worry about it. We buys a few new sets every spring."

Joe locked the stage and tied the brin bag on the front rack of the three-wheeler with the other bags. They got on board and went back up Gallows Cove Road. They took a left-up Carey's Road. They reached the Southern Shore Highway and turned left. They crossed a one-mile stretch of highway known locally as Frog Marsh, they descended into the small community of Mobile. As they passed the regional high school Mobile Central High. Rory looked back; he saw an RCMP cruiser parked beside it. The rear of the vehicle was facing the road. Rory's heart was pounding in his chest. He watched the cruiser but lost sight of it when they went into a turn. Luckily for them, the school was a fair distance from the road. If Butch hadn't been stoned, he would have seen the cruiser. Joe probably imagined himself on a Harley with two bitches strapped on the rear. Rory allowed himself a bitter grin.

The further they went, the more relaxed Rory was. Every mile on the trike was a mile they didn't have to walk. They passed

Tinkers Lounge. There were a few dozen cars in the yard, pretty regular for a Saturday night. Rory thought how enjoyable it would be to be in there now, having a vodka and orange juice or a beer, playing pool, or out in a slow waltz with a hot chick who smelled like a rose.

When they reached their destination, Joe turned off the bike. "B'ys, we made it in one piece."

Rory got off the bike and walked around. His legs and bony arse were paining from the hurried ride. So much for Joe saying he would take his time.

"B'ys, that wasn't a bad run. Never met a car from Witless Bay to here."

"Neither of ye saw the RCMP cruiser in the high-school yard?" Joe spit over the bank on the side of the shoulder.

"RCMP cruiser? Rory, ya gotta be shittin' me."

"No, Joe, there was a cruiser parked in the schoolyard. Arse on to the road."

"Holy Jesus, Rory, if I'd seen that, I'd have freaked right out and most likely gone no farther. Butch, ya want one last draw?"

"Yes, sure, one to finish off the night." Butch could see Rory eyeing him, he didn't care.

Joe and Butch had their draw and a few laughs.

"B'ys, I only got two joints left; otherwise, I'd give ye a draw to take with ye. What's yer plan from here?"

Rory spoke up before Butch had a chance to open his mouth. The last thing he needed was for stoned Butch to start rambling about how they were getting up the Shore.

"We're goin' to walk the highway 'til daylight, bunk down somewhere for the day. Joe, can I borrow your flashlight? I'll replace it sometime down the road?"

"Sure, Rory. I put fresh batteries in it' fore I left the shed."

"Take yer time headin' back home, Joe. Keep an eye out for the RCMP cruiser. Thanks a million for what ya gave us and the ride. Ya knows it could be a few years 'fore our next beer or draw together."

"I feels bad for ye, the fuckin' mess yer in; I'll be keepin' an eye on the news the next few days to see how far ye gets, and what sentence ye gets" Joe shook hands with Butch and hugged Rory.

"B'ys, be careful and remember yer wanted. Don't do somethin' stupid and give 'em yellow-legged bastards a reason to tattoo ye with lead."

"We'll be careful, no worries, Joe. We'll talk about this for years to come." Joe laughed, hopped on his bike, did a power spin, gunned her, and headed for home.

CHAPTER TWENTY-SIX

"Okay, Rory, what's the plan?"

"Well, we can't stay here on the road like sittin' ducks. We gotta be leavin' Bauline by daylight and on the trail to La Manche."

"How far is Bauline?"

"About two or two and a half miles. Didn't ya walk a chick to Bauline one night from Tinkers a while back?"

"Yes, I was so drunk I can hardly remember it. Come to think about it, I don't even remember her name." Rory rolled his eyes and shook his head.

Butch hated walking hated it even more with a buzz on. Even if he was on pavement.

"Can we find a spot to sleep for the night, Rory?"

"No. I have a plan, and we're stickin' to it. Ya shouldn't have gotten stoned. Ya knew we weren't stayin' at Joe's for the night." Rory was bitter cold, cold to the bone, he figured Butch was as well. They should have put on the oilskins before they got on the trike to break the wind. Rory hauled the oil jackets out of the brin bag, he threw one at Butch.

They made their way down Burnt Cove Hill. "This ain't bad, Butch. Easy walk downhill and warmer than the trike ride."

Every third or fourth house they passed had a dog. Most were chained to a doghouse. A few barked for a few seconds as they went by. An Irish setter appeared from behind a bungalow and trotted along behind them for ten or fifteen minutes before turning back. The small church in St. Michael's looked eerie in the dark as they passed it. Rory asked Butch if he knew there was a cemetery to the left, behind the church. The words were barely out of his mouth when Butch took off like a shot. Rory bent over, laughing. A grown man afraid of dead people buried in the ground. When Rory caught up to Butch, Butch called him an arsehole cunt.

They made it to Bauline in a little over two hours. Carrying the extra gear Joe gave them was slowing their walk. As they were about to take a right to go up LaManche Road, which would lead them in the direction of the abandoned community of La Manche, Rory eyed the Bauline community fishing stages. What a place to get in out of the weather to sleep for the night. "Butch, follow me and be quiet."

The building was roughly eighty feet long, painted white, trimmed mountain green. With six individual stages, each with a separate door, which meant six fishing crews, most likely gear belonging to families of Melvin's, Reddick's, and Colbert's, all known as hard-working fishermen. They had their fishing gear in each separate unit. There was a pole light on the side of the building with the doors, which made checking each door easy. The first one was locked with a chain and padlock. Same with the second; the third had a chain on it but no lock. Rory untangled the chain; he pried the green door open enough to allow them to squeeze inside. As soon as they were in, Rory lit the flashlight and said, "Bingo!" On the floor, a massive pile of black twine. Rory could tell from the size of the pile, there was more than one cod trap, maybe two. The inside of the stage was dark, unpainted with a bilgy odour.

"Butch, this is our spot for the next twenty-four hours."

"Ya serious?"

"Yes. Sure, what's wrong with it? A roof over our heads and somethin' half-soft to sleep on. Better than Joseph and Mary in the stable."

"Whose stable were they in?"

"Who fuckin' knows, Butch!"

"Why we stayin' here for s'long?"

"Well, it's late, and we needs a good night's sleep 'fore we walks to Brigus South. It's a fine jaunt from here. There's no cabins between here and Brigus I knows of. There's two maybe three, I believe, at the bottom of Admiral's Cove. And tamorrow is Sunday, and there's always someone down in La Manche for a Sunday afternoon walk, takin' pictures of the stone and cement foundations of the houses and stages that once stood there. So, we stay here 'til dark tamorrow night, then we head for La Manche. When we gets to La Manche, there's an old two-story house still standin' on this side of the gut. We might spend some time in it. I'm thinkin' with a good night's sleep; we could walk to Brigus by Monday evenin'."

"Why's it goin' to take s'long?"

"Well, Butch, there's no crossin' at La Manche. The swingin' bridge is gone since the winter storm of sixty-six. Could be a few hours lookin' for a spot to cross. I'm hopin' the hikers have the trail cut from La Manche to Brigus. I hope for once in yer life yer right about somethin', the hikers and their trail cuttin'. If yer not, we may have no other choice but to walk the highway to Cape Race. If we're forced to walk the highway, our chances of gettin' caught are much higher.

The closer we gets to home, the more cops there will be. The longer we're on the run, the more they will think we're headin' for home. I'm haulin' on the pants of me oil clothes, they'll keep us a bit warmer. Ya should haul yers on. We'll crawl into the middle of that pile of twine and sleep for eight or ten hours."

"Rory, yer not afraid someone will come in here?"

"Tamorrow is Sunday. Why would anyone be comin' in here? Fishermen don't fish or work on Sundays. Most go to clubs for Sunday afternoon entertainment. Most of the fishermen who live down here will be at Tinkers tamorrow afternoon. They won't be haulin' these traps out for mendin' for another week or two."

"Ya sure?"

"No, but we have to take that chance."

"Rory, I'm hungry."

"We're not eatin' 'til tamorrow."

"I'm fuckin' starved, let's have a small mug up."

"Yer not! Ya got the munchies."

"Whatever it is, I got; I'm starved!"

"Go to sleep and no smokin' on the twine. If ya needs a smoke, get up and move away from the twine. Ya drops a cigarette; this will go up like a flare boom on an oil rig."

"Rory, I'm not that stund."

"Yes, ya are!"

Butch woke Rory up in a panic.

"Rory, there's someone at the door. I'm sure I can hear someone pokin' around out there."

"Okay, shut up and listen. Okay, I knows what it is. It's the Irish setter that started followin' us in Burnt Cove." Rory jumped up, opened the door. The dog was on the other side of it, wagging his tail.

"Here, pup, c'mon."

"Give 'im some of the bologna Joe gave us."

"Butch, I'm not wastin' bologna on a dog we don't even own."

"Rory, we gotta feed 'im to settle 'im down for the night. We can't put 'im outside again. He'll keep tryin' to get in. Someone sees 'im pokin' at the door they'll know there's somethin' up in here."

"Okay, give 'im some bologna."

Butch took out the large stick of bologna, cut off a two-inch chunk with the boning knife, he gave half of it to the setter. He ate the other half.

"Once he's fed, he'll settle and most likely go to sleep. Won't ya, boy?"

"Now, Butch, don't go talkin' to 'im."

"Ya think I'm after losin' it to go talkin' to a dog?"

"Butch, ya'd talk to a wet rock when yer stoned."

CHAPTER TWENTY-SEVEN

Rory slept until ten. When he woke, Butch and the dog were as close together, cuddled up on the pile of twine as any man and woman have ever been in a bed. It rained hard for most of the day. When Butch woke, he had a can of spaghetti and shared it with the dog. Rory knew it was a waste of time to put the dog out. He'd only want back in. It was going to be a long day, stuck in the stage in the dark. Butch wanted something else to eat around suppertime.

"Forget it, Butch. We gotta ration our food." They had plenty of saltfish, but it had to be boiled for at least twenty minutes to a half-hour to remove some of the salt out of it. Butch kept talkin' about food; Rory let him open a can of beans and wieners, which he shared with the dog.

"Rory, I needs to shit. Where can I have a crap?"

"Go over in the corner and have it; there's a beef bucket half full of water, use that. There's a half sheet of plywood standin' up against the wall, there's a bag of rags hangin' on a nail. When yer finished, place a couple of rags over the bucket, put the plywood on top of it and lay a few lead weights on it. The weight should seal it and keep the smell down."

"Ya for real?'

"Yes."

Rory's plan was to stay in the stage for a few hours after dark. They couldn't cross La Manche River in the dark. He wanted to be at the river for first light come morning, to head inland to find a spot to cross.

They left the stage around eleven o'clock, they made their way up LaManche Road. This gravel road would lead to La Manche, with the dog following them. After an hour of walking, they reached Doctors Cove.

"Rory, can we stop for a spell and a smoke?"

"No. We'll rest and have a smoke when we gets to the river."

Walking was reasonably easy; the path was fairly level and wide. It was a reasonably bright night. They came to the river and stayed back a few hundred feet from it; Rory figured they would find an old footpath in the morning. They found the old two-story house, the last one standing in the abandoned community. Most likely owned by a Melvin family. Most of the Melvin's on the Southern Shore originated from La Manche. Rory was planning on sleeping in it, it was in too bad a condition to even enter. They found a mossy spot and lay down in their oil clothes, sharing the brin bag with the salt codfish in it as a pillow.

When they woke, it was coming on daylight. The oil clothes helped keep them warm overnight. The sun was rising over the ocean. The Irish setter had pressed himself up against Butch's stomach.

"Even the male dogs like ya, Butch."

"Go to fuck, ya prick."

"Rory, we boil up some fish for a bit of breakfast?"

"Sounds good to me. I'm starved, I'd eat anythin' now."

When they passed Bauline Pond, Rory had topped up the jugs. They would need water before they reached the other side of the river. Butch sat and watched Rory build a fire with the splits they'd taken from the cabin in Bay Bulls.

"Rory put on an extra piece of fish for the dog."

"Ya serious?"

"Yes. We gotta feed the poor animal."

Rory shook his head. He tasted the saltfish to see if it had boiled enough. It was ready. He shared it up with Butch and the dog. The three of them had a slice of homemade bread Joe had given them. After they ate, they lit up cigarettes.

"Butch, I wants to be at Brigus at dusk. Durin' the night, we'll cross the community and be ready to head for Admiral's Cove early in the mornin'."

"How far to Brigus, Rory? How long will it take us to get there?"

"Butch, I got no idea. If I had to guess, I'd say it's six or seven miles. And don't forget, we're not even on the right side of the river yet. How long it will take us to get to the other side. Time to start movin'."

They doused the fire and hauled on the woollen socks and rubber boots. Rory figured the trail would be wet. As they started to walk inland, Rory suddenly dropped to his knees behind some small juniper trees. Butch, startled by Rory's sudden movement, hit the ground beside him.

"What's up, Rory?"

At least, Butch had the sense to whisper. "Look, on the other side of the river: a fella and a dog."

"Jesus, Rory, where did he come from?"

"Who knows. He looks like Gary Grant."

"Who's Gary Grant?"

"A cop that was stationed in Ferryland years ago. One mean bastard that few fucked with."

"How'd ya know about 'im?"

"I saw 'im one time when I was young; he was at the house lookin' for me ol' man for somethin'. I remembers his look. He looked like a fella not to mess with. There was a rumour on the Shore 'im, and John Henry Tee were plannin' on squarin' off. It never happened. It woulda been some battle."

"Who's that?"

"Butch, everyone knows John Henry, he's from Burnt Cove, one tough dude. He hangs out at the Beehive, has a brown Doberman with 'im most of the time, named Crusher. Ya remember the fella Tobin nicknamed Crusher who beat ya playin' pool at Kent's last fall. He named the Doberman after 'im. They're good friends. I believe Grant was transferred to Nova Scotia, gotta big promotion for bein' the top cop on the Dr. Carr drug bust in Tors Cove."

"How'd ya know all that?"

"Heard a crowd at the house one night with the ol' man talkin' about it."

"Do ya think he's a real cop?"

"I got no idea. Butch, keep the dog from barkin'. He barks, and buddy turns out to be a cop, we're finished."

Butch cuddled the dog and talked to him softly. Rory keenly watched the man. He had the height of a cop; his hair was short, and having a German Shepherd with him. It could be a cop taking a chance that the boys were in this area, or it could be a fella out for an early morning stroll with his dog. He strolled around for fifteen or twenty minutes before heading for the path to La Manche Road.

When the man was out of sight, both let out sighs of relief, Butch released the dog.

"Man, that was a rush."

"Yes, Butch, it was."

They stood and started moving inland.

"Rory, what are the two cables hangin' across the river?"

"That's what's left of the swingin' bridge, which linked the north and south sides. There were houses and fishin' stages on both sides of the gut before the 66' storm. Time for a smoke after that scare."

"Rory, how the fuck are the hikers plannin' on gettin' across this river?'

"I guess they'll have to build a bridge. Apparently, the bridge has been rebuilt several times over the years. They might even build a swingin' bridge like what was here 'fore the storm took it."

"Jesus Rory, that'll cost a fortune."

"I guess a grant from the government will help fund it."

"I can't wait to see how they'll cross this river if the trail is ever fully developed."

After their smoke, Rory told Butch to try and get the dog to go back the way he came.

"I'm not goin' fuckin' with 'im, Rory. If he wants to follow us, let 'im. When he gets bored, he'll turn around and go back."

They stayed on top of the cliff on the north side of the gut, walking further inland, back towards the heavy woods away from the ocean. Rory hoped they would find an old footpath from when La Manche was an active community. Sure enough, they came across a well-worn path. In another ten minutes, it led them down from the cliff to the river. They found a spot where the river was shallow enough to cross, roughly fifteen feet across. Rory went first. Carefully jumping on moss-covered rocks, he reached the other side dry. Butch tossed the brin bags before crossing. The dog waded across. Rory bent and filled the water jugs.

"One more obstacle behind us, and a big one, Butch." They couldn't get wet again on this trip. Getting wet would slow them down and make the journey much harder than it was already going to be.

When they reached the Quarry, they lay down for a rest. Rory watched the waves coming in the gut and wished he was on a boat going somewhere no one knew him.

"What time is it, Rory?"

"Nine o'clock, time to move!"

The trail was hard walking in rubber boots. It had many hills and was muddier than the path from the Goulds to Bay Bulls. They made it to Quay's River, with a big waterfall. This river flows from Little Pond. Rory's heart sank on seeing the river. He saw a narrow crossing made of rough planks screwed together a moment later, weighted down with large boulders on both ends. As Rory crossed on these planks, he said to himself, God love the hikers from MUN. On the other side, they had a smoke, Butch knelt to drink from the river.

"Rory yelled, "NO, Butch, don't drink that!"

Surprised, Butch raised his head and looked at Rory. "Why not?"

"Cape Broyle's dump is west of here. I'm not sure where; I

knows it's somewhere between Brigus and the park; I believe it's closer to Brigus. This river could run fairly close to the dump."

"Thanks for the heads up."

"No problem. Probably saved ya a trip to the Janeway."

"Fuck off, ya pig bastard."

"I guess the dog is goin' to Cape Race with us, Butch."

"It looks that way. He seems to have taken a likin' to us. We need to give 'im a name. What about Lucky?"

"What about Unlucky?"

"Why would we call 'im that?"

"Well, Butch, he's the unluckiest dog in the world to get tangled up with us."

The day warmed up. The boys hauled off their oil clothes and put them in one of the brin bags. They left their jackets on.

"What time is it, Rory?"

"One o'clock. Don't worry, we'll be lookin' at Brigus in a few hours. We may as well take our time. We can't cross Brigus in daylight."

The walk was brutally hard, with many elevations and descents. When they reached Roaring Cove River, they had a smoke. Rory reminded Butch not to drink from the river and the possibility it ran close to the dump. After their smoke, they continued on. Around five o'clock, they could see the houses of Brigus. They waited until eleven before crossing the little community from the north side to the south side. Rory told Butch to make a collar for the dog.

"Why?"

"There's usually domesticated ducks and a big ol' graylag goose hangin' around the inside of the gut. If the dog sees 'em or smells 'em, he might make a racket goin' after 'em and draw attention to us."

Butch made a collar from some rope they had taken from the stage in Bay Bulls.

"Butch, keep on my right side and keep the dog on yer other side. We're runnin' from here to the other side."

The boys ran the breadth of the small town in four or five

minutes.

"Butch, did ya see the ducks asleep on the slip?"

"No. How'd ya know about the ducks?"

"Me and Brock drove down here a few weeks ago for a look around and saw the ducks and the goose swimmin' in the gut. I knew they'd most likely be here tanight. Good thing we were goin' so fast, the dog never noticed 'em either."

They walked for twenty minutes, glancing back, they could no longer see the community's lights. They called it a day and made a small fire.

"We should've grabbed a few of 'em ducks to eat."

"They would have made too much noise squawkin', Butch. But yer right, they woulda made a nice change from the fish."

They had bologna and bread toasted on the open fire. Rory begrudgingly gave the dog bologna and half a slice of bread. Butch gave him one of his slices of toast and some bologna.

"Are ya losin' it, Butch? Givin' that much food to a stray dog?"

"He's not a stray. He's ours, and he has a name, Lucky. I bet he'll go all the way to Cape Race with us."

"Not likely. We're not responsible for that dog or any dog for that matter."

"Don't be so cold-hearted. He needs the company, and so do we." Butch put his arms around the dog and rubbed his face.

"Butch, ya've lost it. I thinks Brigus South is the most picturesque community on the Shore. I loves to come down here for a look around."

"First time I've ever heard ya say that."

They had a few smokes, hauled on their oil clothes, and let the fire burn out. Rory limbed a thick spruce tree with the boning knife, they settled down on the branches for a night's sleep. The cold weather was the last thing on Rory's mind before he drifted off. He was tired, he didn't care if it was the month of February. The last sight Rory had of Butch, he and Lucky were cuddled up and snoring like drunken buddies.

CHAPTER TWENTY-EIGHT

The dog's barking woke Rory. It was coming on daylight: two crows had landed in the spot where the fire had been the night before. Rory hated to get up, knowing what he had to face. It was cold and damp. They still had thirty-five or forty miles to go before they reached the drugs, he hoped were still buried. He made a fire, boiled the kettle before waking Butch.

"Butch, get up. Kettle's boiled; we can't stay here all day."

"What's for breakfast?"

"Not a thing."

"Jesus, Rory, we can't walk all day on an empty stomach."

"Well, Butch, we only have so much grub, which we have to spare. We have to find the cabins at the bottom of Admiral's Cove; I knows there's a couple there. The plan is to break into one of 'em tanight and stay there for a while. Hopefully, we'll find some more grub, and we'll get a decent night's sleep."

After Butch finished his second cup of tea, they quenched the fire and started walking.

"Rory, I hears geese."

"That's not geese, that's snipe. The sound they make is called winnowin', though it does sound like geese. They're called Wilson's Snipe in North America. In Europe, their called Common Snipe. C'mon, we got at least four miles to go to get to Admiral's Cove. Ya can stop and listen to the birds if ya wants, 'cause we can't break into a cabin 'til dark."

Half an hour later, they came across a wide path that veered off to the right in the direction of Admiral's Cove.

"We take this, Rory?"

"No, we don't know where it leads. At least by stickin' to the headland, we're guaranteed to come out in the next community. The path we're on is dry, and by the looks of it, the hikers have worked on it. I'd say our best bet is to stay put on this one."

"Rory, what do ya think that other path is?"

"Could be a woods path, for hauling firewood and logs on in the winter. Or it could be a part of the old Southern Shore Highway, who knows?"

When they reached Tar Cove Beach, they descended a steep and narrow path through the alders to the beach. They gathered up enough driftwood on the beach to boil the kettle. They shared four cans of sardines and two slices of bread with the dog. The weather was decent; it warmed up during the day, not overly warm, but decent all the same. They waited on the beach. An hour before dark, they made a move towards Admiral's Cove. Rory's instincts and good sense of direction led them to a dirt road called Crane's Lane, which led them to a cabin. It was a reasonable distance from the few pole lights they could see at the bottom of Admiral's Cove.

They approached the cabin with unease, checked the door: it was locked. Finding an old oil drum behind a shed, rolling it over to a window at the back of the cabin. Rory got up on the barrel and gently pried open the small plastic framed window with his pocketknife. He couldn't break the window, hoping to make a fire; once they got inside, a broken window would hamper any chance of getting some heat. With the window open, he squeezed his small frame inside, landing headfirst on the floor. He got up, turned on the flashlight, unlocked the door and let Butch in. Butch turned around and called the dog.

"Are ya serious, bringin' that dog in here?"

"So what? It's a fuckin' cabin, not Newfoundland Hotel."

Rory held his tongue. It was easier to have the dog inside than it was to argue with Butch. The cabin had three rooms, a kitchen, two small bedrooms with a set of bunk beds in each. Luckily all the bunks had blankets on them. It was painted in bright colours, yellow in the kitchen and two different shades of green in the bedrooms. An older model kerosene lantern sat on the small round wooden kitchen table; it was full of fluid. Rory lit it and laid it on a small shelf above the table.

"Not a bad spot, hey, Rory?"

"Looks fine to me. Better than the community stage we stayed in, in Bauline. There's even wood here for a few fires. Butch, light the fire while I have a look around, see if I can find anythin' that would be of useta us."

"Why can't you light the fire, and I'll look around?"

"Butch, light the fire."

It was no use to argue with Rory. Rory had given him a bit of leeway about the dog. He wasn't going to push it and make him crooked.

"Butch, look, there's a little pantry with enough grub here for the rest of the week. Cans of beans and wieners, Irish stew, a few cans of Vienna sausages and a few different cans of soup. Look at what else I found: a flask of Screech."

"Did ya find any mix?"

"I did, ginger ale."

"Rory, I can't drink Screech with ginger ale."

"Well, I can—more for me."

"I guess I'll try it."

"Butch, I'd drink it with water if I had to."

The cabin warmed up in no time. It would be spaghetti and fish for supper. After eating, they had a few drinks of Screech mixed with ginger ale.

"It's time to turn in for the night, Butch; it's near midnight. I'm goin' to stoke the fire and go to bed."

Rory woke several times during the night. He was nervous sleeping with a roof over his head, a roof they should not be under. He woke around seven o'clock; Butch was still asleep; he would stay that way for a few more hours. After a cup of tea, Rory decided to have a look around. The night before, he'd found a key ring with five or six keys on it. He figured they'd give him access to the two sheds on the back of the property. Upon opening the door, a cold, harsh day was beginning.

The first shed he entered had a red fifteen-foot canoe with paddles and lifejackets. The second shed was a woodshed with no firewood in it. He found five or six large saltfish and a brin bag with a couple of dozen salted capelin and salted vins in plastic bags inside, hanging from the beams. Perfect; grub for the rest of the trip. Butch was going to complain about having to eat more saltfish, but grub was grub. Fuel for the body. Rory went back to the cabin, he sat at the window, watching. There was always a chance someone could come from the direction of Admiral's Cove to check on the cabin.

Butch opened his eyes around ten. "Rory, isn't that heat some nice?"

"I gotta agree. We could be enjoyin' heat like this every mornin' only for yer idea of a get-rich-quick scheme."

"All right, Rory, don't go harpin' on it, especially this early in the marnin'. I knows I screwed up."

"Butch, yer life is yer path to walk; you decide which direction it goes. You are the maker of yer own decisions and destiny. It's ten o'clock. Anyway, I got good news."

"What is it?"

"Well, I found some more food to take with us."

"What kind of food?"

"Food I likes, food yer not too fond of."

"Jesus, Rory, don't tell me ya found more bloody saltfish?"

"Yup, enough to get us to Cape Race."

"I'll turn into a goddamn codfish 'fore this is all over."

"Not only salt cod. Found some salted capelin and vins, two of me favourite things to eat."

"Rory, only old people are s'posed to like grub like that."

"Well, I must be old at heart, 'cause I loves rough grub. I got more news."

"What is it?"

"There's a canoe in one of the sheds."

"Yeah, so what?"

"Well, I got an idea."

"I don't think I'm goin' to like what yer about to say."

"We cross Cape Broyle Harbour comin' on dark this evenin'."

"I knew I was not goin' to like it: Rory, yer off yer head. I can't swim. I'm not gettin' in a fuckin' canoe on the ocean. Ya might get me in one on a pond, but not on the ocean. Don't ya remember what I said standin' on the Cliff in Bay Bulls? I said I would not get in a canoe. Especially on the ocean."

"Relax, Butch, it's a harbour, not an ocean. There's three lifejackets, two are extra-large."

"I told ya, I'm scared of the water."

"Okay, but hear me out. It's not that windy, and here's no sea on. I say we cross the harbour just 'fore dark. And by goin' 'fore dark, we can keep the lights of Cape Broyle on our starboard as we cross."

"What's keepin' the lights of Cape Broyle to our right got anythin' to do with crossin' the harbour?"

"Well, here to Lance Cove Beach is a mile or a little more. If we keep Cape Broyle lights on our right, it will be like a compass in case the fog rolls in. I'm not expectin' any fog to roll in as it's too cold for fog. I don't foresee the wind changing in the time it takes us to reach Lance Cove Beach. I'd say we'll be across in thirty minutes or so."

"What if the canoe is leaky?"

"Looks fairly new, fifteen-footer, small keel on it which will help with stability, has a few superficial scratches on it."

"I'll tell ya what, Rory, look around for a radio. I'm sure there's one here somewhere. Everyone has a radio in their cabin. If the weatherman says the wind is easterly, northeasterly, or southeasterly, I'll get in the fuckin' thing. Any Screech left?"

"There's about three good drinks left in the flask."

"I'll be downin' that for a bit of courage 'fore we leave, that's if I go at all. So, don't dare drink it!"

"Butch, Cape Broyle is a big community rockin' with nightlife and drugs. One of the most happenin' places on the Shore.

The cops will be lookin' for us there for sure."

"Rory, I wish the canoe was a dory."

"Butch, it's a canoe, not a dory. That's all we can do."

"Why don't we paddle into Cape Broyle and rob a dory from a collar or a stage-head? Everyone leaves their oars in their dory's?"

"Butch, that would take up too much time. And there's a chance we could be seen and get caught. And besides, there might not be any dories in the water yet. It's still a few weeks 'fore the trap fishery starts."

"Whatever, Rory, 'I'm gettin' somethin' to eat and havin' a nap."

CHAPTER TWENTY-NINE

"Get up, Butch, and get somethin' to eat. I found a small spring comin' out of the bank behind the cabin."

"Did ya have anythin' to eat while I had a nap?"

"I had a can of beans and wieners, with saltfish and a few capelin with bread. Some of it is still in the fryin' pan if ya wants it. I'm goin' to have another look for a radio."

"Rory, what I wouldn't give for a feed of bacon and eggs with a few toutons covered in molasses."

"You and me both, it would be nice, a decent feed." Rory turned the place upside down; he found a small transistor radio with batteries with some life left in them.

"Butch, I found a radio. And two full cans of Export 'baccy with the seals still on 'em and a couple of packs of Embassy rollin' papers. I also found four brand-new batteries that will fit our flashlight. I was hopin' to find a bottle of java."

"Strong baccy, we can't complain. I guess we'll have to roll 'em by hand like the old fellas did years ago when our rollies are gone. A smoke is a smoke. And what the fuck is java?"

"Coffee, Butch, in some parts of the world, that's what it's called.!"

"Oh, okay."

"It's ten after twelve; the weather will be on at half past the hour."

They huddled in front of the radio, waiting for VOCM's weather report. Before the weather came on, the announcer gave a report about the robbery. Saying the RCMP were continuing with roadblocks on the Southern Shore in an attempt to locate Rory O'Ryan and Butch Hynes from Cappahayden. Both are wanted for questioning concerning an armed robbery at Scotiabank in the town of Goulds on Thursday, May 6. A reward of one thousand dollars was being offered for information leading to any assistance in apprehending the two wanted individuals. People were advised not to approach these two individuals.

"Who'd have ever thunk it, Rory, two lads from Cappahayden havin' their names mentioned on the radio?" Butch was grinning from ear to ear.

Rory wasn't smiling. The heat was still on; Cape Race was a reasonable distance from the north side of Cape Broyle and still a few days away. According to the weather report. The wind was blowing from the northeast; it would switch to a southeasterly coming on dark. Rory turned off the radio.

"Okay, Butch, the weather is perfect, blowin' on land. We can't fuck it up."

"Rory, do ya know where this beach is on the other side?"

"No, I don't. If we leave 'fore darkness sets in, I'm sure we'll see it from the water. If we don't find it, the worst-case scenario is that all we gotta do is head in the harbour. I'm sure there's a few small beaches along the other side of the harbour to land 'fore we gets too close to the community."

"Where are we goin' to launch this canoe?"

"We'll have to go back to the beach where we boiled up 'fore we got here. It won't take us long to carry the canoe back there. A canoe weighs no more than seventy or eighty pounds."

"Sweet holy fuck, Rory, that's two or two and a half miles back. That'll be a hard slog, carryin' a canoe."

"Yes, Butch, it will be a little workout. Sure, in 1877, a team of rowers, all fishermen from Placentia, carried their shell on their shoulders from Placentia to row in the St. John's Regatta. They walked a trail such as we'll be doin'. They won the Fishermen's race. They put the shell back on their shoulders and walked home. So, us carryin' a fifteen-foot canoe two or three miles will be nothin' in comparison to walkin' from Placentia to St. John's with a shell on their shoulders."

"I guess yer right. What time should we start headin' for the beach?"

"About an hour and a half 'fore dark."

As Butch finished the beans and wieners, Rory put on a pot of vins. How he wished he had some drawn butter to go along with them. After he ate, he roasted a dozen capelin on top of the stove.

"Ya wanna' few capelin, Butch?"

"Like the fuck., the smell of 'em is enough for me."

"Butch, did ya know Capelin are called breakfast fish."

"Never heard that 'fore."

Rory went out to the woods for a crap. Butch removed the calendar from the wall with sailboats on it, he hunted around for a pen and found one in a drawer; he printed BH/ROR/May82 on the back of the calendar. To the right of the date, he wrote the number two and circled it. Placing it back on the wall.

When Rory returned, he said, "Okay, Butch, here's the plan. We'll take all the canned food with us. Take two life vests."

"How many vests did ya say were in the shed?"

"Three."

"Okay, perfect, I'm wearin' two."

"Ya serious?"

"Yes, better chance of survivin' with two on."

"If it makes ya happy, wear two."

"Another question. What's the plan when we hit the beach on the other side?"

"We spend the night in a cabin, some b'ys I know from Calvert use for huntin' in the fall."

"Do ya know where it is?"

"I don't. I'm sure if we follow the paths, we'll find it. It shouldn't be hard to find. Must have a path beaten to it if it's bein' used. I knows it's beyond Lance Cove Beach on the Cape Broyle side of the headland."

"What will we do with the canoe when we're finished with it?"

"Hide it in the woods."

"Why?"

"Well, if someone sees a canoe on Lance Cove Beach this

time of year, it won't take 'em long to figure out it was probably us who left it there. And report it to the cops. Not many people paddlin' around Cape Broyle Harbour in a canoe this early in the spring."

They hauled the canoe out of the shed and laid their gear in it. Locked the sheds. Rory crawled out through the window he came through to enter the cabin and closed it tight, hoping no one would come there for at least a week. They started walking back along the trail towards the beach. It wasn't as hard to carry as Butch expected.

When they arrived at the beach, they made their way down the path through the alders.

"When are we leavin', Rory?"

"In a half-hour or so. It's a little too early yet. Don't wanna' bring any attention to us."

"Did ya remember to take the radio?"

"Yes, I got it."

Butch gulped the Screech and tossed the flask in the alders. He looked at Rory with a sad face. "Is Lucky goin' with us in the canoe?"

"No way. It's too dangerous. He's too big. He could act up and cause us to overturn."

Butch said nothing. As much as he wanted the dog to continue with them, he was more afraid of the water. What Rory said made sense.

"Time to start movin', Butch. Tie the water bottles to the back of one of yer lifejackets with the nylon string I found in the shed. If we turns over, we'll still have our water bottles. We'll need 'em if we plan on makin' it to Cape Race."

"Oh, thanks. That makes me feel better, talkin' about turnin' over."

"Butch, the chances of turnin' over are slim to none. If we do, we'll need these bottles. We can make it the rest of the way without food; we won't make much headway lookin' for rivers and ponds to drink from every few hours. It'll kill our travellin' time.

Now let's move!"

Butch knelt; and hugged the dog. It broke his heart to leave him behind. He didn't want to drown.

"I'm gettin' in the stern, Butch—you get in the bow."

"Why?"

"Have ya ever been in a canoe any time in yer life?"

"No, I haven't."

"Well, pick up the canoe and start walkin'. We have to walk fifteen or twenty feet out into the water 'fore we get aboard. If not, she'll ground on the bottom."

They dragged the canoe across the sandy beach, launching it without a hitch. The dog waded out after them for several yards before turning back. He stood at the water's edge, barking non-stop. Butch wanted to look back, he couldn't. It would hurt too much. Maybe he shouldn't have let him follow them in the first place. He hoped the dog was smart enough to find his way back to Burnt Cove.

"Butch, pay attention, do as yer told."

"Rory, whatever ya tells me, I'll do."

Butch, must be scared to death. He waited for Butch to tell him to fuck off, Butch stayed quiet. The trip across the harbour was uneventful until they got to the middle. Suddenly, a strong current took the canoe. Butch started rowing like a madman.

"BUTCH! Settle down, scull three times on the port side and twice on the starboard side," Rory yelled.

"What the fuck does scull mean?"

"It means row."

"Why couldn't ya say row, you and yer big fuckin' words."

The wind was against them on the port side. Both were breathing heavily, paddling harder than they ever imagined they could. They could see pole lights starting to come on in Cape Broyle.

"Butch, keep an eye out for the beach. It should be between two rocky outcrops."

Ten minutes later, Butch shouted, "I sees Long Beach, a little to the left."

Rory stroked the canoe left. The water was starting to get a little rough. They could make it to the beach in five minutes with some luck. It was almost dark; the land appeared black between the sea and sky.

"Butch, look for the sea stacks. Paddle—paddle hard!" If they didn't reach the beach before it was dark, their chances of ever finding it would be slim. If they couldn't find the beach, they would have no choice but to head inland towards Cape Broyle, something Rory did not want to do.

"I sees one, Rory! It's right in front of us."

Rory's eyesight was not as good as Butch's. Everything on the coastline looked the same to him.

"We're there, Rory!"

Rory could just make out the outline of a wide beach with the two rocky outcrops on both sides. "Paddle, paddle hard, Butch—I wants to go up on the beach as far as we can."

They landed on the beach. The lifejackets came off and were thrown in the canoe along with the paddles. Butch knelt and kissed the sand. Rory thought about the Pope, John Paul II, who did the same thing every time he got off a plane in a different country. It was his way of showing respect to the country he was visiting.

"That was my last boat ride, Rory."

"C'mon, Butch, pick up the bow. We gotta hide this in the woods."

They hauled the canoe up a steep embankment. Crossed a path, it looked like it was part of the trail the hikers were cutting; they stepped off it into heavy woods, they dragged the canoe a hundred feet or more into the heavy woods. They returned to the path.

"I'm some fuckin' happy we're on land."

"That wasn't a boat."

"Fuck off, prick jaws. Ya knows what I means. I wonder how our dog is doin' on the other side."

"Butch. He never was our dog."

"He was. He was with us long enough to call 'im ours."

"Relax. He's smart enough to get back home."

"I hope so. I liked 'im; I liked 'im a lot. Okay, now, trusted leader, where the fuck is the cabin ya told me about?"

"Let's head towards Calvert. I was told it was on this side of the headland, beyond the beach. We shouldn't have much difficulty findin' it."

The flashlight told Rory the hikers had worked on this section of trail. It had been pruned and widened, stepping stones had been placed in a couple of wet areas. They walked carefully in the dark, trying to find a beaten path that would lead inland away from the path they were walking on. Finally, after walking for thirty minutes, they found a path, it veered off to the right. It was well-worn; Rory figured it had to be the path to the cabin. Sure enough, there it was, sitting on three-foot poles, about three hundred feet from the main trail, partially hidden among tall coniferous trees. It was a fair bit bigger than the one they had stayed in the night before, one window with peeling clapboard painted a dull orange. When Rory turned the doorknob, it wasn't locked, which was the main thing. Most Newfoundlanders don't lock shacks in the country in the rare chance someone gets lost and has to get in out of the elements. It could be the difference between life and death.

Two kerosene lanterns hung from the beam over the table. Rory shook them; both were full of fuel, he lit one. By the light of the lantern, they had a look around. It was more of a shack than a cabin—one unpainted room, which wasn't too clean. There were six bunks with blankets. They had been lucky; all the cabins they had been in had blankets. There was enough wood in the cabin for days. Butch lit the stove, Rory poked around some more.

"Butch, I found more grub under the bed. We'll be as fat as two spring heifers in calf by the time we're finished this journey. I wouldn't bet on it. By the time we reach Cape Race, we'll be lighter than when we started. Let me rephrase that, Butch: ya'll be lighter. I'm about as small as I'll ever be, ya still gotta few pounds of baby fat to lose."

Butch didn't reply. His nerves were still rattled from the trip across the harbour. Being safe on land again, he was thinking about his sidekick he had to leave behind.

After they ate, they turned on the radio. The news broadcast did not mention their names.

"No news is good news," Rory said. "But rest assured, roadblocks are still goin' up. The RCMP aren't stoppin' 'til they get their men. But they won't get us 'til we're ready for 'em to get us."

The weather report predicted heavy rain, with southerly winds overnight, with the possibility of thunder showers for most of the next day and night.

"I knew the weather was brewin'."

"How did ya know, Rory?"

"I saw the stratus clouds to the south as we were crossin' the harbour. We gotta stay here for two nights. No wonder George Calvert fucked off to Maryland with this weather."

"Rory, what's a stratus cloud?"

"They're one of the three clouds that produce rain!"

"Who's George Calvert?"

"Calvert was one of the first settlers in Ferryland."

"Ya mean Calvert?"

"No, Ferryland."

"Did he have anythin' to do with Calvert?

"No, in 1922, a parish priest, Alfred Maher, renamed Capelin Bay to Calvert. In honour of George Calvert."

"And where is Maryland?"

"A State in the US, below Boston, right next to New Jersey."

"Ya serious about stayin' another night?"

"We're hardly goin' to walk to Calvert in the rain with the report they gave out. Walkin' a wet trail is a lot harder than walkin' a dry trail. Newfoundland weather sucks. That's it when ya live on a rock in the middle of the North Atlantic."

"How far is Calvert from here?"

"I'd say eight or nine miles to the highway by Harold Power's store from here."

After a cup of tea and something to eat, Rory found a deck of cards and a crib board shaped like the number twenty-nine. They played crib for a few hours, listening to the wind pound the south side of the cabin as they enjoyed the heat.

"Wouldn't it be nice to have a bottle of Screech and a big ol' dirty ghetto blaster? What a night we'd have."

"Yer days of drinkin' Screech are over for a few years."

Rory beat Butch twelve times, skunking him twice. Butch won four games.

"Butch, yer lousy at crib."

"Ya can't beat me at pool."

"I just beat ya at crib; that's good enough for me. What I wouldn't give for a shave, a bath and a book."

"A piece of pussy would be better."

"Ya'll get all the pussy ya wants when Bubba gets hold of ya in prison."

"Who?"

"Bubba. Ya'll meet 'im first week yer on the inside."

"Who the fuck is Bubba?"

"Go to bed, Butch."

Rory stoked up the fire, turned out the lantern around one in the morning. They crawled in the bunks; they lay awake, chatting and listening to the rain. Thankful, they weren't out in it.

"Ya know, 'cause of yer antics at the bank, we're goin' to miss Run on the Rock."

"What the fuck is Run on the Rock?"

"A motorcycle rally bein' held at Raymond's Field in the Goulds in July. A couple of different chapters of the Hells Angels are comin' in from across the country for it. The 13th Tribe from Halifax is rumoured to be comin'. There could be hundreds of Harleys."

"Where's Raymond's Field?"

"Across from The Hayloft, up in the woods."

"How the fuck were ya goin' to a motorcycle rally when ya don't own a motorcycle?"

"Lots of people go to rodeos that don't own a horse. It woulda' been a great weekend to push some weed and hash."

"I guess yer right."

"Butch, what are ya hummin?"

"A song I'm makin' up in me head. About all the women I've banged."

"Butch, yer burnt. But it makes sense. Ya've fucked every slut from the Goulds to Trepassey."

"Rory. Yer only jealous 'cause I gets the women, and ya can't."

"Butch, most of the chicks ya've banged, I wouldn't touch with a ten-foot pole. How many have ya banged?"

"All of 'em."

"No, seriously, how many?"

"I dunno, maybe thirty-five or forty."

"Ya serious?'

"Yes, why?"

"I never thought it was that many."

"I've had a few more, but they wouldn't bang me, either 'cause they were on the rags or not on the Pill. I guess I am after gettin' ten or twelve blowjobs from the ones who wouldn't put out."

"Ya never started a serious relationship with any of 'em?"

"No, I don't wanna' steady, I wouldn't be able to be faithful."

"Ya don't have much respect for women."

"Rory, they're all sluts, except Momma. Listen, women always want it, and men are always lookin' for it."

"Yer burnt. Here's a verse ya for yer song:

Ferryland for women,
Calvert for style.
Ya want yer skin,
Go to Cape Broyle."

Butch laughed. "Rory, where did ya hear that?"

"I heard it a long time ago. I dunno who I heard it from."

"I likes it."

"Good. Now fuck off hummin', I wants to go to sleep."

"Rory, a question. Are we Irish?

"Yes, Butch, ya stund cunt!"

"Why am I a stund cunt 'cause I dunno something?"

"Yer a stund cunt, ya don't have any common sense or a level of clarity, ya learned that in elementary school."

"Well, I guess I must have missed that day."

"Hynes and O'Ryan are Irish names. Some families dropped the O' in front of their surnames when they arrived here, centuries ago. Any name on the Shore that starts with an O' is Irish. The Shore is eighty percent Irish; the rest are either English or Scottish. Most of the Irish on the Shore came from County Waterford and County Kilkenny, southeast Ireland. A bit of history for ya: Cappahayden was originally called Broad Cove up until 1913, a Catholic priest named John Walsh renamed it after his birthplace, Cappahayden, in County Kilkenny. Now fuck off and go to sleep."

"Why did he do that?"

"'Cause he wanted to. Remember, back then, everyone considered Priests as God. Whatever they said was Gospel and still is taday to some degree."

"Ok, another question. Why are there Ryan's and O'Ryan's?"

"Some families put the prefix back after bein' here for generations."

"How do ya remember so much?"

"Anythin', I have an interest in, I remembers. Now go to sleep."

"Night, sweetheart."

"Fuck off, Butch—yer pushin' it."

"I La Lu!"

"What the fuck does that mean?"

"A little girl named Sandra, I spoke to with her mother while hitchhikin' in Bay Bulls last year said it to me, it's 'I love you.' She can't pronounce her words properly yet; she's only two, blonde curly hair, cute as a kitten. It's cute, ain't it, Rory?"

"Fuck off and go to sleep!"

CHAPTER THIRTY

"Rory, Rory, wake up! I hears someone at the door."

"Settle down: that's rollin' thunder. The weather broadcast gave out for thunder overnight."

"Rory, that ain't fuckin' thunder, rollin' or not."

Rory listened hard. Butch was right: it sounded like someone trying to get in.

"Holy fuck, Butch. Who the fuck can it be?"

"I dunno, I been listenin' to 'em at the door for a few minutes, and it's pourin' out. Rory, it can't be a human fuckin' bein'. The door isn't locked. Get up, Rory, and see what it is."

"I ain't movin'!"

Butch got out of bed, grabbed the flashlight from the table, he slowly made his way to the door. He put his ear to the door and suddenly threw it wide open.

"Jesus Christ, Rory!" By now, Rory could hear the dog prancing around the cabin.

"Rory, get up! It's Lucky."

"I knows, I can hear 'im. And smell 'im. Wet mutt."

Butch knelt beside Lucky; he buried his face in the wet coat of the dog he never owned. He hoped the wind and rain were loud enough so Rory wouldn't be able to hear him being emotional. He bit his lip, waiting for his emotions to pass. He was beyond happy. He lit the lantern and checked Lucky out.

"Rory, how'd he find us?"

"I have no idea."

"Rory, I'm some happy he did. Can I give 'im a can of somethin' to eat?"

"Sure. He deserves it."

Butch gave him a can of corned beef hash and a can of cam. Lucky wolfed both down in less than ten seconds.

"Butch, run yer fingers through his coat and taste 'em, see if ya can taste salt."

Butch ran his fingers tips down the dogs back and licked them. "I can't taste salt."

"Well, he never swam across the harbour. He knew if he went towards Cape Broyle, he would find us. Butch, he's a smart dog. I bet he's a good bird dog. Whoever owns 'im will be disappointed he's gone."

"Fuck whoever owns 'im. We owns 'im now."

"Ya might; I don't. I got enough troubles of me own without havin' to take care of a dog. Remember, Butch, we're on our way to a federal prison for at least two years. Who is goin' to take care of 'im when we're locked up?"

"I dunno, I'm sure we'll find someone to look after 'im. We'll have to find someone."

"No, ya'll find someone."

"Rory, the three of us are on this journey together. We can't abandon 'im when it's over. You might, I won't."

"Get a blanket, Butch, put it on the floor for the dog."

"Like the fuck. He's gettin' in the bunk with me."

Rory woke at nine and got up. He glanced towards the other bunk, shook his head at the sight of the setter on Butch's bunk with a blanket over him. The blanket was dry, which told him the dog was now dry.

The weatherman was right on the mark: it was raining cats and dogs out, sheets of rain blowing sideways from the south. Rain with a southerly wind can last for days on the Avalon Peninsula, especially on the Southern Shore. Rory could hear the sea rolling; it had come up since they crossed the harbour. Even though they were a fair distance from it, it was still sounding powerful. Rory had a cup of tea, smoked two cigarettes, banked up the fire, and crawled back into the bunk.

When he woke at twelve, the rain had let up a bit. The dog was at the door, trying to get out. He needed to relieve himself. Rory did as well. He hauled on his oilskin coat, went out behind the cabin. There was an old green dilapidated outhouse, which some old-timers still call a privy. Rory did his business in the rain. He wasn't chancing going into the outhouse and ending up in a shit pit if the floor was rotting and couldn't hold his weight.

When he got back to the cabin, the dog was on the step. Rory let him in; Lucky jumped up beside Butch and curled around him. Another good hand to sleep, a perfect buddy for Butch.

He put the kettle and some saltfish on to boil for dinner. He started contemplating how they were going to make it the rest of the way. He figured they were over halfway. He knew he was gambling on the trail being opened by the hikers the further south they went. He figured less of it would be pruned and widened the further away they got from the city. For the most part, it was open to some degree as a means of travelling between communities eighty or a hundred years ago and for hunting sea ducks. Moose and other animals helped keep the trail open as well.

When they hit the highway in Calvert, they'd look for the trail somewhere below the Squid Jigger Lounge. He figured they would come out somewhere by Baltimore High School in Ferryland. They'd cross the highway, get up on the old railway track, which would bring them to the highway. They'd cross the road and walk in Freshwater Road to the end. The trail should start somewhere at the end of Freshwater Road. Rory was surmising and hoping he was right.

But where in Aquaforte did the trail exit? Most likely at Spout River, the river crossed the road by the Ultramar bulk storage tanks close to Vivian Grahams' old food-store building. Spout River was wide; the hiking group wouldn't have the funds to build a bridge over it, not yet anyway. A makeshift bridge would never last, with ice washing down the river in the spring runoff. He figured they'd pick up the trail, past South West River on the south side of Aquaforte. If there was even a trail by this river, it would bring them into Port Kirwan on the north side of Fermeuse. Rory doubted it. Aquaforte to Port Kirwan was a long-distance by way of the coastline.

Kingman's Cove Road is on the south side of Fermeuse. It's where the trail would start to go towards the north side of Renews. The trail going into Renews would come out somewhere near the public wharf on the harbour's north side. When they made it to Renews, they'd figure out how to get to Cappahayden and the rest of the way. It was hard going, one community at a time. Their luck had been good thus far.

Butch finally crawled out of bed at two o'clock.

"Butch, ya looks like shit."

"Fuck off, I already told ya, I'm not a mornin' person."

"It's not mornin'. I figured ya'd be in a better mood with yer sidekick next to ya."

"He never moved all night."

"He didn't, did he? I was up earlier and let 'im out to piss. Some dog lover ya are, ya couldn't even get up to let the poor dumb animal out to do his business."

"Fuck off. Any water there for a cup of tea?"

"Yes, there's a drop. One of us will have to go look for water sometime taday. We're gettin' low."

While the kettle boiled, Rory said to Butch, "I tossed and turned all night. It's like a dream; we got caught in Renews."

"Jesus Rory, don't say that."

Rory gave Butch a rundown on the route that would get them to Renews. Butch agreed and nodded. Rory knew areas of the Southern Shore better than he did.

"Butch, did the hikers happen to say if they did any work beyond La Manche?"

"I can't honestly say. The bar was three parts full; I was wired, the jukebox was blarin'. I was hustlin'. All I can tell ya is they told me they were a couple of years openin' up trails on the Shore from Fort Amherst to Cape Race."

"Well, they haven't let us down yet. But the big question is, how far beyond Renews or Cappahayden will we get on the trail? If it ends in one of those communities, we could be in trouble.

We can't walk the highway, well, if we must, we will. After midnight and off the road before daylight. Walkin' the highway will take us at least two nights to make it to Portugal Cove South from Cappahayden. We might do it in one night if we put the push on. There's a fine lotta miles between those two communities. Here, Butch, I'll get yer tea for ya."

Rory hauled on his oilskins, grabbed the water jugs, he headed towards Calvert. There was no river between Lance Cove beach and the cabin; there might be one in the opposite direction. After walking for fifteen minutes, headfirst into the wind and rain, he came upon a small stream. He knelt, filled the jugs and headed back to the cabin.

Butch had taken one of the pens he'd found in the last cabin with him. While Rory was gone, he took the full-length calendar with half-naked models down; he printed on the unpainted wall, "BH & ROR were here May82 (3)". When he replaced the calendar, he wondered if this would be their last cabin. These cabins had been a godsend.

"Rory, ya weren't long."

"No, I found a small stream on the trail towards Calvert. The water will need to be boiled; it's brown with runoff from the rain. It's pourin' out. The trail is all mud; I'm mud to me balls. We'll have a wet slog makin' it to Calvert."

"Rory, give Lucky a drink of water."

Rory poured water into an old saucepan, laid it on the floor and called Lucky. The dog jumped off the bed, drank and returned to the bunk.

"Butch, while I was out gettin' water, I gave some more thought to us walkin' from Cappahayden to Portugal Cove South. There are many cabins on the highway, a dozen or so on Old Shoe Cove Road; maybe we could break into one and spend a night, two if the weather is bad. If we do, we won't be able to light a fire durin' the day."

"Why not, Rory?"

"Well, all the cabins are on the highway or reasonably close to it. Someone sees smoke comin' out of one of the cabins with no car or truck parked next to it, they'll figure out who may be in it. We'll be caught in no time. Not only that, but the cops will also be cruisin' around lookin' for us, checkin' out places like cabins and sheds. We'll wing it, play it by ear. Butch, I'm havin' fish and the last of the vins and a few capelin for supper. What're ya havin'?"

"It won't be saltfish, capelin or vins. I'll get a can of somethin'."

"Fine with me. I'm goin' to stretch out 'fore supper, like the rest of ye."

All three dozed off for a few hours. When Rory woke, he put on the fish and vins. Shortly afterward, Butch got up, put on a can of tomato soup. He soaked stale crackers in it, which he'd found in the cabin. Rory said they were getting low on bread, so it was only one slice each for supper.

"Why don't we break into a convenience store? Every community has two or three. We're goin' away for the armed robbery and the dope—fuck it if we gets caught."

"Butch, that's too foolish to even talk about. If we breaks into a convenience store, the cops would be all over that community; they'd figure it was us who did the B and E. That would put the chances of gettin' caught much higher."

"I guess." Butch was dying for a coke, a decent smoke, and a raisin square. He was sick of the rollies. What Rory was saying was right. He was always right, not that Butch would ever tell him.

They played cards until it was time to turn in. Rory won most of the games, which pissed Butch off—he hated losing. Before they turned in, they listened to the weather report. The rain was forecasted to end overnight, with sun and warmer temperatures predicted for the following day.

They turned out the lantern and turned in. Rory listened to the rain pounding on the roof. What a beautiful sound, especially when you hoped you'd be waking up to sunshine.

CHAPTER THIRTY-ONE

When they woke, the rain had let up. Rory let the dog out, and stoked up the embers and hove in some dry wood. He threw on a small saltfish to boil. Butch toasted a slice of bread on top of the stove, said how much he'd enjoy partridge berry jam on his toast if he had it.

"What's the plan, Rory?"

"We'll leave around noon to walk to Calvert. We needs to be at North Side Road 'fore dark. We'll have to wait 'til at least midnight 'fore attemptin' to walk to the highway."

"What do we do when we gets to the highway?"

"I'm thinkin' the trail should start somewhere below the Jigger. I'm hopin' it brings us somewhere past the school."

"What do we do when we gets to the school?"

"We'll cross the road, get up on the old railway track. We'll walk the track, go down Goose Well Lane by the old cemetery, this side of the white bungalow belongin' to the Whites."

"More damn cemeteries!"

"Relax, Butch. I won't be mentionin' cemeteries anymore. I promise. More on me mind than havin' ya runnin' around like a lunatic." That's all they needed, Butch running around like a chicken with its head cut off, followed by a barking dog. "The track will bring us to the highway. I figures we cross the road, go in Freshwater Road. I'm hopin' the trail starts somewhere in that area. It's the most logical place for it to start to head towards Aquaforte."

"Where will that bring us?"

"I dunno, I'm thinkin' we'll break out somewhere 'fore Spout

River. There's no way for us to cross that river, it's too wide, and the current is too powerful. We should hit the pavement somewhere around Vivian Grahams' old food store buildin', across the road from the Ultramar bulk storage tanks."

"What do we do after that?"

"That's as far as I have given serious thought to. When we gets to Aquaforte, we'll have to find the trail on the other side of South West River. I swam in that river dozens of times when I was young, in the swimmin' hole called Salmon Pool. Me ol' man useta take me out there on Sunday afternoons."

"How'd I miss that?"

"Ya weren't allowed to go. Yer ol' man was afraid of water, he wouldn't let ya go swimmin', afraid ya'd drown. That's why ya can't swim. If yer father had let ya go, ya'd know how to swim. And ya wouldn't be so afraid in a boat."

"I guess I'm too old to learn now."

"When we go up-along to a federal penitentiary, ya'll be able to take swimmin' lessons."

"They have swimmin' pools in prisons?"

"No, ya, chucklehead!"

"What the fuck does that mean?"

"It's an old sayin', grandfather useta say it, it means idiot."

"Quit tormentin' me. How would I know there aren't any swimmin' pools in prison?"

"Butch, everyone knows that."

"Well, I didn't."

"Go figure, ya didn't know somethin'."

"Rory, please tell me there's pool tables in prison."

"I don't think there are."

"Why not?" Butch's face was so long he looked like a bloodhound.

"Too dangerous. If a riot broke out, prisoners could break the cue sticks in half and use 'em as impalin' weapons, and the pool balls could be put in socks to beat someone about the head with."

"Fuck, Rory, I'll be some rusty by the time I gets out."

After they ate, they went behind the cabin and brought in

firewood to replenish what they had burned. In Bay Bulls and Admiral's Cove, no wood was there to replace what they burnt. After lugging the firewood in, Rory swept the floor with a birch broom and swept the dirt out the door.

"Butch, hopefully, no one will ever notice we were here. I doubt if anyone will ever know we were here. Could be weeks or months 'fore someone is here." Butch thought to himself. I did leave our initials.

The rollies Joe had given them were almost gone. They took turns rolling cigarettes by hand. Most of them looked like poorly rolled joints.

"Okay, Butch, time to start movin'. We gotta long, arduous walk ahead of us, walkin' in mud after all the rain the past two days and nights."

Rory double-checked with Butch to make sure they had everything in the brin bags, especially toilet paper. Bad enough shitting in the woods, worse shitting in the woods with no toilet paper.

"Butch, I'm puttin' on me oil pants and jacket. The trails open, but it needs a lot more work. Ya should put yers on, too —brushin' up against scrub, and the drip from the overhangin' branches is goin' to soak ya if ya don't."

They walked for two hours into a mild head-on breeze, a long, strenuous, weary walk, before stopping to rest. The path was pure mud with pools of water every couple of feet. They were exhausted; the trail was hilly and a challenge to find at times. Lucky was the only one enjoying the hike, disappearing for up to twenty minutes at a time.

"Another three or four hours, I suspect, Butch, 'fore we makes it to Stone Island Road. C'mon, let's keep at it."

The boys could hear the ocean pound the coastline as they made their way. The wind had the sea stirred up from the heavy winds the previous two days. The brin bags slowed their walking; they contained ten or fifteen pounds of saltfish, plus a dozen cans of tinned food. By the time they reached the road, they were soaking wet with sweat. They sat on a deadfall tree and watched the emitting light of Ferryland Lighthouse to the south.

"Rory, I guess we'll wait here. What time is it?"

"Quarter to six."

"Rory, we got five or six hours 'fore we even attempts the walk to the highway. I'll be bored out of me mind."

"Well, it's time ya got used to boredom. Ya gotta couple of years of it ahead of ya."

"Rory, why are ya remindin' me of what we gotta face?"

"Cause we wouldn't be standin' here on the north side of Calvert sweatin' like elephants, beat to a snot if not for you. Now shut the fuck up, I'm in no mood to listen to ya. Go find a spot for you and yer sidekick to bide the time. I'm havin' a nap right where I'm sittin' after I haves a smoke."

They slept till ten-thirty.

"Rory, I can taste salt in the sweat that's gettin' in me mouth. It must be from all the saltfish I'm eatin'."

Rory laughed. "It's the sea spray. We've been walkin' next to the ocean since we left the Goulds."

"Ya serious?"

"Duh. Put the collar on the dog, tie a rope to it. Hold 'im tight as we walk to the Jigger. We can't chance 'im wanderin' into someone's yard and gettin' every dog in Calvert barkin'. Anythin' different or strange goin' on in any community will be reported, especially this hour of the night."

They took off their rubber boots, hauled on their sneakers. They walked a fast pace up the north side of Calvert towards the highway. It was after one when they reached the highway. By the time they hit the highway, they were huffing and puffing like two eighty-year-olds.

"Butch, when I gets to prison, I'm quittin' smokin'."

"I'll probably smoke more in prison. Where do we go from here, Rory?"

"Towards the Jigger. The hikers should have the trail cut somewhere below the Jigger; if not, we'll have to walk the highway to the track. Walkin' to Ferryland on the highway is not a good idea, especially with the RCMP detachment in Ferryland, and more than likely, with extra cops workin' out of it tryin' to catch us."

They walked the shoulder of the highway, going up the steep hill. Using the flashlight looking for an opening in the trees. And there it was, about eight hundred feet from the Jigger. They ducked into the woods, went down a steep decline towards the ocean.

"Butch, this has to be the trail. It has been trimmed and pruned recently, by the look of it. Who would do it, other than the hikers? But the big question is how far this section goes. Hopefully to the school."

They walked carefully, coming out close to the school in forty-five minutes. Rory never mentioned when they passed a cemetery; all he needed was Butch running around Ferryland like someone demented, bringing every cop at the detachment their way. The graveyard was Catholic, also used by Calvert. They crossed the highway and made their way to Sunny Hill Road, which put them on the old train track.

Rory gave Butch a quick talking to. "Butch, under no circumstances can ya let the dog get loose or bark. Anythin' that gets the attention of anyone livin' around here will have the cops on this track within minutes, with a dog or two."

The boys walked fast; they wanted out of Ferryland as fast as possible, away from the RCMP detachment. They passed Ron Hynes' old homestead, a member of the Wonderful Grand Band and the Stone Gothic Style Holy Trinity Church, which sat below the track. They made their way along under the hill known as the Gaze and went down Goose Well Lane, and hit the highway. They crossed it and made their way in Freshwater Road.

"Rory, I needs a rest."

Rory replied in a low, angry voice. "Keep walkin' and be quiet. We'll rest when we hits the woods at the end of this road. Another ten minutes or so."

When they reached the tree line, both dropped to the ground, exhausted from the pace they had been keeping since they hit the highway in Calvert.

"Rory, give me one of 'em rollies. How far is it to Aquaforte?"

"At least three or four miles. It's three now; we'll walk for ten or fifteen minutes, find a spot to sleep for a few hours."

Ten minutes later, they found a grassy knoll just off the path. They hauled on the oil pants and jackets; Butch opened a can of spaghetti, he shared half with Lucky. Rory had a can of ravioli; he gave the dog a little.

"Don't be so miserable; give Lucky some more."

"I don't own 'em, why should I feed 'em?"

"I'll tell ya why. He's a livin' breathin' animal who's with us, like it or not. He's walked as far as we have, and he's as hungry as us."

"Oh, for fuck sake. Have what's left in the can."

As Rory lay on the ground awaiting sleep, he smiled, staring at the stars. Wouldn't the RCMP be livid, knowing they were technically walking past the detachment. Rory fell asleep quickly. Before he drifted off, he thought of how hard a hike they just had, the most challenging workout since the beginning, when they'd run down Shoal Bay Road like two scalded cats.

CHAPTER THIRTY-TWO

When they woke, the sun was shining, the temperature had gone up a few degrees. Having slept in their oil clothes, they were covered in sweat again. Lucky was nowhere to be seen.

"Rory, I gotta go back and look for Lucky." Butch's voice was full of panic.

"Like the fuck! Ya serious? Someone sees a stranger walkin' the roads, the cops will be called. Don't worry about the dog. He made it from one side of Cape Broyle Harbour to the other side. He'll come back. Sure, he's probably off chasin' a rabbit."

"I s'pose. Are we goin' to eat?"

"Not 'til we gets closer to the highway in Aquaforte. Which I'm thinkin' is about two or three hours from here. Let's haul off these oil clothes, have a smoke and get underway."

The walk was brutal. Speaking was limited.

Roughly a mile and a half along the trail, they came to a summit. From there, they could see Ferryland Head to the north and Spurwink Island on the south side of Aquaforte Harbour.

"Rory, these hills are killin' me."

"Yer own fault for bein' overweight."

"Fuck off, Rory. I can't help it, I'm a big man."

"A big shit."

"Keep it up, Rory. I'll turn around and walk the other way."

"Fine with me. Enjoy whichever penitentiary yer put in. Don't worry, we're nearly there. In less than an hour, we should break out somewhere this side of Spout River. Let's sit down for a bit."

They came to a small river. Rory knew it wasn't Spout River. The flow was too low for it to be Spout River.

"Rory, me knees are gone. Look—it's Lucky!"

The muddy dog, whining with pleasure, ran to Butch, knocking him off a downed tree he was sitting on.

What noise from the two of them, like a couple of youngsters. Rory shook his head in disgust. "C'mon, Butch, time to start walkin'."

Within a half-hour, they could hear another river. The path veered off to the right. Rory figured it would lead them to the highway. Twenty minutes later, they walked out of the woods, seeing the highway.

"Right where I figured we'd break out. I knew the hikers couldn't have built a bridge over Spout River. Buildin' wooden bridges is costly, with a lot of labour involved. A bridge, or should I say bridges, are a long way down the road for that crowd if they ever do get government fundin'."

They went back into the woods, found a spot to make a small fire to boil some fish and heat a few cans of whatever they had with them. Rory collected some dry wood and started a fire.

"What I wouldn't give for a few thin slices of bologna and a bag of plain chips to make a Newfie sandwich. I loves 'em, I do. Rory, turn on the radio, see what the news is sayin' and what the weatherman is givin' out."

Rory tried every radio channel, all he got was static. He wasn't surprised. He knew the farther they got from St. John's, the less chance there was of picking up radio stations, especially on a cheap transistor radio. He'd been surprised, they got reception on Cape Broyle Head.

"Butch, it's three o'clock now. We're not leavin' here 'til midnight or later. We gotta walk two miles or more on the highway, the riskiest travel since we travelled from Witless Bay to Burnt Cove Hill. Tie on the dog while we gets a nap."

"No way I'm tyin' on the dog. It's cruel, there's no need."

"Suit yerself. But don't go snottin' and bawlin' if he goes to the highway and gets hit by a car or don't come back." Rory wasn't going to fall out with Butch over a dog. The end of everything was getting closer, might as well keep the peace.

They found a decent spot to nap in among some young spruce trees. Before Butch hauled on his oil clothes, he told Rory he had to go have a crap. He opened up one of the brin bags to get toilet paper, he saw the boning knife. Taking it out, he carefully slid it down his rubber boot, making sure Rory didn't notice him do it.

When he was finished doing his business, he found a thick, snotty evergreen and engraved "BH/ROR May82" on it. He figured someday after he got out of prison, he'd come back and find the inscription. Or maybe others will see it. Butch imagined what would be said if people found their names on the trees or in the cabins. Maybe, the trail builders will find them. He figured it would cause some interest if reported to the RCMP, which he suspected it would be.

When he got back, Rory opened one eye and asked Butch what had taken him so long.

"I couldn't do anythin'. I'm constipated from eatin' so much saltfish."

Rory laughed, rolled over, and went to sleep. They slept till eight. When they woke, the dog was beside Butch in the same position he'd been in when they dozed off.

"So, Butch, yer bum still bound up?"

"Fuck off, arsehole."

"Nothin' wrong with me, arsehole," Rory said with an evil grin and a laugh. "How'd ya get so much turpentine on yer hands again?"

"I tried to limb a few evergreens with the bonin' knife for the fire. Fuckin' knife is useless."

The boys rolled and lit smoke after smoke and chatted. Rory said, they'd be able to run the Tely 10 if they had still been home for it. Said they were in good enough shape to run it; with all the walking they had done. Butch asked, "what's the Tely 10?"

"It's a ten-mile road race from Paradise to Bannerman Park in St. John's, started in 1922. Ben Dunne from Renews won it in 75."

Butch said, "he wasn't a runner." Rory laughed. "Ya ran

down Shoal Bay Road pretty fuckin' fast."

"Yes, Rory, I did, but that was different."

"Well, Butch my advice to ya, in case ya ever decide to run the Tely 10 when ya gets home from up along, pretend the cops are chasin' ya."

Butch ignored Rory, got up and stretched. "I'm itchin' to get movin', Rory."

"No way. Too risky to move 'til midnight or later, less traffic."

Midnight finally rolled around; they made their way to the highway. The bulk storage tanks were lit up brighter than the powerhouse in Witless Bay.

They walked fast, trying to get away from the lights. Butch had the dog leashed. Rory was surprised he did it without having been told to do it.

They passed a cemetery on their left, with a road running alongside it, a road that was part of the old Southern Shore Highway. Rory had forgotten it existed and the name of it.

"Butch, we're goin' to walk this road. It'll be safer than walkin' the highway. Less chance of bein' seen, I'm sure the cops are stickin' to the highway."

As they veered off to the left to set foot on the old road, they heard a car coming towards them from the south at high speed. A car with plenty of horsepower, by the sound of it.

"Run, Butch!"

They sprinted in the old road, which was lined with large trees which hid them from view. Lucky didn't make a sound; Rory had expected him to start barking when he yelled, and they started running. To a dog, it was a bit of excitement. A couple of hundred feet in the road, they stopped and looked back just in time to see two RCMP vehicles, a car and a Suburban, fly past.

"Man, that was close. I knew it was goin' to happen. I knew it; the closer we gets to Cappahayden, the higher the chance we'd run into cops and most likely plenty of 'em. We have to be on our toes from here till we gets beyond Cappahayden. I'm sure Cappahyden is not crawlin' with cops. Keep yer eyes open and speak quietly. As I said earlier, someone calls the cops about two suspicious characters walkin' through their community, we're finished. There'll be a posse of cops on us like Ali's gloves on flesh."

"Okay, let's go. We have to separate. You first with the dog, I'll follow in ten minutes."

When they reached the highway, they crisscrossed the highway from side to side, trying to stay out of the glare of the pole lights. Aquaforte was incorporated in 1972, which is why street lights were lining the highway. They kept a fair distance apart. One car passed them, they could hear it coming, they took cover in the alders in the ditch lining the road. Butch reached the bridge at South West River. He waited in the trees for Rory to catch up. When Rory arrived, he told Butch to follow him. They ducked into the woods, left of the highway, crossed an old, dilapidated cement bridge. At the other end of the bridge, they found an opening going into the woods, where Rory figured the hikers would have started cutting a trail going into Port Kirwan.

They walked for ten minutes, looking for a decent spot to sleep. Rory knew what they were facing the next day. The walk into Port Kirwan was going to be at least nine or ten miles. They had to walk from the bottom of Port Kirwan back to the highway and walk the highway to the start of Kingman's Cove Road. Three long and gruelling walks.

They were famished, too exhausted to fetch water or light a fire. They had a few gulps of water of what they had left. They settled down and slept until seven.

When Rory woke, he grabbed the jugs, went back to South West River, went under the old bridge, and filled them. He lit the fire and put on some fish to boil. When Butch woke, the kettle was boiled. He liked that, to wake up and have a hot mug of tea in his hand in a minute or two.

Rory told Butch what was in front of them, Butch listened attentively. When Rory finished talking, Butch said, "I got an idea. And 'fore ya goes shittin' on me, please hear me out. Sure, isn't it just as easy to walk to Kingman's Cove Road from here as it is to hike to the bottom of Port Kirwan and have to walk back to the highway? Walkin' the highway from here to Kingman's Cove Road is much shorter and easier, ya knows how hard it is walkin' the trail."

"Butch, let me contemplate it for a few minutes."

Butch lit up a smoke. He watched Lucky nosing around in the undergrowth. Rory sat in silence, pondering what Butch suggested.

"Butch, I hates to agree with ya. I believe ya are exactly right. I always wanted to see Berry Head Sea Arch. I guess I'll see it another time. I agree it would be much shorter. It makes a hell of a lot more sense to walk to Kingman's Cove Road from here than to walk the coast and back up out of Port Kirwan. We would be killin' two birds with one stone. We gotta change the way we've been travellin'. We'll have to space ourselves even more. We can't stay together walkin' through Fermeuse. We needs a longer distance and time between us than we had walkin' through Aquaforte."

"Why?"

"Well, Butch, we will not be walkin' till one or two in the mornin' or later. Even though it will be late, there's always a chance someone is lookin' through a window. There's a few pole lights on the highway goin' through Fermeuse. This is what we'll do: ya'll walk first with the dog, I'll follow an hour or an hour and a half later. I'll carry all the gear. You walk like a perfectly normal person. I'll keep to the woods and ditches as much as possible. I'm smaller and quicker than you. Under no circumstances can we be seen together. Two people walkin' through a community, any community on the Shore that hour of the mornin' will bring the heat in a hurry. Even if ya are seen, the dog will throw people off. No one, especially the cops, would be expectin' us to be travellin' with a dog."

"Sounds like a plan, Rory."

In the afternoon, they walked out the coast as far as Gallows Cove for something to do. When they got back, they boiled the kettle, ate, and had a few smokes before settling down for a nap.

CHAPTER THIRTY-THREE

When they woke, it was pitch black and had gotten colder. They boiled the kettle for one last mug of tea. They waited, boredom sitting heavily on them. Finally, it was time to make a move. Both pissed on the fire to out it. Butch put the collar and leash on the dog.

"Walk normally. Don't raise yer voice to Lucky. If ya meets anyone, if they speaks, say 'hello' and keep walkin'. Do not run under any circumstances. If we gets separated, that's the end of our chance of gettin' to the stash together."

"Rory, I gotta tell ya, I'm scared to death."

"Relax, ya managed to rob a bank in broad daylight. That must have been pretty scary."

"I gotta agree, it was. But for some reason, I'm shakin' like a leaf. I could shit me drawers."

"Listen to me, ya'll be fine. Walk straight and fast, real fast, and like I said, no runnin'."

"What do I do if I sees a car comin'?"

"Keep walkin' straight ahead with yer head down. Don't release the dog for any reason. The chances of seein' a car or anyone walkin' this hour of the mornin' are slim to none. If the cops happen to stop and ask yer name, say yer Jeremiah Kenny from Fermeuse. Fermeuse is full of Kenny's. If they question ya, say yer home from Toronah, and ya spend half yer time here and the other half in Toronah. And yer out exercisin' yer dog. Remember, even if they stop to talk to ya, we don't look like ourselves. We haven't shaved in over a week. There's a good chance they won't recognize us, especially you. They're usin' yer grade seven school picture. Also, if a cop stops, he's most likely not even stationed in

Ferryland. Seconded for the great Southern Shore manhunt. And as I said earlier, the dog will throw them off."

"Rory, I sees a cop car; I'll seriously shit me drawers. I'm shit baked!"

"That's twice yer after sayin' that, shit 'fore ya leave!"

"I can't, I'm too fuckin' nervous, and I'm still bound up."

"Ya won't be bound up for long if ya sees a cop car," Rory said with a laugh.

"Butch, it's either one or the other, either ya shit, or ya don't gotta shit."

"I'll shit when I gets there!"

"Relax; ya'll be fine. Like I said 'fore, we'll be talkin' about this adventure when we're old with our grandchildren. Now get movin'. I'm leavin' in an hour or a little more. Ya should be on Kingman's Cove Road by the time I leave here, with yer stride."

"What do I do when I gets to Kingman's Cove Road?"

"Walk a little slower. I'll catch up with ya 'fore ya reach the bottom. See ya in a couple of hours."

Butch headed south towards Fermeuse. His palms were sweaty, his heart was pounding, he kept a steady pace. Whenever he approached a pole light, his heart pounded like it was going to burst through his chest.

As he passed Southern Strand Lounge, he could see a light behind the bar through a small side window. A Black Horse Beer sign illuminated. What he wouldn't give for a cold beer or two, for the sweat he was working up and for his nerves. Breaking in crossed his mind; if he got caught, Rory would flip.

He kept moving, climbing the steep hill by Brophy's Ultramar, which was a workout. He was doing what he was told, keeping a consistent pace. He was dying for a piss, but it would have to wait. Getting off the highway was more important than relieving his kidneys.

He reached the turnoff to Kingman's Cove without a car passing him in either direction. He was relieved to be off the highway. He tied Lucky to an alder and had the best piss of his life. It was better than the best orgasm he ever had. He wondered what time it was; he didn't have a watch. Never wore one in his life. He lit up a smoke and ambled down the road, looking behind occasionally, wondering how long it would be before Rory caught up with him. He was on his third cigarette with still no sign of Rory.

He sat on the gravel road to wait for Rory. He started to doze off, Lucky started barking. Butch figured it was either Rory, another dog, or a moose. He decided to let Lucky off the leash; he ran back up the road in the direction they had come. Ten minutes passed, twenty minutes, the dog didn't come back. Butch's nerves were beyond the fraying point. He started to pace in circles. He heard a faint voice in the distance. He figured it had to be Rory.

"Rory? Rory!"

"Butch, that you?"

"Yes!"

"What took ya s'long?"

"Here, take the gear—I'm beat. I was makin' good headway 'til I saw a car comin' toward me, I had to lay down in the ditch. When I got back on the road, I spotted an RCMP cruiser under a pole light comin' towards me. I wasn't takin' a chance, I beat it in behind Windsor's Rock, waited there for twenty minutes or so 'fore I started walkin' again. I'd say the cruiser was most likely comin' back from Cappahayden. Did ya see anyone?"

"Not a soul."

"I told ya not to release the dog."

"I never, till I thought I heard ya. He was goin' wild barkin'. I guess he heard ya walkin'. I gotta admit, I was frightened to death."

"Okay, no big deal. I'm thinkin' we should be at the end of this road in less than an hour."

A quarter-mile past the last house on the road, they flopped down on a grassy bank.

"What's the plan from here, Rory?"

"I got no idea. I'd like to find a cabin, but findin' a cabin in the dark, not knowin' if there are cabins anywhere in this area, would be like lookin' for a needle in a haystack."

They lay where they were, rolled cigarettes and smoked until they fell asleep. When they woke, it was daylight.

"Get up, Butch! Us here asleep on a right-of-way, sure anyone could come along on a three-wheeler or a dirt bike."

They picked up their gear and headed for the woods. As they entered the woods, they could see the wreck of the SS Ilex. The SS Ilex left St. John's on the morning of October 27th,1948. She was en route to Kingston, Jamaica, with a shipment of saltfish. When an approaching storm forced the ship to seek refuge in Fermeuse Harbour. Shortly after the crew tied the ship off to the wharf in Kingman's Cove, a fire broke out in the engine room. Firefighting efforts followed, but by morning the ship was destroyed and beyond salvaging. The vessel was ran aground in its current resting place.

They walked for ten minutes, lit a fire, and had something to eat.

"We're goin' to walk to Renews while it's daylight. I hope the original trail is passable. I'm thinkin' it most likely is, as there are a lot of duck hunters in Renews usin' the shoreline which should have it well beaten."

"Rory, I needs more sleep. That was a long and stressful walk from Aquaforte."

"It's only five or six miles to Renews. We'll be there in a few hours. Ya can sleep then."

"We gotta be extra careful when we approach Bear Cove Point Light Station. One of the two staff, either Jim Chidley or Raymond Fennelly, are guaranteed to be on site."

They had a leisurely walk on the well-used path to Bear Cove Point Light Station, compared to some of the paths they had been on.

"Rory, where's this road go?"

"It's Bear Cove Point Road. It goes right into the heart of the north side of Renews."

"We should walk it."

"Ya serious? We're s'posed to be stayin' away from people and communities. Not walkin' into a population."

They left the path and stayed in the heavy trees and alders, crossing Bear Cove Point Road a couple of hundred feet back from the light. They made their way back to the coastal path. As Rory suspected, the path was well beaten down; men from Renews most likely used it for hunting sea ducks. Renews men are known duck hunters, especially saltwater ducks. At South Point, they had a few smokes.

Dark was coming on. They kept trudging along; this path was the best path they had been on. They reached a large open meadow near Renews public wharf. Rory was a little nervous about staying in this location, with no trees to conceal them. They got down out of sight on the leeward side of a large boulder embedded in the ground, which protected them from a cool breeze blowing in off the ocean. They were facing the community; if they noticed anyone coming, they could get back to the tree line reasonably quick before being spotted.

"Rory, I'm starved."

"Eat away, but it will be cold. We can't light a fire here, too exposed. Besides, there's nothin' here to burn. Here's the plan for the night. The same as last night. Ya leave here at around one with the dog, I'll follow an hour or so later."

"Ya serious? I nearly shit meself walkin' through Fermeuse last night."

"There is one salvation: it's a much shorter walk than last night and relatively level as Renews is fairly flat. Ya can walk the beach on both sides of the harbour rather than havin' to stay on the road. Butch, we're all but there. Cappahayden is the last community left to go through to get to Portugal Cove South. I'd say we'll be on Cape Race Road in two days or so, three days in a worst-case scenario."

"I can't wait to get to the other side of this harbour. I'm hungry and tired."

"Sure, Butch, we may as well sleep now. We can get five or six hours of decent sleep 'fore it's time to move. Tie on the dog — can't have a strange Irish setter runnin' around Renews. Guaranteed, someone would catch 'im and keep 'im in no time. Most likely, a bird hunter."

Butch leashed the dog, he put the rope around his ankle. They leaned back against the rock and slept solidly.

CHAPTER THIRTY-FOUR

Rory woke first, rolled a cigarette, lit it, waiting for Butch to wake up. He thought how he'd like to go say a prayer at Our Lady of Lourdes Grotto. Built between 1927 and 1928, it sits behind Holy Apostles Church. Renews Grotto is one of three in Newfoundland. It had been some time since he'd done that. Walking through the community would be too risky. Rory wasn't a big churchgoer; he had faith. St. Patrick's Church in Cappahayden closed in 1965, three years after Rory was born. He occasionally went to church in Renews.

As he sat and waited for Butch to wake, he could smell the spring greenery coming to life, the pleasant smell of alders in the spring when they started budding. He was going to miss going into his favourite fishing hole, Mont's Pond behind Capphayden in the spring, to savour the woodsy smells. But he knew to right their wrongs, they had to face the consequences.

"What time is it, Rory?"

"Eleven o'clock. Butch, we're kind of like the Masterless Men. The only thing is most of 'em were never caught."

"Who were they?"

"A group of Irishmen led by Peter Kerrivan back in the mid-1700s who ran away from their English masters and vessels, they lived at Butter Pot Mountains in the Avalon wilderness area. Kept it up for years, huntin', fishin', and pilferin' from nearby communities rather than bendin' to the English. They were outlaws, same as us."

"Rory, roll me a smoke? I hates rollin'."

"I s'pose b'y."

Rory looked at his watch. "Time to start movin'. Butch, when ya gets over a little hill from here, the road forks off in two directions. Go left, which puts ya on Front Road. When ya gets beyond the wooden breakwater, get off the road and walk the beach. Stay on it till ya gets to Boat Cove Road when ya comes back to Front Road. Keep walkin' 'til ya meets the highway. Beyond the bridge, there's a little road—Murphy's Drive, I believe is the name of it—it goes off to the left. Stay on this road 'til ya comes back to the highway again. Walk 'til ya reach the beach, get off the road and walk it. It's narrow at high tide, ya won't be seen below the road. There's a few houses on that side of the harbour; some are close to the highway, as ya know. When yer on the side opposite of the harbour from where we are now, go in Cutler's Road, it will bring ya to the woods. Stop at the turn in the road, below the guardrail, stay there, wait for me. Don't let the dog off the leash. Like I told ya last night if ya meets anyone and they say hello, reply the same, and keep movin'. I'll be on the other side in roughly an hour. Keep lookin' behind ya every fifteen or twenty seconds. Like I said, it's gettin' riskier the closer we gets to Cappahayden."

"Rory, can ya repeat it all. I'm so nervous I could hardly take most of it in."

"Calm down. Ya'll get there all right."

After Rory repeated everything a second time, Butch was less nervous. It was a bright night; he could see the lay of the land as he made his way. Walking the beach was far more relaxing than walking the road. The sound of the sea rolling on the beaches was soothing. He reached the other side in roughly forty minutes.

Thirty minutes after Butch left, Rory set out. He stopped to drink from the watering hole that legend has it the Mayflower picked up water from on its way to Plymouth Rock. He filled the two jugs.

An hour and a half after Butch sat on the side of the dirt road, Rory showed up.

"I never saw a soul, did you, Butch?"

"Not a soul."

"Butch, I got an idea. I say we walk to Cappahayden tanight. There's no traffic on the move, the moon is almost full."

"I'd love to. I'm sick of walkin' in the woods. Fightin' our way through on paths that are hardly passable. Mud up to our balls. Walkin' on pavement last night, and tanight was so easy. I'd walk to Portugal Cove South non-stop rather than have to walk the coastline again."

"Butch, we can't go fuckin' around in Cappahayden. We stay close to the shoreline. By doin' that, we'll pass both of our houses. Which is where I would expect the cops to be staked out. Staked out a distance from 'em with binoculars and high-powered scopes. Waitin' for us to show. Kinda like a standoff in reverse. Standoffs, the authorities are usually waitin' for someone to exit a house. Their waitin' for us to go in. But we're smarter than that."

"Rory, to think we have pogey checks home waitin' for us, and we can't go get 'em. I'm sure me ol' man and yers are after bein' to the mail."

"Butch, we can't even think about that. There's no way we could change 'em anyway, and we'd have nowhere to spend it. I guarantee ya, there's cops at our houses, sittin' there in their cruisers or ghost cars. Staked out in barns or sheds or in the woods. God knows where they're at.

As much as we'd like to go home, we can't. Goin' home would get us caught, not after makin' it from the Goulds to where we are now to get caught by bein' stupid. They'll have us in a few days anyway. As soon as we gets to the stash and moves it in a different spot, we'll be turnin' ourselves in. Ya rested enough to hit the road again?"

"Sure, after I haves one more smoke. Ya know, Rory, we'll be tellin' our grandkids about this adventure someday."

"Butch, ya might not live long enough to have kids let alone grandkids, if ya keep pullin' stunts like what ya did at the bank."

"Here's the plan. When ya gets to Bear Cove Beach, stop at the picnic tables. When I gets there, we'll get on the pole line 'til it reaches the coastline, we'll stay on the coastline 'til we gets to Lawlor's Garage, we'll head to the woods for the rest of the night. Have a boil up or two, our last. Relax with a few smokes and get some sleep. We can't attempt the coastline beyond Cappahayden. I doubt if the hikers got anythin' opened or even cut beyond Cappahayden. Not only that, but I'm also willin' to bet the connection between Cappahayden and Portugal Cove South a hundred years ago was a path over the barrens, not on the coastline. Time will tell.

Okay, Butch, get goin'. Keep the dog on the leash. I'll be roughly an hour behind ya. There's not many houses between here and Bear Cove Beach."

Butch made it back to the highway. It took him an hour and a half to walk to Bear Cove Beach. He was sitting on a picnic table, about to light his second cigarette, when Lucky started barking. Butch prayed it was Rory.

"Butch, did ya see any cops or any cars? I didn't see a thing."

"Me neither. Why don't we go to Brock's house, get 'im to bring us to Portugal Cove South?"

"Definitely not, too risky. Cops are most likely checkin' every car and truck moving in Cappahayden. And I wouldn't want Brock gettin' caught with us in his car. He'd be in trouble. Not doin' that to 'im. He's too good a friend to do that too. Two of us goin' to the slammer is enough. Time to get goin'. Haul on yer boots, the coastline will be damp."

They kept a steady pace; morning was creeping upon them. They couldn't get a visual of their homesteads with the overgrown trees. Their houses were on the west side of the highway: they were on the east side of the highway. They cautiously crept through Cappahayden. When they reached Lawlor's Garage, they walked in Freshwater Road into heavy woods. Fifteen minutes after passing the garage, they dropped to the ground, both exhausted. After a rest, they built a small fire, boiled the kettle, and downed some grub.

"Butch, May twenty-fourth weekend is this week. I guess we won't be gettin' down to La Manche Park to party. Streetheart is playin' at Memorial Stadium the end of June. Trooper is playin' there in July, so much for a good time. Raymond Jordan told me a few weeks ago at the Petrel, he was tryin' to get the Wonderful Grand Band to play a few gigs over the summer. I was lookin' forward to seein' them, wanted to hear a few tunes of their new album "Living in a Fog."

Butch didn't reply. He knew if he did, there would be an argument; he didn't want to piss Rory off. He could tell Rory was getting more agitated the closer they got to the stash in the last day or so.

"What's the plan from here, Rory?"

"Portugal Cove South, I'm guessin' is twenty miles from here. I figures we could walk it in one night, but we'd have to be on the road by seven or eight o'clock."

"Are ya serious? Go all the way to the Cove in one night?"

"Why not? Didn't I tell ya the other night in Aquaforte, Ben Dunne won the Tely 10 in 75. His time was fifty-six minutes even. So, at our age, if we can't walk from here to Cape Race Road between dusk and dawn, there's somethin' wrong with us. I know we're not in the shape Dunne is in. We're in decent shape with all the walkin' we've done the better part of two weeks. We leave here at seven this evenin'. We don't gotta take any grub, rubber boots or oil clothes with us. We'll hide our stuff; the only thing we'll be carryin' is the jugs. We'll wear our jackets; if we gets too warm, we'll toss 'em in the ditch. I'm thinkin' we should be at the stash early tamorrow mornin', sometime between daylight and eight or nine o'clock. It will be a good workout, the last big push, we can do it. Our first day goin' down Shoal Bay Road was our first big push; we'll end it with a big push."

"I guess I'll have to take yer word for it, Rory. I'll need a good nap first and a big feed."

They cut spruce boughs to sleep on, hauled on their oil clothes, lay down and dozed. Rory woke every half hour expecting a cop or two to be standing over him, ready to throw the cuffs on them. Cappahayden was not the place to be for two wanted people who happen to be from Cappahayden.

Rory contemplated walking to Cape Race Lighthouse along the coastline. It would be safer than the highway, much but longer. The coastline route would not be easy, even if the hikers had worked on it. They would have to cross Chance Cove River, forty feet wide, four or five feet deep. When they got to the lighthouse, they would have to walk in Cape Race Road to get to the stash, roughly ten or twelve miles. Rory knew this was the best route to take, not the safest, but better than the coastline. Rory always wanted to see where the SS Anglo Saxon went aground in Clam Cove. The SS Anglo Saxon went aground on April 27th/1863, with the loss of 237 lives. Clam Cove is approximately four and a half miles north of Cape Race Lighthouse.

CHAPTER THIRTY-FIVE

When Rory woke, embers were still smouldering. He stoked them up, added wood and boiled water had a mug of tea with a few smokes. He was paranoid on a big scale, kept looking around constantly in case anyone was sneaking upon them.

Butch was snoring it up, with the dog beside him. After the second cup of tea, Rory decided to walk the coastline towards Chance Cove Park to see if the trail was open beyond Cappahayden.

Rory walked as far as Freshwater River, about a half-mile from the garage. It was as he surmised: nothing in the way of a trail. There was an old footpath; it was too narrow to walk on; it looked like it hadn't been travelled on for years, if not decades.

When he got back, Butch and Lucky were awake.

"Mugga tea, Butch?"

"Sure. Thanks."

"How'd ya sleep?"

"Like a baby! Where were ya?"

"I went about a half-mile up the coast towards the Park. No trail cut beyond here. There's an old footpath which would be too hard to walk on. I guess the hikers haven't gotten this far down the Shore yet. It's four-thirty. We'll eat now, and our food will be settled by the time we start walkin'."

"I'm gut-foundered. What I wouldn't give for a feed of moose or stew fish."

Rory laughed. "Ya'll get all the moose ya wants when ya gets incarcerated." Butch pretended he didn't hear him. "I'm confident we'll be on Cape Race Road come daylight. It will be a hard workout gettin' there."

Both dozed off after eating. Rory woke around seven o'clock.

"Time to hit the road, Butch. Same as last night. You go; first, I'll catch up with ya when we're out of town. We gotta be extra careful. I'm sure the RCMP in Trepassey are lookin' for us, we'll see a car comin' a mile or two away on the barrens."

Rory hid the brin bags in the alders. He figured he might come back and retrieve them in a few years.

Butch hit the pavement and started walking. Twenty minutes later, he was on a barren landscape, with not a tree in sight. Rory caught up; they walked on the pavement and shoulder. The shoulder was easier on the feet, but they made better time on the pavement. They let Lucky run free. Two cars passed, both heading north. They jumped in the ditch and lay flat. Butch lay on top of the dog to keep him out of sight of the headlights.

"Are we halfway yet?"

"I'm not sure, Butch. I dunno if the entrance to the park is the halfway point or the Rocky Downs is. We must be close to halfway by now. It's almost midnight, we're walkin' almost five hours. We'll have a spell and a smoke or two."

"Where's Rocky Downs?"

"I believe it's a couple of miles south of the park. Between Brousey Island Pond and Clam Pond."

They trudged along at a steady pace, breathing heavily, soaking with sweat, determined to be off the road and on the barrens heading towards Cape Race Road by daylight. It was perfect weather for walking; the road was flat compared to all the hills they had encountered on the trail. Butch's long stride enabled him to keep pace with Rory. They passed the gate to the park. At two sharp, they stopped, had two smokes each.

"I guess we won't be spendin' a night in any of these cabins we're passin'."

"No, Butch, ya knows the plan. The plan is to walk to the stash in one night, and that's what we're doin'. I suspect we're more than halfway there. We can do it. I knows it's harder walkin' for you than for me."

"Fuck off, Rory."

They found a river shortly after they had their smokes. They both knelt and drank copious amounts of water. Rory filled the jugs, which they took turns carrying. They slung the jugs over their shoulders or around their necks. Being careful not to let the nylon string get under their collars, which would cut into their skin. As Rory walked, his mind was racing; he was anxious and nervous at the same time. Anxious to get to the stash, hoping and praying it was still there. Nervous about going to jail.

As they passed Cape Race LORAN-C transmitter.

Butch asked, "how tall it was?"

"Butch, I've told you about that tower a few times!"

"Well, I forgot it, remember we're not all as smart as you."

"Yer gonna have to give up smokin' drugs, yer fryin' yer brain cells. It's thirteen hundred and fifty feet, built-in 1965, it was the tallest structure in Canada 'til the CN Tower was built in the seventies."

"Where is the CN Tower, and how tall is it?"

Rory shook his head. "Toronah, it's over fifteen hundred feet."

As they walked along, Butch asked Rory if he knew exactly where the dope was buried.

"Me and Perry tied hunters tape on a few tuckamores close to the stash. Hopefully, the tape is still there. If it isn't, I should be able to figure it out from the landmarks."

They finally saw the lights of Portugal Cove South off in the distance.

"Butch, in ten minutes, we'll be hangin' a left and hittin' the barrens!"

"Rory, we should wait 'til daylight. I knows from huntin' partridge over the years how hard it is to walk on the barrens. Hard enough in daylight, never mind darkness."

"Yer right, we'll wait."

They sat on the shoulder of the road. Butch removed his sneakers, he squoze puss from two large blisters on his right heel and one on the left ankle. He complained to Rory how his feet were killing him. Rory said, "suck it up, buttercup," turning his back to him. Butch told Rory he was one saucy prick. They smoked in silence, awaiting daylight. When it was bright enough to walk the barrens, they left the road, headed east in the direction of the ocean.

As soon as they hit the barrens, Lucky started running back and forth with his nose held high.

"Rory, look at Lucky workin' the ground for partridge. Not his first time on the barrens."

"Too bad we won't be home in the fall to take 'im birdin'."

Walking on the barrens was much slower than walking on the pavement or the shoulder of the highway. The scrub was wet with morning dew. Rory regretted not taking their rubber boots and oil pants. They were soaked within minutes of leaving the highway. They walked for twenty minutes before veering off to the right, heading southeast towards Cape Race Road. They were starved and exhausted, and they stank. They hadn't had a wash since they left the Goulds.

When they finally made it to the gravel road, they walked for a couple of hundred feet east. Rory said, "Butch, here's the spot, over this knob, right around here somewhere. Go lie down for a bit 'til I figures out exactly where it's buried."

The location looked right, but Rory didn't see any orange hunters tape. This made him nervous. He went back to the road and walked back and forth for five minutes. He got off the road and went further into the tuckamores trying to find the grubber and shovel. They were nowhere to be found, no tape, no grubber, and no shovel. His palms started sweating, he felt sick to his stomach. He walked to the spot where he figured they'd buried the drugs, rooted around, looking for the moss Perry had put over the buried drugs. Ten minutes later, he hollered to Butch.

"Found it, I found it, Butch!"

"Ya serious?" Butch was lying back on his elbows, leaning back on a large flat rock. Lucky was napping beside him, with his head resting on Butch's crotch.

"Yes, yes, this is it. I found the loose piece of moss; Perry covered the hole with."

Rory kicked the moss aside; he saw the freshly disturbed soil. He knelt, breathing heavily, blessed himself and faced the sky. "Lord Jesus Christ, please let my drugs be here. If they are, I'll go to the chapel every day and go to mass every Sunday while I'm in prison, I promise ya, Lord Jesus Christ." He blessed himself again and started digging with his bare hands. He dug madly for a few minutes, he stopped, out of breath.

Butch walked over to Rory. "Get out of the way, let me have a go at it." Butch dug longer than Rory had; there was still no sign of the plastic bags or the tin can. Rory had told Perry to put the money in.

"Okay, Butch, move out of me way. If this is the right spot, I'll know pretty fuckin' soon."

Rory started digging with a vengeance. Sweat ran into his eyes from his forehead, snot ran over his top lip, saliva ran down his chin. Breathing heavy, two minutes later, his hands touched plastic.

"I got the drugs, Butch—I got 'em!"

He dug for another minute or so, he started pulling on the plastic. A bag came clear of the soil, Rory held it up.

"Jesus, Jesus, Jesus—the fuckin' thing is empty."

He dropped the plastic bag and started digging again, faster, and harder, pulling more plastic bags free of the soil, empty plastic bags.

Rory started cursing, he fell over on the ground. "Perry is dead, he's dead, he's fuckin' dead. The cocksucker, I'll kill 'im. I'll kill 'im with me bare hands. See what ya did, Butch!"

"What d'ya mean, what I did?"

"If ya didn't have to rob the fuckin' bank, my drugs would be here!"

"Fuck off, Rory, I didn't rob yer fuckin' drugs!"

"No, ya didn't. But Perry knew it was only a matter of time 'fore the cops got me. So, I guess he said fuck it and decided to have a field day with my dope and money. God fuckin' knows what he's after doin' with it. Not like I can go knock on his door and demand he give it back. I'm ruined. I'm not only goin' to a federal prison for God knows how long, and when I gets out, I owes me dealer for fifteen pounds of weed and a pound of hash. All 'cause of you, ya stupid prick!"

"I never imagined it being a big deal. Figured I'd walk into the bank and rob a few thousand dollars, no big deal."

"No, but ya involved me!"

"Rory, you bein' involved was an accident."

"An accident? If ya were goin' robbin' banks, ya should've done it when ya were by yerself, not when ya had to pick me up immediately after."

"I guess all I can say is I'm sorry, ya got tangled up in all of this."

They didn't speak for some time; Lucky came bursting out of the alders and leapt on Butch, who shoved him off.

"Can I say somethin', Rory?"

"Ya may as well."

"Think there's a chance Larry may have taken the drugs?"

"That never crossed me mind. Ya could be right. Whoever took it, they have it, and I don't. Most likely, Perry and Larry did it together. Fuckin' Perry, I was good to 'im, unthankful bastard, he'll have his fuckin' day."

"I wish the weed had been there. I was so lookin' forward to a few draws. Haven't had one since we were with Joe. So, what're we goin' to do now?"

"The only thing we can do is turn ourselves in."

"When?"

"Some time taday. I hope the cocksucker enjoys 'imself, partyin' on my drugs and money. I hope he fries his brain so bad he won't be able to spell his own name. I hope he gets lung cancer from smokin' it. I hope his tongue swells so fuckin' big he can't breathe. I hope his trachea rots."

"Jesus, Rory, I didn't know weed done all that to ya."

"It don't, ya stund imbecile."

"So, where we turnin' ourselves in?"

"Ferryland!"

"Why, Ferryland?"

"Well, it's the detachment closest to Cappahayden. By turnin' ourselves in at Ferryland, the RCMP will think we've been in Cappahayden all along. They'll never know we were in the Cove. We both know Campbell to some degree; he might be able to help us. God knows we needs all the help we can get."

"How we gettin' to Ferryland?"

"I guess we'll hitchhike. If we don't get a run, we could always go in somewhere, call the cops, tell 'em where we are. I'm sure they'd come pick us up free of charge."

They smoked and discussed what they'd tell the cops.

"Butch, armed robbery and possession of drugs for the purpose of traffickin' both carry federal sentences. Yer goin' to have to own up to doin' the armed robbery, I'll take the rap for the drugs. Hopefully, the judge will go easy on us as this is the first time we've ever been in trouble with the law."

Rory was more pissed about losing his drugs than what he had to face with the law. He was going to have a big issue to deal with when he got out of prison. Paying his dealer for drugs he hadn't sold and barely had a chance to smoke. "Let's start walkin', Butch."

They walked along the dirt road, which hugged the ocean. The wind was blowing on land from the southeast with fog on the horizon. "Butch, smell the beautiful salt sea air; it'll be a few years 'fore we get to savour that scent again."

They made their way in Harbour Road, took a right onto O'Leary's Loop Road to get to the Southern Shore Highway. Rory was nervous being out in public, having avoided the public for over a week and a half.

"Butch, a man who runs eventually, finds he has no place to go. To end this saga, we have no other choice but to turn ourselves in. As much as I hates the thought of bein' caged like an animal for a few years. That's what we must do to start over. It's like resettin' the program of our lives. These charges will not go away 'til we start doin' our time. We'll use the strength of this experience and journey goin' forward."

Butch agreed. The two worn-out, dejected souls had walked and made their way from Goulds to Portugal Cove South in twelve days for absolutely nothing but memories.

CHAPTER THIRTY-SIX

When they reached the highway, they sat on the pavement for twenty minutes. Butch squoze the blisters on his feet again. Lucky was curled up, sleeping on the shoulder. A beat-up, black 74 Dodge Ram pickup was heading south. The truck hauled in on the opposite side of the road.

The old fella driving rolled down his window. "Where ye goin', lads?"

"Ferryland," Rory replied.

"Jump in, I'll dart ye to Ferryland. Ye could days waiting for a run. Not much traffic this far down the Shore."

Butch opened the passenger door and asked if they could take their dog.

"No problem," said the driver, "heave 'im in the back. I'll take me time. I loves dogs, got a couple of Irish setters meself."

Butch picked Lucky up, he gently laid him in over the tailgate. They got in, the driver made a U-turn and headed north.

"Thanks, mister, for goin' out of yer way, bringin' us to Ferryland. Sorry, we smells bad—we've been on the road a few days, haven't had a wash in a while."

"That's all right. I was young once and hitchhiked a lot. I fishes for a livin', so I've smelt worse than ye. B'ys, yer in some mess of gravel, what were ye at to be in such a state, diggin' worms with yer bare hands? And yer jeans and sneakers are soakin'."

"Long story." Replied Rory.

Rory asked, "where were ya headed?"

"I was goin' to Trepassey, to the hardware store. Ye lads from

Ferryland?"

Rory hesitated a moment. "No, we're from Cappahayden."

The driver looked at them. "Jesus, b'ys, don't tell me yer the two lads from Cappahayden who robbed the bank in the Goulds? B'ys, the cops are goin' around in circles lookin' for ye."

Rory looked straight ahead. "Yes."

"Holy mother of sweet Jesus in the fuckin' garden. How the fuck did ye get to the Cove?"

Rory said, "It's a long story."

"Do ye know the Shore's been crawlin' with cops since ye did the armed robbery? There's after bein' at least twenty roadblocks between the Goulds and Trepassey and a few over by the turn-off to St. Shott's. Almost guaranteed a roadblock or two a night somewhere on the Shore. B'ys, they wants ye bad, real bad. Tell me, how'd ye get this far without gettin' caught?"

"We'd rather not say anythin' 'til we talks to a lawyer and give our statements to the RCMP."

"C'mon, b'ys, I won't tell anyone, I promise."

"Sorry, we can't. We're goin' to the RCMP detachment."

"I tell ya what, I'll drive ye right to the cop shop. Not every day, ya gets to hang around with the two most wanted fellas in Newfoundland, who got the cops running around in circles for nearly two weeks. Ye b'ys are goin' to be famous. How the two of ye ever got this far from the Goulds without gettin' caught is beyond me. Hasn't been a manhunt on the Shore like this since they were tryin' to recapture Peter Kerrivan and his band of Masterless Men."

"We got no money on us to give you for gas; we'll return the favour someday, down the road."

"Don't worry about it. It's a pleasure to drive ye two lads to Ferryland. But why are ye turnin' yerselves in, in Ferryland? There's an RCMP detachment in Trepassey. I'm sure the cowb'ys there wouldn't turn ye away."

"We knows there's a detachment in Trepassey. We both knows an officer in Ferryland who might help us with the tangle we're in."

"I hope for yerselves he does, 'cause you two are in big trouble, and I mean big fuckin' trouble. Ye'll need all the help ye can get."

"Skipper, do ya smoke?"

"I do."

"Could we bum a few smokes off ya?"

"Sure—here's a full pack, smoke to yer heart's content."

The boys faces lit up when they saw the pack of Player's Light Regular, the brand they both smoked.

"We appreciate the smokes, mister. We haven't had a decent draw in a while."

"B'ys, I gotta ask ye again, how the devil did ye make it all the way to the Cove? Not only how did ye get here, but why? Sure, yer from Cappahayden—what brought ye this far from home?"

"Sorry, we can't say anythin' about what has happened since the incident in the Goulds."

"Okay. I'm thinkin' ye went out the Trans-Canada Highway and came in through St. Mary's Bay. But the old curiosity is killin' me, who brought ye this far? I guess ye were tryin' to get back to Cappahayden?"

Rory ignored the man's many questions, leaving Butch to chat with him while he pieced together what he would tell the cops. Two charges were pending. The armed robbery was a given; the big question was, who would they try and pin it on? The car was registered in his name, so they would most likely try to nail him for it. He didn't mind taking the rap for the drugs; he wasn't going to be nailed with the armed robbery. Either way, he was going to the big house up on the mainland for a few years. He would have to do all the talking at detachment.

The last half of the drive to Ferryland was quiet. Rory knew the interrogation and drilling was getting closer, and it was going to be gruelling.

As the truck made its way into Cappahayden, they met an RCMP cruiser heading south. The driver grinned.

"B'ys, they're still lookin' for ye."

Rory asked the driver to slow down as they approached Gerald

Goffman's house.

"Skipper, would ya mind droppin' the dog off at that house on the way back? Tell the owner, Gerald Goffman, Rory O'Ryan owns 'im, and his name is Lucky. Please tell 'im I'll be in contact with 'im in a day or two."

"Okay, me, son. Why don't we drop 'im off now?"

"My house is next door to his, and I don't want the possibility of bein' arrested where me father can see it. Besides, if we were seen gettin' out of yer truck, ya'd be arrested too, for aidin' and abettin'."

"Well, in that case, I'm some fuckin' glad we're not stoppin'."

As they exited Cappahayden, Rory asked Butch how many cop cars he'd seen.

Butch said, "three in total if ya count the one we met 'fore we entered Cappahayden."

"I counted four, Butch, includin' that one. There was one in my yard, one in yer yard. And one parked at Lawlor's."

"I missed the one at Lawlor's."

As they entered Renews, the driver turned on the radio. It was on VOCM; as luck had it, the news was coming on. The talk show host Bill Rowe said, "We'll be right back following the news and weather report." The first thing the news anchor said was the RCMP were scaling back their man hurt for Rory O'Ryan and Butch Hynes, both of Cappahayden, wanted for questioning in relation to an armed robbery at Scotiabank on May 6th, in the town of Goulds. The driver grinned and said, "I guess, now, it's technically over, hey b'ys?" The boys didn't reply.

The truck sped through Renews. Rory wished he could stop at the grotto to say a few prayers and make his confession, to pray to his maker; the law would go easy on him and his best friend.

As they approached the RCMP detachment in Ferryland, both thanked the driver again for the lift and the smokes. Rory repeated the promise to return the favour someday.

"Don't worry about it. By the way, I'm Hedley Sharpe from the Cove. Can't wait to watch the news tanight, b'ys. Everyone will go mad when they hears ye turned yerselves in. Yer celebrities, everyone in Newfoundland and probably Canada is rootin' for ye. I even saw yer story on the CBC National News one night the week. The two of ye are more popular than Trudeau and Peckford. Yer the first story on the news every night since the day of the robbery."

"Skipper, could ya please keep quiet about where ya picked us up 'til we're sentenced? We'd appreciate it. We're pleadin' guilty, so we should be sentenced in a week or two."

The man laughed. "Sure, I never saw ye in me life! I look forward to havin' a few beers with ye someday down the road. And findin' out why the fuck ye were in the Cove."

"I'll tell ya what. Ya, keep quiet till we're sentenced, about pickin' us up and bringin' us here. And we'll tell ya the whole story over a few beers someday."

"Ye got yerself a deal, lads!"

Sharpe pulled the truck onto the shoulder of the road near the detachment; The boys shook hands with him and got out. Rory watched as Butch went to the back of the truck, let the tailgate down; he lifted Lucky down on the ground. He knelt, put his arms around the dogs neck, the dog whimpered and licked his face. As Butch held Lucky, he could sense Rory's impatience. Before he let the dog go, he whispered, "I love you." Butch had never said that out loud to anyone in his life. And no one had ever said it to him.

Sharp said, "heave 'im in the front with me." Butch picked up Lucky and laid him in on the seat. Before Butch closed the door, Rory elbowed him aside, patted the dog on the head. Lucky licked his hand.

"Mister, don't forget to tell Gerald I'll be in touch in the next few days."

"Sure thing—take care of yerselves, lads. And God bless ye!"

The truck drove off with Lucky standing on the seat, staring back at them through the rear window. Butch was staring at him with tears in his eyes. Rory put his arm around Butch.

"Butch, don't worry about Lucky. He'll be in good hands with Gerald. He loves animals and cares for 'em, like children. He's a decent fella."

"I hope yer right, Rory."

"I knows I am. If I didn't think he'd take good care of Lucky, I wouldn't have sent 'im there."

"Thanks, Rory. That means a lot."

They turned and looked at the brick building several hundred feet down the road. Their long, drawn-out arduous journey was over.

"Butch, ya knows what both of our stories are. You admit to the armed robbery; I'll own up to the drugs. And remember, I do all the talkin' for both of us. And we're not sayin' a word till we gets lawyers."

"We're gettin' lawyers?"

"Legal Aid lawyers. The cops have to let us call a lawyer. If they separate us, say nothin', and I mean absolutely nothin.'

"Okay."

"We'll each need our own lawyer. I dunno if it would be in our best interests or even if we're allowed to have the same lawyer."

"Ya ready?"

"As ready as I'm ever goin' to be."

"One more thing, Butch. Sorry for losin' it and raggin' on ya earlier."

"Okay, no worries."

"Let's go."

As the boys walked across the yard towards the building, the sun broke through the clouds. Rory looked up and hoped if it was a good omen. The first time they had seen the sun in many days.

CHAPTER THIRTY-SEVEN

There were eight police vehicles parked in the yard of the detachment, to the left of the building: five cruisers, a ghost car and two Suburbans.

"Eight rigs, Butch. This detachment only ever has three police vehicles parked in the yard at any given time. I guess they manned up."

Butch grinned. "I guess so."

They opened the double doors and walked in. Campbell was leaning on the front counter doing paperwork. He raised his eyes to meet theirs.

Rory smiled. "Good marnin', officer."

Campbell was taken aback; he stared at them. He turned around and addressed an officer who was standing near a window. "Go get Staff Sergeant Coady, immediately!"

The officer went through a door and was back in no time with the Staff Sergeant.

"Sergeant, these are the two young men from Cappahayden we've been trying to locate."

"These two punks? Then you'd better arrest them."

Campbell walked around the counter and told both they were being arrested, what the charges were, and they had the right to contact a lawyer. He ordered both to put their hands on the counter and not to move. He ran his hands over them, from top to bottom; he had them remove their sneakers, which he turned upside down and shook.

"The two of you stink. I wouldn't want to be the person who has to drive you to town."

He led them to a holding cell, guided them inside and locked the door. Half an hour later, he returned with ham and cheese sandwiches and Cokes.

Rory said to the officer, “Officer, could get a couple of smokes of ya.”

“I don’t smoke.”

“I’m sure someone around here must have a smoke or two to spare.”

“Maybe so; I’ve got better things to do than go hunt up cigarettes for criminals.”

“Never mind about the smokes. I needs a pen and a sheet of paper if ya don’t mind. We picked up a stray dog on our travels. We wants my friend to take care of ‘im while we’re on holidays. I needs someone to get the note to ‘im.”

“So, there were three dumb animals on the loose, were there? I’ll get you a pen and paper and make sure your friend gets the note.”

When Campbell left, Rory looked at Butch, “I always thought he was a decent fella, I guess, I’m goin’ to have to change me mind on that one. I guess if yer a cop, yer a prick, and if yer a prick, that makes ya a good cop.”

“Rory, I thought he was the best kind.”

“No worries, we still got some ‘baccy and papers left.”

Campbell came back with a notepad and pen. Rory thanked him.

Dear Gerald,

As you read this letter, you should be in possession of an Irish setter whose name is Lucky. Butch and I befriended this dog in the past few days. Long story! Butch, for some reason, loves this dog. I need a favour. As you know, by now, we are in police custody here in Ferryland, soon to be transported to St. John’s. I want you to take care of this dog while we are in prison. We could be gone away for a few years. We’re hoping we’ll get a break on sentencing—first offence for both of us. I enjoyed our night of drinking and look forward to a few more drinks in the future. Please give this dog whatever he needs in food and vet bills. I promise I will square up with you big time when I return home. I forgot to bring over the brace and bits that you wanted to borrow to build your boxcar. The brace is resting on the beams in my old man's barn, there should be a box of bits with it. Root around, you'll find it. Tell my old man I said you could borrow it. Thanking you in advance for taking care of Lucky. I'll write you from prison. Take care!

Rory,

P.S. Please tell my father I'll call him when I get settled in prison.

After Rory finished writing his letter, he read it aloud to Butch. Butch smiled when he heard the part about the brace and bits. He knew Rory had hidden drugs in his father's barn, and he was giving Gerald a hint about where to find them.

Rory called out through the bars. Campbell appeared.

"Officer, here's me letter. It's for Gerald Goffman, who lives next door to me. I'm sure ya knows my house by now. Gerald's is the blue saltbox, with the small brown barn behind it. I would appreciate it if ya could get it to 'im taday or tamorrow. It's concerning takin' care of Butch's dog."

Campbell took the letter. "You're lucky I'm an animal lover, O'Ryan."

Shortly after, the two were taken to the health clinic nearby to be checked by Dr. Peter Morry. Dr. Morry saw them immediately. He gave each of them a clean bill of health. Half an hour after returning to the detachment, Staff Sergeant Coady and another officer appeared in front of the cell and unlocked it. The junior officer entered the cell, handcuffed, and shackled the prisoners' legs, he led them out in front of him. Coady said, "you're going to

St. John's."

Rory asked, "Why aren't we goin' to court in Tors Cove?"

Coady replied, "Court in Tors Cove is every second Thursday. We're not holding you here until then, and besides, these charges are serious and have to be dealt with in St. john's."

Outside, two cruisers were backed up to the door, waiting. Rory stopped dead.

"Officer, me and Butch wants to travel together goin' into town. We also wants officer Campbell to accompany us."

Coady pushed Rory forward towards the vehicle. "I don't care what you two want. If you ever thought of anyone but yourselves, you wouldn't be in the mess you're in. You never gave one thought to the people in the bank, did you?"

CHAPTER THIRTY-EIGHT

The run down the Shore in the cop carrier wasn't as enjoyable as cruising in the '68 Charger. Listening to Bob Seger or The Kinks. Rory's gut was aching for more food; he felt small and alone in the back seat by himself. Rory hoped Butch wasn't snottin' and bawlin' or letting his mouth run away with him. Butch, he wasn't strong like Rory.

As the Suburban passed the Credit Union in Witless Bay. Rory wished Butch had done his armed robbery there. If he had, they probably wouldn't be heading to the city to face a judge. The worst thing was passing the Sou' Wester and Soundbone, knowing Angus was likely in one of the bars selling dimes of weed belonging to him, weed he'd never see the money for.

When they arrived at the courthouse, which housed the lockup in the basement. There were several reporters at the entrance, along with two TV camera crews. Rory was curious who had tipped off the media. It must have been the fella who had given them the run from the Cove to the detachment. No big deal. They would have found out eventually.

The two cruisers backed up to the lockup doors below the court building, to the left of the steps. By the time the police officers opened the vehicle doors, four guards had moved the media back a fair distance. Rory stole a glance at Butch: he looked like a lost dog. They were moved inside as quickly as their shackles would allow. Their restraints were removed. They were photographed and fingerprinted. Given fresh clothes, razor blades and brought to the showers. After the wash-up and shave, they were put into cells. Butch's cell was a fair distance from Rory's. There was no way they could make any real kind of connection.

Rory asked to speak to a Legal Aid lawyer. A call was made to Legal Aid, Rory was brought into a small office, the guard handed him a telephone and left him to have a conversation in private. When the conversation ended, he was brought back to his cell. An hour later, Rory was escorted into a room that was painted a flat gray, with a table and four chairs, where a lawyer awaited him. The lawyer was overweight, balding, who looked like he hadn't missed a meal in years. The lawyer got up from his chair, shook hands with Rory, introduced himself as Berkley Bennett. They both sat, the lawyer on one side of the table, Rory on the opposite side.

"I'll be representing you in court; if that is your wish, my colleague John Small will represent your friend."

Rory took a long look at Bennett. Bennett was wearing an expensive suit; the man had an intelligent face; he reminded Rory a little of Gerald Goffman. Rory said, "I'm fine with that, Mr. Bennett."

"Mr. O'Ryan, I have been informed that you are charged with armed robbery and possession of drugs for the purpose of trafficking. Each of those is a serious charge, as you know. Want to tell me about it?"

Rory sat back in his chair and expelled a long breath. "Well, it's plain and simple. I won't butter-coat it. I'll tell ya exactly what happened. Butch can confirm what I say. We knows we gotta take the punishment we're given for what we did. Here's what happened. I had a quantity of weed and hash stashed on Shoal Bay Road in the Goulds. We went to the stash to pick up some of it. When we got there, Butch said he needed to go to the washroom to do number two." Bennett looked puzzled. "He had to have a shit!"

"Oh, okay."

"I told 'im to go to The Hayloft, which is a nightclub below the turnoff to Shoal Bay Road, which is in the lower end of the Goulds, towards Big Pond. I told 'im to go there to use the washroom. Long story short, he never needed to use the washroom at all. He went directly to Scotiabank at Bidgood's Plaza and robbed it usin' a wig, a fake mustache, sunglasses, a baseball hat, and gloves. He passed the teller a note demandin' all the money in her till. In the note, he said he was armed, he wasn't. The teller gave 'im what money she had. Butch left the bank and headed back towards Shoal Bay Road. On his way back to Shoal Bay Road, he met an RCMP cruiser pullin' out of Keith Drive with lights and siren on, which he suspected was headin' for Bidgood's Plaza. He met another RCMP cruiser on Ryan's Bridge. That cruiser turned around and chased 'im down Shoal Bay Road. He came to a screeching stop, where the road gets bad and started runnin' down the road towards me. As I said, I was in the woods gettin' a little bit of weed and hash from me stash. I hears the siren, next thing I sees Butch runnin' towards me like a madman. What do I do but start runnin'? Why I ran, I have no idea. Why don't ya get me and Butch together with his lawyer? He can confirm the story."

Bennett said. "Not a chance. The RCMP is separating both of you for questioning."

Rory says with a seriousness about him. "Here is how this is goin' to happen, if they keep us separated, Butch, will not speak, not a word. I do all the talkin' for both of us. When the cops come in here, ya' tell 'em if they wants cooperation on these charges, for 'em not to separate us, not for five minutes, when dealin' with the cops. Butch stays with me durin' this whole procedure. If not, he doesn't speak. I wants no one harassin' or puttin' pressure on Butch. You understand?"

Bennett said, "I suspect they'll charge both of you with armed robbery and possession of the drugs for the purpose of trafficking. Are you going to fight these charges or plead guilty?"

When Bennett stopped speaking, his pager went off; he ignored it. He apologized for the interruption.

"I'm takin' the rap for the drugs, and Butch will take the rap for the armed robbery. If we take a charge each and plead guilty or fight it and lose, then both of us will be charged with armed robbery, and both of us will be charged with possession with the intent to traffic. We figure we'd plead guilty to one charge each, and hopefully, the judge may go along with it. He might go easy on us, as neither of us has a criminal record. Both of us wants this court action over the sooner, the better. Can ya ask the prosecutor to have us sentenced as soon as possible if the judge agrees to it?"

"It all makes good sense to me," said Bennett, "but the big question is, what will the prosecutor be looking for. I will call the prosecutor's office this afternoon or first thing in the morning to see which prosecutor is assigned to your case. Small, and I will be requesting a meeting immediately. The prosecutor's office opens at eight-thirty, court starts at ten. I suspect both of you will be the first called, with the charges read against you. We will ask for a one-day postponement.

When you appear in court in the morning, we will be after talking to the prosecutor. We'll know what the prosecutors' plans are. After court, we'll meet you down here."

"And make sure Butch's lawyer knows what I'm sayin'?"

"Of course. But will the prosecutor go along with a single charge each? We'll know before court. And if the prosecutor won't agree to a single charge each, we'll have to argue our case before the judge. Judges take everything into consideration when making a decision, and most judges give people a break who admit and own up to their crimes. We might get away with a single charge each."

Bennett took a breath and asked, "Any more questions?"

"No, I've said everythin' I wanted to say."

Just as Rory stopped speaking, two tall RCMP officers walked in. One was carrying a file folder. They were not the officers the boys had dealt with in Ferryland. Bennett shook hands with the officers, they did their introductions. Both officers hauled chairs back from either end of the table and sat. The first officer to enter the room spoke first, said he was Sergeant Gillman, and his partner was Sergeant Crocker. Gillman opened the file folder and started to speak.

Bennett interrupted him, asked if he could speak first; the officer said, go ahead. Bennett announced reassuringly, both prisoners would be pleading guilty to a single charge each. Hynes for the armed robbery, O'Ryan for the drug charge. And O'Ryan is speaking for both.

The officer acknowledged what the lawyer said. "We need to know all the details concerning what went on, on the day of the armed robbery. We also need to know where these two individuals have been since Thursday, May 6th, the day of the armed robbery. We also need to know how these two men made it from Shoal Bay Road to the RCMP detachment in Ferryland."

When the officer stopped speaking, Rory looked directly at the officer. "Officers, on a go-forward basis, we will not be givin' a statement. I believe there is no need for it, as my lawyer told you, we will each take a charge. What went on the day of the armed robbery and where we have been since the robbery, I believe, is not relevant. The important thing is, we turned ourselves in and admitted to the crimes at hand. We're here to take our punishment."

Gillman looked at Rory and said, "We need to know this information. Furthermore, if you don't co-operate with us, it will not help you in your dealings with the court."

Rory looked at the policeman. "Officer, both of us will take our chances in front of the judge."

Bennett spoke up, "I believe this meeting is over."

The two officers looked at each other, rose from their seats and left.

"You spoke well to the officers, but the judge may have a problem with neither of you giving a statement to the RCMP."

"What good would it do? It wouldn't change anythin'." Frustration added an edge to Rory's voice.

"We're here; we are goin' to take our medicine. Even if we're both charged with both offences, we're still not givin' statements. End of story!"

Bennett stood, "I'll see you in the morning. Try to get a good night's sleep." Bennett knocked on the door to let the guards know he was finished. When the door opened, he told the guard they were finished. "Take good care of these two young men.

This is their first encounter with the law."

The guard gave the lawyer a skeptical look, he assured him they'd be fine.

Rory was taken from the meeting room, led down the corridor to where the cells were. As luck would have it, the cell he was put in was next to Butch's. The boys chatted through the bars for the rest of the evening and into the night.

"Rory, I did like ya said. I told them you spoke for me and kept my mouth shut. My Lawyer was fine with me not speakin'. The two cops didn't like it much. I kept sayin' over and over, you spoke for both of us. How did the meetin' with yer lawyer go?"

Rory said, "Good, but the ball is in the prosecutors hands. What charges and against who is the question. Pleadin' guilty is the smart thing to do. With any luck, the prosecutor and the judge will agree to the guilty pleas and give us the minimum sentences possible."

Supper was brought in at five-thirty: fried bologna and mashed potatoes with baby carrots plus a slice of banana cake. Butch downed his in minutes. Home-cooked grub. Last week he was dreaming about this kind of food. Rory ate only half of his. He was too wrapped up in his head about what was going to happen in the morning.

"Rory, did ya eat all yer supper?"

"No."

"Can I have what's leftover?"

"How the hell am I goin' to get it to ya? The tray or the plate won't fit through the bars."

"Scrape it in yer mug after ya drinks yer tea."

When Rory finished his tea, he stuffed what was left of his meal into the tea mug he passed it through the bars. It looked like mush. Butch thanked him and ate it from the mug with a spoon. He passed the empty mug back to Rory.

Shortly after supper, a guard approached their cells to tell them they were celebrities. Saying their story was the first thing on the news, on all local cable channels. Both had a chuckle over it. They had more to worry about than being local celebrities.

"Butch, I'm beat. I'm goin' to turn in early. Please don't wake me over somethin' foolish." Butch grunted assent.

CHAPTER THIRTY-NINE

Rory woke before daylight. Butch was still snoring away, as usual. Rory read a couple of old newspapers a guard brought him. Papers from the past two weeks. Every paper had a story on the armed robbery and the suspects who could not be located. On May 7th and May 8th, the first two papers had their pictures, school pictures from Baltimore, Joe Walker had told them about. The heading in one of the papers asked, with a question mark after it, "Where Are These Two Individuals?" with the subheading "wanted for questioning concerning an armed robbery at Scotiabank in the town of Goulds on May 6th." Whoever wrote the article summarized, the two were most likely still in the area or somewhere in St. John's. Rory chuckled to himself. If the reporter, along with everyone else, only knew what they had been through since they ran down Shoal Bay Road.

At seven-thirty, a guard brought in two large breakfasts, along with that days newspaper.

Rory called out, "Butch, get up and eat yer breakfast."

"Rory, that was the best sleep in a long time." "Go figure," said Rory. "Sleepin' on the cold ground some nights wasn't what ya'd call comfortable this time of year." After Rory finished his breakfast, he unfolded the newspaper. There they were, again, Baltimore High School pictures on the front page. The heading read, "Untraceable for twelve days." O'Ryan and Hynes walk into the RCMP detachment in Ferryland. It went on to say, the RCMP were mystified, how both suspects got from Goulds to Ferryland without being seen or reported. And how they made it to Ferryland without being apprehended, as there were dozens of extra officers brought in from across the Province to search for the two wanted suspects. And why they turned themselves in at the detachment in Ferryland. A news briefing was scheduled for two that afternoon with Staff Sergeant Coady of the RCMP. Rory read the article out loud to Butch. When he finished, he passed the newspaper through the bars to Butch. Butch looked at the pictures; he kind of roared and laughed at the same time.

At ten minutes to ten, two guards unlocked a cell each; they told the boys it was time for court. Leg shackles and handcuffs were placed on the prisoners, they made their way from the basement in an elevator to the courtroom. Before getting to the courtroom doors, reporters with cameras flashing blocked the entrance, all roaring questions to the prisoners. The boys couldn't understand any of the questions as they came fast and shouted all at once. The four guards had to push their way through, to get to the doors of the courtroom. When they made it inside the wooden panelled courtroom, their Legal Aid Lawyers waited for them at the rail in front of the first row of seats. The courtroom was packed to capacity. The prosecutor was there, seated to the left of the judge. There were six uniformed RCMP officers plus three RNC officers in attendance. Guards removed the handcuffs. Bennett beckoned the prisoners to come forward to the rail to confer with them. Bennett spoke first.

"Everything is looking good. I don't have time to get into it. We'll be downstairs to speak with you immediately after the charges are read."

As the Lawyers and the prisoners took their seats, the judge entered the chamber. "All rise," the Court Clerk intoned loudly. It reminded Butch of mass, with everyone standing in unison.

Rory didn't like the look of the judge. He was an older man, overweight, and wearing eyeglasses with a stern look.

"Please be seated," said the judge, who addressed the prosecutor first.

Rory sized up the prosecutor. She was blonde, short and runky, mid-forties with a serious look.

"Good morning, Madam Prosecutor, and good morning counsel. Madam Prosecutor, would you like to fill me in on what we have here this morning?"

The prosecutor stood and read from a paper.

"Your Honour, we have two nineteen-year-old individuals from the Southern Shore community of Cappahayden. One Mr. Joseph Seamus Hynes, the taller of the two, and a Mr. Rory Maxwell O'Ryan were involved in an armed robbery on Thursday the 6th of May, at Scotiabank in the town of Goulds. The bank in question is located at Bidgood's Shopping Plaza. This plaza has a busy supermarket along with an Elizabeth Drugs drug store. The drug store is next door to the bank.

After the armed robbery in question, a police chase by the RCMP ensued through town in a southerly direction. The pursued vehicle is registered to Mr. O'Ryan, a yellow1968 Dodge Charger with a green vinyl roof. The car chase ended and turned into a foot chase. The foot chase, which was unsuccessful in apprehending the car's driver, ended on Shoal Bay Road. This road is located on the south end of Goulds. Marijuana and hashish were discovered by a K-9 unit on this road, amounting to three pounds of marijuana along with eight ounces of hashish. The marijuana was bagged in individual bags, weighing an ounce each. We believe these drugs were to be trafficked on the street. The hashish in question was a single block. Your Honour, neither suspect will give a statement as to what went on, on the day of the robbery or where they hid for twelve days or how they made it to the RCMP detachment in Ferryland from Goulds. Your honour, this creates problems for us."

As soon as the prosecutor identified the amount of drugs in question. Rory was confident the weed he had stashed in the beams of his father's barn was still there. The dogs never found it if they even checked the barn. Rory was confident they had, after what Joe had told them.

The prosecutor continued, "These drugs were in the process of being buried. RCMP investigators believe they were being reburied. Fingerprints taken from the bags of marijuana and hashish matched up with fingerprints found in the vehicle used as the getaway vehicle from the armed robbery. These prints belonged to Mr. O'Ryan. We found a second set of prints on the steering wheel and door handles of the vehicle. We've since discovered they belong to Mr. Hynes.

I will add Your Honour before I conclude. There was no weapon involved in this robbery. The note the robber passed to the teller said he had a weapon. As you know, Your Honour, threatening to have a weapon in an armed robbery is considered armed robbery in Canada under the Criminal Code. All monies from the robbery was located in the vehicle. Both men are pleading guilty to a single charge each. Hynes for the armed robbery and O'Ryan for the drugs. Both want to be sentenced as soon as possible to start their sentences. That's all I have to say. Thank you, Your Honour."

As soon as the prosecutor sat, Bennett stood, "May I address the bench."

The judge said, "Go ahead."

"Your Honour, I am here this morning representing Mr. O'Ryan, and my colleague Mr. Small is representing Mr. Hynes. Your Honour, both counsels met with Madam Prosecutor this morning, and we have another meeting scheduled for this afternoon. I respectfully ask that you put this case off until tomorrow morning. I believe we can come to a speedy disposition on these charges outside this courtroom."

The judge looked at the prosecutor and asked, "Are you in agreement with this request?'

The prosecutor rose. "Yes, Your Honour, I see no problem in further discussion outside of this courtroom on these charges."

The judge spoke up, "As I am allowing both parties this request, I am expecting results when we reconvene. This case will be back here at ten in the morning. I will honour the prisoners request to be sentenced as soon as legally possible."

The judge rose, the Court Clerk announced, "All rise." Everyone stood, the judge left the chamber.

Bennett turned to the prisoners, "We'll see you downstairs in fifteen minutes."

Guards put the handcuffs on the prisoners. If there were six or seven reporters on the way in. Now there were at least ten or twelve on the way out. Most were roaring questions in the direction of the prisoners. The loudest question and the one repeated the most often was, "Where did the two of you hide for the past twelve days?" Others shouted, "Was it your dope?"

The prisoners kept their heads down as camera flashbulbs flashed every few seconds. When they got downstairs, they were led into the same meeting room Rory had been in the day before. They were surprised at all the media attention they were getting.

Butch turned to Rory. "What's got the media so interested in us. Was it the armed robbery or the amount of dope they got or that we had the cops runnin' around in circles like hens with their heads chopped off?"

"I figure it was 'cause of the manhunt," Rory replied.

A different guard opened the door and asked, "Is there anything I can get for you?"

Rory said, "Two smokes would be appreciated."

"I'll see if I can get a few for you," said the guard. He returned about three minutes later with two smokes, Rothman's, not their favourite. They were not going to turn them down, in the predicament, they were in.

"Thanks, boss," they both said in unison.

Five minutes after receiving the cigarettes, both lawyers walked into the meeting room.

"How are ye doin'?" asked Bennett.

"Good," replied Rory.

Small looked at Butch and repeated the question to him.

Butch said, "I'm good. Great sleep last night after a hearty supper and a decent breakfast this mornin'."

"How were the guards overnight?"

"Everythin' was good, guards were great, decent fellas."

Bennett said, "good to hear, after what you both have been through for the last number of days. I'm not going to ask where the two of you spent your time since the robbery. Or how the two of you got from one location to the other without being apprehended. That's not our department. Our job is to look out for your best interests in the court of law. Okay, boys, this is where we're at. The prosecutor agreed to Butch taking the rap for the armed robbery and you, Rory, taking the rap for the drugs. That's the good news. Here's the bad news. Both of you will most likely be going to a federal penitentiary. The prosecutor said she will be asking the judge for federal sentences."

Rory asked, "What is the worst and or best sentence we could get for both charges?"

"It's two years plus a day for both charges, armed robbery and trafficking drugs. But you must do the full two years with programs and no probation when released. How do you both feel about that?"

Rory said, "no big shock to us. We figured we were gettin' federal time."

"But let's not rush this," said the seasoned lawyer. "All this depends on what the judge agrees to. The prosecutor can only put this minimum sentence request in front of the judge. It's fully in his hands. He may go with it, he may not. Armed robbery and trafficking in drugs are serious offences under the Criminal Code. Based on both of your ages, plus the fact neither of you have ever been in trouble with the law before. It looks hopeful. You turned yourselves in, which will help, even if it was twelve days after the fact. There is a good chance the judge will accept this. I can't promise you he will, but if he does, he may attach several stipulations."

"What kind of stipulations are we talkin' about?" asked Rory.

"For one, as I said, he will most likely order both of you go into a drug treatment program and for both of you to further your educations."

"Are ya serious?" asked Rory.

Bennett said, "It's either that for two years or three or four with no programs and probation for a few years after you serve your sentence. Rory, do the math, you are not a stupid man."

Rory shook his head, "Yes, I guess whatever sentence we're

given, we'll have to agree to."

"He may separate you and send you to different prisons due to the fact that two police forces in this province couldn't find you for twelve days. Having you together increases the risk of escape. He may not even mention it. I'm preparing you for the worst-case scenario. In the morning, the prosecutor will put this in front of the judge. He may agree to it immediately, or he may ask for a day or two to think it over to look at case law. If he asks for some time to think it over, it will be a good sign. He will most likely agree with the prosecutor's legal opinion. So, everyone understands everything we have discussed here?" asked Bennett.

Rory said, "I'm cool with everythin'."

Small spoke up and asked Butch, "Do you understood everything we discussed and agreed to?"

Butch said, "Yes, this is what me and Rory talked about and expected to happen."

"Boys, I picked you both up a pack of smokes each. I didn't know what brand you smoked, so I took a guess."

"Thanks a million," Butch piped up.

"If there are no questions, we're finished. We'll see you in the morning."

The boys thanked the lawyers. They spent the rest of the day chatting back and forth between the bars.

"Rory, what do ya think a federal prison will be like?"

"I dunno, I guess if we keep our noses clean and find a few Newfies to hang out with, we'll be fine. I'll say one thing to ya. Ya can tell me to go fuck meself if ya like. We knows ya never done much with school when ya were in Baltimore. This is a great opportunity for ya to finish high school and get yer high school diploma."

"I never thought about it Rory, but it does make sense."

"There won't be much else to do. I might do a trade," said Rory.

"What do ya got in mind for a trade?" asked Butch.

"I dunno, maybe weldin'. There should be plenty of work for

welders comin' up in the offshore oil industry, or maybe sheet metal work. I'm sure we'll find out what's available to us when we gets there."

Both lads turned in early after supper, anticipating what they had to face in the morning. They both woke early, ate breakfast, and enjoyed a few smokes before guards arrived to escort them to court. They went through the same procedure, leg shackles and handcuffs.

When they arrived at the courtroom doors, there were two more guards there, anticipating their arrival. Most of the reporters from the previous day were seated when the prisoners entered. The boys took their seats behind their lawyers.

The prosecutor didn't look in their direction to acknowledge them, as she had the morning before. This made Rory a little nervous.

The judge came in within minutes of the prisoners arriving. "All rise" was announced by the Court Clerk.

"Please be seated," said the judge. "Good morning, Madam Prosecutor, good morning counsel. Madam Prosecutor, the floor is yours."

"Your Honour, two days ago, the two gentlemen before you walked into the Royal Canadian Mounted Police detachment in Ferryland and admitted to being involved in the armed robbery on May 6th and owning the drugs in question. Your Honour, having looked at these charges, case law, and taking the ages of the accused into consideration and the fact neither has ever been in trouble with the law before. This is where we are at this morning. Your Honour, concerning the first offence of armed robbery, Mr. Hynes will plead guilty to that charge, and to the second offence of drug trafficking, Mr. O'Ryan will plead guilty to that charge. After serious consideration, I recommended the two accused be sent to a federal penitentiary for the minimum sentence possible. Which is two years, plus one day." She thanked the Judge and sat.

"Excuse me," the judge said. "May I ask why you are asking me to consider a minimum sentence for such serious crimes."

The prosecutor rose from her seat. “Your Honour, as I said previously, we have two crimes before us this morning. We have two people who are admitting to these crimes. If we go to trial on these charges, Your Honour, there is a high probability we could end up with the exact outcome after two lengthy trials. We have no way of proving both were involved in the armed robbery, and we cannot prove both owned the drugs in question. These men are young, neither has a criminal record. They have a long future in front of them. I will add, these crimes were not violent crimes. Thank you, Your Honour." The prosecutor sat.

"Who would like to speak first, Mr. Bennett or Mr. Small?" asked the judge.

Bennett rose and said he would speak first. The judge said, “Go ahead.”

“Good morning, Your Honour. I respectfully ask you to please give serious consideration to what Madam Prosecutor is recommending. I have met with my client on two occasions; he knows the seriousness of his crime and knows he must take his punishment for it. With some ordered programs while my client and his friend are incarcerated, I believe both will come out of incarceration much more responsible, more mature, and better persons than when they entered prison.” Bennett sat when he finished speaking.

“Thank you, counsel, “said the judge. “Would you like to add something here this morning, Mr. Small?”

Small stood. “Your Honour, all I will say is, I agree with what both Madam Prosecutor and my co-counsel have said. A long prison sentence will do nothing for the future of these two young men, who know what they did was wrong, and who are taking full responsibility for their actions. Thank you, Your Honour, that is all I have to say.”

The Judge cleared his throat, he sipped water from a tall glass. “Here is where we are with this case. I want all involved back here in the morning at ten thirty, between now and court tomorrow morning. I want both young men assessed by a caseworker and a one-hour session with a psychiatrist. I leave this in your hands Madam Prosecutor, to see it will be done this afternoon with written reports in my chamber at nine in the morning for me to review before sentencing."

The prosecutor stood. "I would like to assure you, Your Honour, your requests will be taken care of this afternoon."

The judge rose and left the courtroom. The lawyers turned to their clients, saying they would see them downstairs in ten or fifteen minutes. The prisoners were returned to the interrogation room to await their lawyers, who showed up roughly twenty minutes later.

CHAPTER FORTY

When the lawyers walked in, Bennett threw two packs of Player's Light Regular on the table along with a box of matches.

"God love yer cotton socks," Butch said.

"Here is where we're at. We had a quick meeting with the prosecutor. She has a caseworker meeting with both of you at two this afternoon. At seven this evening you will meet with a psychiatrist. Both meetings will be one-on-one here in this room. The reason for the caseworker is to find out what level of education each of you has. And to see if either of you may be interested in furthering your education or learning a trade."

Rory spoke up. "I have my high school diploma."

Butch chimed in with, "I went to grade seven, did it twice, but never finished it. I'm interested in finishin' high school."

"I would be interested in doin' a trade while incarcerated," Rory added.

"Excellent," said Bennett.

"Why does the judge want a psychiatrist to meet with us?" asked Rory.

"To see if both of you are mentally fit to be incarcerated in a federal penitentiary. Especially how young both of you are."

"If either one of us is not fit for a federal penitentiary, what's the other option?" asked Rory.

"You would either have to stay at Her Majesty's Penitentiary here in St. John's or more likely be sent to the West Coast Correctional Centre in Stephenville. Rory, as your lawyer, I would advise that both of you agree with going to a federal penitentiary. Butch can finish high school there. When he's done, he can learn a trade. Rory, you could do a trade. You might even have time to do two trades. So, don't be nervous about meeting with these people. They're only doing their job. They're just like you and me. Be open and honest with both. We'll be here at nine forty-five in the morning to speak to you to see how your meetings went before court."

"Will ya meet with the prosecutor 'fore court in the marnin'?" Rory asked.

"No, there's nothing to discuss. We've said everything that has to be said between us. The prosecutor will not see either of the written reports; neither will we. So, it's just to appear before the judge for sentencing. Any questions before we leave?"

"No," both prisoners said.

Both lawyers stood. Bennett said, "we'll see you in the morning." Small knocked on the door, a guard opened it, the lawyers said their good-byes and left.

The prisoners were escorted back to their cells, awaiting their meetings. When their cell door closed, Butch ask Rory what he thought of everything.

Rory said, "I wasn't surprised at what the judge requested. With the prosecutor askin' for minimum federal sentences, the judge has to get professional advice on our mental states to see if we are candidates for programs. Butch, remember, prison is not just a place to lock up people. It's a place for rehabilitation to ease prisoners back into society. And if doin' a few programs is what they wants, fine. Besides, what else are we goin' to do for two years? This will give us somethin' to be at, to pass the time. I got no problem doin' somethin' to better meself. Whichever way we cut it, we're both lucky; we could be goin' away for four or five years."

Butch said, "I guess yer right. I had a few things I wanted to do in the next few years."

"No worries, Butch. They'll be on hold for a few years. We'll fulfill 'em when we gets out. We're not dyin'. This is only a hiccup."

Both were pleased with their meetings with the caseworker and psychiatrist. Both thought everything went smoothly. The boys spent a long evening, awaiting the sentence they would be given to them in the morning. Both settled down early to sleep. They were woken around three a.m. by a loud drunk being processed in another room thirty feet away. The prisoner looked like Relic from the Beachcombers TV show. He smelled worse than they did when they walked into the detachment in Ferryland. After the prisoner was processed, he was put in the cell to the right of Rory's. He was so loud the boys couldn't get back to sleep. This was all they needed—a night with little sleep, facing the most important day of their lives.

The prisoner said he was Gill Sampson from Tors Cove. He asked Rory who he was and where he was from. Rory told him his name. As drunk as the prisoner was, he immediately knew Rory's name from the news reports in the last few weeks. "Holy Jesus, yer the two lads from Cappahayden. Ye knows the two of ye are famous. Both of ye are more famous than that Dr. Carr fella, do ya remember 'im?" Rory said, "he had heard the story a few times over the years from his father."

Dr. Arthur Carr was caught aboard the yacht Carrero near Tinkers Point between Mobile and Tors Cove on June 25th,1974, offloading forty-two hundred pounds of marijuana onto Kearney's Beach, worth 1.2 million dollars. It had been picked up in Columbia. The RCMP had the drugs brought into Tors Cove in a trap skiff owned by local fisherman Gus O'Driscoll, offloaded at the public wharf and brought to St. John's in a truck owned by Martin O'Brien, owner of Tors Cove Fisheries. Twin Hills Lounge was used as a makeshift post by the RCMP during the bust and investigation that followed.

The drunk said, "Yer pretty smart for a young trout. How many people has the cops runnin' around lookin' for 'em for nearly two weeks, and they don't even get 'em. They ends up turnin' 'emselves in. B'ys since ye two have been on the run; there has been dozens of roadblocks all over the Shore. Someone said they had roadblocks all the way from the Goulds to Cappahayden. And apparently, some narc lookin' fellas were noticed hangin' around the nightclubs in Bay Bulls and Witless Bay. B'ys, tell me where ye were. I promise I won't tell anyone."

"Sorry, Gill, we can't say."

"C'mon b'ys. I promise I'll keep me mouth shut."

"Sorry, we can't."

"Well, can I give ye some advice? Why don't one of ye write a book about yer days on the run? I loves crime stories, I do. I'm sure everybody in Newfoundland would buy it. And I wouldn't be shocked if someone made a movie about it.

"I'll tell ya, the first time I ever smelled or smoked weed was in 75 or 76. Me and me, buddy Rock, got it from the hippies that lived down in the Quays in Bay Bulls. Ya know where the Quays is, do ya?"

Rory smiled, said, "yes."

"What a weird lookin' bunch. Most of 'em wore 'em poncho things ya hauls down over yer head and tie with a piece of rope, and all of 'em, even the women, walked around barefoot all the time. They had this huge white horse; I believe it was a stallion; they rode it bareback all the time. They even had a small cave shovelled out of a bank. I was in it once, smokin' it up. I'd say they hid their dope in it."

The prisoner took a five-minute break from talking, giving Rory hope for a bit of shut-eye, before starting again.

"I apologize for talkin' so much. I usually don't talk this much. I've been on the beer for a week or more. Some prick in Burnt Cove stole me Irish setter. His name is Red. Someone told me they saw Red with 'im in his truck two weeks ago. I got up taday and got drunk again. I loves that dog. Got 'im in Portugal Cove South last year. Great bird dogs come out of the Cove. I went up and demanded me dog back. Buddy stuck his head out his kitchen window and told me to go fuck meself. Said he never saw my dog. I said buddy give me, me dog back before the war starts. Ya don't know who yer fuckin' with. He laughed at me, told me to go fuck meself a second time and closed his kitchen window.

I beat every window out of the front of his house with rocks. I jumped in me truck and went home. I woke up two hours later with the barrel of a gun in me face. Cocksuckers put the cuffs on me, and here I am. I asked 'em why I wasn't bein' brought to Ferryland. They said I was most likely goin' to that Mental Hospital for an assessment. I said, for what? They said, for beatin' the windows out of buddy's house. I said to them, wouldn't ya do the same thing for yer dog? Cocksuckers told me to shut up. The fuckin' cops in Ferryland brought me Cousin Harry out to that mental hospital thirty years ago. Poor ol' bastard hasn't seen daylight since."

Rory smiled and said, "Mister, I feels bad for ya, losin' yer dog and endin' up in the tangle yer in."

"Thanks, that means a lot. Yer, a fine young man."

Rory bit his lip. If the drunk only knew the poor bastard in Burnt Cove with no windows in the front of his house hadn't seen Red/Lucky in two full weeks. That's if he ever saw him.

Finally, after talking none stop for two hours, the prisoner passed out. Rory asked Butch if he was asleep. Butch never answered. Solid asleep, as Rory expected. You'd need more than a drunk to keep Butch awake.

CHAPTER FORTY-ONE

When the boys woke, the drunk was dead to the world, stinking like a urinal in a bar. A late breakfast was delivered, a little cold, they didn't complain, given what they'd had to eat for the past twelve days. Besides, they had more on their minds than food. Their lives for the next number of years were on the line today.

At nine-thirty, two guards unlocked the cells and told the boys they were bringing them to the meeting room to await the arrival of their lawyers. Just as they sat, Rory said to Butch that he had something to tell him after court. They smoked a cigarette each while they waited for their lawyers. The lawyers arrived as the boys finished their smokes.

When the lawyers entered the room, they asked how their meetings went with the caseworker and the psychiatrist.

Rory said, “Both my meetin’s went well. The one with the caseworker was much shorter than the one with the doctor.”

“How did yer meetings go, Butch?” asked Small.

“Good as far as I was concerned. The caseworker talked mostly about what I did in school, or should I say, what I didn’t do in school. And asked me if I was interested in finishin’ high school. I said I would do whatever was recommended and advised. The psychiatrist recommended; I speak to the psychiatrist on staff at the prison when I gets there. Said I might have a learnin’ disability.”

Bennett asked, “Do you have any questions before court?” Both boys shook their heads, implying no. “Okay, we'll see you upstairs." As they were leaving, Bennett added, "Remember, the sentences and which prison you are going to will be based on your meetings with the caseworker and doctor. There's nothing more we can do for you."

When the Prisoners arrived at the courtroom, they were flanked by four guards. Not one news reporter was outside awaiting them. When they entered the courtroom, they were shocked by the crowd of people within the courtroom. Every seat was occupied, with fifteen or twenty people assembled along the walls on both sides of the room. As soon as they entered, Rory eyed Brock, who was standing on the right side of the room. They made eye contact and smiled at each other. The prisoners took their seats, behind their lawyers to the right of the judge. When they sat, Rory asked Butch if he saw Brock. Butch said no; Rory nodded his head in Brock's direction. Butch eyed Brock, both smiled at each other.

Butch whispered to Rory, "That's some nice of 'im to come out here, taday."

"Yes, it is."

The judge entered within minutes. "All rise," came the call from the Court Clerk. "Be seated," the judge said as he sat.

"Good morning Madam Prosecutor and good morning counsel. And a good morning to both gentlemen from Cappahayden. Before I start, I want to explain why I am allowing people to stand in my courtroom. This case has garnered a lot of attention. I usually don't allow people to stand in my court out of respect for the court system. But I am allowing it here this morning,"

"Young men, I have to tell you, Cappahayden is a beautiful place. I have stopped there many times for a picnic on a Sunday afternoon, driving around the loop. A beautiful spot for a retirement home."

Both prisoners smiled. Rory's mind raced, hoping this was a good sign. The judge saying good morning and mentioning their hometown. He hadn't said anything like this on the first two appearances.

"I will start by talking about the crimes in question. Armed robbery is a serious crime. Not only a serious crime but a dangerous crime. When one enters a bank or retail business to rob it forcefully, it puts many people in the line of harm, not only the person who meets face to face with the robber and or robbers in question. They don't know if the person in front of them is armed. Even if a weapon is not involved, the chances are the person being robbed could go into cardiac arrest. Some people who come face to face with an armed robber feel the impact for the rest of their lives and never recover mentally. Or a bystander might intervene and try to apprehend the robber and or robbers, resulting in injuries or death. When the robber leaves the bank or business they robbed, there's a high probability they may cause a serious accident by driving above the speed limit to get away from the location they robbed.

I have read both reports on each of the individuals from the caseworker and the psychiatrist. I have taken their professional opinions into serious consideration as I sentence you both here this morning. I will mention, I am not comfortable with neither of you giving a full report of your activities on the day the crimes were committed or for the days afterwards before you turned yourselves into the police. These issues are not my concern; they are the concern of the police. This morning, it could factor in here; I will not allow the issue to cloud my legal judgment. Since May 6th and up until the day you turned yourselves in, you committed no other crimes; that in itself speaks volumes. I see neither of you has a criminal record."

The judge stopped for a moment to take a sip of water.

"Madam Prosecutor, would you like to add anything here this morning before I hand down the sentences?"

The prosecutor rose, "no, Your Honour. I gave my legal opinion on the days the prisoners appeared before you previously. I still agree with co-counsels on what the punishment and sentences should be. That will be all for me, thank you."

"Mr. Bennett or Mr. Small, would you like to add anything here this morning?'

Bennett rose and said, "I echo what Madam Prosecutor has said." When Bennett sat, Small stood, he repeated what Bennett had said.

"Young men, please stand," said the judge. "I am going to go along with the prosecutor's recommendations, But it is not as cut and dry as you would like. Both of you will receive the minimum federal sentence, which is two years plus one day. The sentences I will impose here this morning will start immediately. I agree with Madam prosecutor on this sentence. Both of you are young and have never been in trouble with the law before. I read both reports from the caseworker and the doctor who met with you last evening. Based on what they wrote, I am sending you, Mr. Hynes, to Dorchester prison for two years plus one day. And as for Mr. O'Ryan, I am sending you to Springhill prison for the same duration as Mr. Hynes. Why am I separating you? Dorchester has a much better teaching facility for prisoners to get their high school diplomas. Springhill has much better programs to assist prisoners in getting a trade. I know you don't want to be separated. Both written reports tell me you have been close since elementary school. I would rather not do this, but I am looking out for both of your futures. I hope both of you will take advantage of the opportunities available to you at these federal institutions. There is no reason why both of you can't return home in two years with a trade and be ready to be gainfully employed. I will recommend, if and when Mr. Hynes gets his high school diploma, both of you be brought back together in the same penitentiary, which most likely would be Springhill. I will recommend that both of you be put into protective custody due to your ages before easing you into the general population.

Young men, I hope you have learned your lesson. Taking two years of your life away is not an easy decision for me to make at the prime of your life. I have given you the minimum federal sentence possible. Hopefully, you will learn from these mistakes and go on to lead lawful lives when you are released. Does anyone have anything to add?" asked the judge.

The prosecutor rose, and said no, and thanked the judge for his decision.

When the prosecutor sat. Bennett rose and thanked the judge for giving his client the minimum sentence possible; he thanked the prosecutor. Small repeated what Bennett had said.

"Court is adjourned," said the Court Clerk. "All rise."

When the judge left the courtroom, Bennett turned to Rory, shook his hand, and said, "I believe we got the best we could get." Small said the same to Butch. All hands smiled at each other.

"We'll be down to see you in a few minutes," said Bennett.

As the cuffs were being put on the prisoners, both looked at Brock, neither of them smiled. The prisoners were led out of the courtroom. The media that had sat through the sentencing were outside waiting. Camera flashbulbs were going off at a steady pace. Reporters shouted many questions. Both kept their heads down and ignored the questions.

When they were brought into the meeting room, the handcuffs were removed, they high-fived each other.

"That worked out great, Rory, but I dread the thought of bein' separated."

"Butch, if ya apply yerself in gettin' yer high school diploma, there is a good chance we could be back together at Springhill in a year or less. The end of this," Rory continued, "it will be the start of our new beginning, don't give up on yer dreams. We still have a full life to live."

"Yeah, I agree, but two years is a long fuckin' time lookin' at the same walls."

"Ya stop noticin' time after a while." Rory said, "goin' away is only endin' up somewhere else. Cappahayden will be there when we gets out."

Ten minutes later, the lawyers walked in. They all shook hands and sat.

"Boys, what do you think of the sentence?" asked Bennett.

Rory said, "As good as we hoped and expected, and startin' our sentences immediately is a bonus. Let's get this time behind us. We don't like that we're goin' to be separated."

Bennett said, "don't worry about it. They'll have you in protective custody wings. Most likely, with prisoners your age, with similar crimes and sentences. There's plenty of Newfoundlanders in federal prisons. You'll find them the first day you're there, and you'll be friends fairly quickly. Remember, Newfies stick together."

"When will we be transported," asked Rory.

"They usually do it within days of sentencing. If they have an RCMP plane heading west, they usually take anyone who has been sentenced in the week previous with other prisoners. And if there is no RCMP plane going out of the province with prisoners within a week of sentencing, they put you on a commercial jet, usually with two members of the RCMP as escorts."

"So, we could be out of here in a matter of days?" asked Butch.

"Yes, usually within a couple of days, no longer than a week."

Rory asked, "will we stay here or be moved to the penitentiary?'

"They'll keep you here unless the place fills up. So, you'll most likely leave for the airport from here."

Bennett asked, "Is there anything else you need to know?"

Rory said, "I have no other questions."

"What about you, Butch?" asked Small.

"No, I'm good." Replied Butch.

They shook hands and thanked the lawyers for their advice and assistance, especially getting them the minimum possible sentences.

After they left, Rory said, "I guess it's over. I guess the fat lady can finally start singin'."

The prisoners were returned to their cells. The drunk from Tors Cove was gone, which pleased Rory. He wanted so badly to tell Butch the story about Lucky.

"Butch yer not goin' to believe this, the fella they brought in last night, loaded drunk. He's Lucky's dad!"

"Rory, what ya talkin' about?"

"Butch, buddy was from Tors Cove, his name is Gill Sampson, he said he lost his Irish setter two weeks ago. Someone told 'im a fella in Burnt Cove had 'im. He went up to buddy's house yesterday afternoon, drunk, demandin' his dog named Red back.

The fella said he had never even saw the dog; he told 'im to go fuck 'imself. The fella from Tors Cove beat all the windows out of the front of his house with rocks. Cops arrested 'im, told 'im he was bein' sent to the Waterford Hospital for an assessment for beatin' out buddy's windows. He was almost cryin' tellin' me how much he missed and loved his dog Red. I was almost cryin' also, listenin' to 'im and feelin' so guilty. I thought about tellin' 'im where his dog was and to go get 'im. I knew if I did, ya'd flip."

"Rory, yer fuckin' right, I would've flipped. He's my dog. If buddy loved 'im so much, why was he walkin' the roads so late at night? Coulda been killed by a car. We probably saved his life. He's my dog, end of story, so fuck 'im. He's safer with Gerald than with that drunk."

"Butch, listenin' to buddy, I was thinkin' I shoulda let ya keep the rabbit dog we came across on Deans Road in Witless Bay. And the poor ol' property owner in Burnt Cove would still have his windows, and the poor drunk wouldn't now be in the Waterford and headin' to jail. I agrees with ya. He's safer with Gerald. It was painful listenin' to 'im. All over, poor Lucky."

"Rory, drop it!

They never spoke much for the rest of the day. They let everything that had happened to them in the past few days sink in.

Butch asked Rory, "What's it like in prison?"

Rory said, "Keep yer nose clean, and it will be easy doin' time."

"What do ya mean, keep yer nose clean?"

"Don't buy drugs or get a front from anyone, 'cause down the road; they might want a favour in return."

Butch asked, "What kind of favour?"

Rory explained. "If ya owes someone money for drugs, they may want ya to beat someone up who owes 'em even more than you do. It could lead to other shit. Stay away from drugs, and ya'll stay out of trouble, especially hard drugs like cocaine and heroin. Once ya start doin' those drugs, ya could take a likin' to 'em and get hooked. If ya get hooked on either of those in prison, it could make doin' time much harder and longer. Remember, yer dealin' with hardened criminals. People belongin' to gangs and fellas from motorcycle clubs. Butch, don't go in there with a weak mind, show some grit, be strong!"

Butch said, "I'll try and keep me nose clean."

Rory replied, "Make a promise to me."

"I promise."

"Another thing, Butch, don't count the days, weeks, or months. It will make doin' time harder. I'm goin' to get ahold of Brock, keep in touch with 'im while in prison. I wants 'im to get the brace and bits back off Gerald. Ya knows the ol' man, how anti-social he is, he'd never ask for it back."

Butch chuckled to himself. He knew what Rory meant. Get the drugs and sell them.

"Butch, I'll call 'im once a week or at least every two weeks. The first time I gets ahold of 'im, I'm goin' to ask 'im to inquire about what's involved in gettin' the charger back from the cops. As I said earlier, I believe cops keep confiscated vehicles for a year 'fore they're auctioned. Ya should call 'im every now and then."

"Rory, me and Brock are not tight, like you and 'im. He thinks I'm half nuts."

"I know. But keep in touch with 'im. To get the news and local gossip of what's happenin' on the Shore while we're away."

"Well, when ya first talk to 'im tell 'im, I might call 'im once in a while."

"I'll tell 'im. I'm interested in asking 'im if the cops tracked 'im down for questionin' about us. Everyone knows we're close. I doubt it; if he even gave them any info, ya would think it woulda come out in court. But knowin' Brock, I bet he didn't say much. He's not a talker even on a good day."

"I hope yer right, Rory."

They said good night to each other and turned in.

The next morning, after breakfast. An older guard wearing a full guards uniform with a peaked service hat approached the prisoners' cells.

"Good day, men. I have news for both of you. Mr. Hynes, you will be leaving here at six-thirty tomorrow morning for a direct flight to Greater Moncton International Airport, New Brunswick, aboard an RCMP plane. From there, you will be driven to Dorchester Penitentiary to serve your sentence. Mr. O'Ryan, you will leave here the following morning at eight o'clock on a commercial flight. You will be escorted by two members of the Royal Canadian Mounted Police to fly to Halifax International Airport. From there, you will be driven to Springhill Penitentiary to serve your sentence. Do both of you understand this?"

Rory said, "Yes, but why aren't we travellin' together?"

"That is something you do not need to know. Are there any other questions?"

Rory wanted to tell the guard to go fuck himself for not answering his question but decided against it. He didn't want his sentence to start off bad.

The guard said, "Good day," turned, and left.

Butch said, "There's a prick of a screw if I ever saw one."

"Butch, he's two pricks! The shit has started already. Cocksucker walkin' in here with his chest stuck out. Don't he know the lowest form of life is the keeper of man? Fuckin' conk on 'im like Lincoln. No big deal, Butch. I kinda figured we wouldn't be travellin' together as we're goin' to different provinces and different penitentiaries. I guess we may as well settle in and start our sentences. This journey started on Shoal Bay Road; it will end when we lands back here. 'fore ya knows it, we'll be on a plane headin' home. Hopefully, both of us will have a trade. I tell ya what we'll do when we gets back here. Why don't we get an apartment in town? There's nothin' on the Shore for us. If we stay in the city, we'll stay out of trouble."

Butch said, "Sounds like a plan. There's not much on the Shore. As much as I loves the Shore, I got to agree with ya. We have to leave it to get somewhere in life. The fishery has been downhill for a few years. Trap crews are gettin' less and less fish every year. Salmon are as scarce as hens' teeth. If we don't leave the Shore, we'll be back behind these bars again 'fore we know it."

"Right ya are, Butch," said Rory.

"If we gets an apartment in town, will we still go to the shack every now and then?"

"Sure, Butch, probably more than we ever did!" That reassured Butch. He loved the shack. Always did since he was a kid. "Butch, it's not about what they're takin' away from us for the next two years. It's what we do with what we learn on the inside and implement into our lives when we're released that will make the difference. It will give us a decent livin' and quality life. It will be a new beginnin'. Peddlin' drugs on the Shore was no future. We were bound to get caught. Not many pushers avoid prison time."

"Rory, I gotta agree with ya!"

"Another thing, Butch, hit the gym when ya get settled away. Exercisin' releases endorphins in the brain, which gives ya a positive feelin'. It's easy to get depressed on the inside, which is why most prisoners turn to drugs. Ya gotta keep yerself busy with school and goin' to the gym. Start readin'; it's a great way to pass the time. We're only facin' two years, not ten."

"Rory, I'll try to keep busy. I know it's goin' to be hard; I guess I got no other choice but to come to terms with it. Get me head around it and look towards a positive future."

"Exactly, Butch!"

The boys chatted well into the night. They mostly reminisced about growing up in Cappahayden, stuff they did as kids and teenagers. And what federal prison would be like. Rory knew Butch was nervous about going to jail for the first time, and being separated was not going to be easy. It was playing on his mind. Rory reassured him, no one would mess with him due to his size. Rory told Butch, the first fella who fucks with him, to kick the shit out of him, then everyone else will know not to mess with you. They will respect you.

"Butch, there's an ol' sayin'. Anticipation causes anxiety, placement creates contentment. I knows yer nervous and anxious. Don't let yer conscience punish you. Once ya gets there and gets settled into a routine, ya'll be okay."

"Rory, I hope yer right."

"Butch, when we talks on the phone, hopefully sometime next week. Ya'll be sayin', everythin' is fine, and the grub is the best ya've ever eaten. Did ya hear what the fella from Tors Cove said?"

"No, I got sick of listenin' to 'im ramblin' on in his drunken stupor and fell asleep."

"Buddy said, one of us should write a book about bein' on the run. I'm seriously thinkin' about it. I have read several books over the years about fellas escapin' prison and bein' on the run for weeks or months. I must say I enjoyed 'em a lot. I believe we have an interestin' story to tell. Two young fellas, last seen runnin' down a dirt road in the Goulds, and mysteriously seen for the first time, twelve days later on the side of the road in Portugal Cove South. With two police forces lookin' for 'em, and one of those forces, the RCMP, one of the most revered police forces in the world.

I'll tell ya what I'll do. I'll start writin' it in the nights after trade school. Sure, there'll be nothin' else to do. It will take me at least two years or more to write it. I should have it written by the time we get released. I'll get ya to read it and add anythin', ya think should be in it. Ya can fix any mistakes I've made and make sure our timelines are correct."

"Rory, I thinks it's a good idea. We might even make a few dollars of it. What will the name of it be?"

"One of the names of the trail, the hikers mentioned to ya. Somethin' like Escape on the Atlantic Coastal Trail, or On the Run-on the Southern Shore Walkin' Trail or Workin' The East Coast Trail. Who knows, by the time we're out of prison, they might have an actual name picked out for the trail. And whatever name they use, we'll go with the same one for our book. Our book would promote the trail, and the trail will promote our book. And hopefully, while we're in jail, they may have gotten their government fundin' to start buildin' it.

Also, Butch, we might get a job buildin' the trail. I might even do a carpentry course. I'm sure whenever they starts developin' and buildin' it, they'll need carpenters. There's bridges to be built, steps to be designed and put in place. And God knows how much boardwalk will need to be laid down."

"That makes sense, Rory."

"It might be a few more years 'fore they gets the fundin' they're lookin' for, so at least we'll be ready whenever it starts," said Rory.

"Rory sounds great. Sure, we walked at least half of it or more. I'd say we're the first ones to walk as much of it as we did. Other than the crowd cuttin' it."

"Butch, I'm turnin' in early. We'll chat in the mornin' 'fore ya leaves."

"All right, sounds good. Good night."

Both slept undisturbed. No prisoners were brought in overnight, so there was no noise to keep them awake. A guard woke Butch at five to let him shower before his flight. When he was returned to his cell, Rory was awake. The guard told Rory they were bringing breakfast early to Butch, asked if he wanted his as well. Rory said, sure.

They sat in silence. Rory was never one to struggle for words. Deep down inside, he was blaming himself for the mess they were in. If he had never started to sell drugs and bought a car he had to share with Butch, none of this would have happened. They'd be getting ready to go to work in the fish plant, not heading to federal prisons.

Breakfast arrived at five-thirty. They chatted while they ate. Butch only picked at his. This was strange for Butch, as he usually ate like a bull moose. Butch, not asking if he had anything left over, told Rory he was too nervous to eat.

At six twenty, two guards approached the cells, telling Butch it was time to leave.

Rory watched Butch exited his cell. As the guards put leg shackles on him.

Rory asked if he could get out of his cell to say goodbye to his best friend.

The guard said, "We normally don't allow it, as there are no other prisoners here, we'll make an exception."

Rory's cell was opened. Rory walked up to Butch. Butch would not make eye contact with him.

Rory raised his voice, "C'mon now, Butch, shape up and look at me. This will be over 'fore we knows it."

Butch looked down at Rory. Rory could see the tears welling up in his eyes. Rory put out his arms to hug him. Butch slowly raised his arms and embraced Rory. They squeezed each other for what seemed like minutes. Before they released each other, Butch said, "I loves ya, and I'm sorry."

Rory released his grip, and looked up at Butch and said, "don't let this define who we are. We're good people. I loves ya too, man, and ya have nothin' to be sorry for! Remember, we're a team. We'll be back together in no time. We can call each other at least once a week. Butch, I'm only a phone call away. Ya needs me, have 'em contact me. Even though I'm also in prison, I can't see no reason why I can't be yer next of kin."

Rory backed up as the handcuffs were put on Butch. When the cuffs were in place, the guards walked Butch down the corridor towards the exit. Butch turned and looked back. Rory could see tears flowing as they stared at each other. Rory entered his cell and sat on the bunk. He cried like a baby. His tears were for his best friend. He knew Butch like no one else did. As big and tough as he was, deep down inside, he was a child.

ACKNOWLEDGEMENTS

Thank you to my editor Susan Rendell and my copy editor Robin McGrath.

Lorna Yard - cover designer and for formatting this document for uploading.

Author Liz Graham - for walking me through the self-publishing process.

thebookgremlins for beta/proofread.

My proofreaders before editing for finding my mistakes and errors and for their positive critiquing and constructive advice. Tina Wakeham Ryan, Ronnie Dunne, Donny Graham Jr, Perry Howlett, Wanda Ronayne, Millie Bishop.

Writing historical fiction takes more than just the author putting pages between two covers. In order to get this manuscript to print, I have contacted many people up and down the Southern Shore for dates, timelines, physical locations and landmarks. I have to single out two people: Cliff Doran, Lighthouse Keeper at Cape Race and Donny Graham Jr. I've messaged these two many times since I started researching and compiling this book in January 2014. Their knowledge of the Southern Shore answered many questions. They helped more than they will ever know. People answering my questions in the smallest detail helped send me in the right direction to find answers. Thank you to each and every one of you. If I omitted anyone from this list, I apologize.

Jimmy Boland, Jim Chidley, Mrs. Rosemary Chidley, Mrs. Ann Coady, Gerard Cummings, Billy Glynn, Della Jordan, Keith Kenny, Teddy Lee, Wayne Maloney, Frank Martin, Rosie Mullaley, Ted O'Connor, Joe Ryan, Carolyn Shannahan, Gerard Swain, Paddy Wakeham, Glenys Williams and Sheila Williams.

ABOUT THE AUTHOR

Christopher P. Ryan was born in 1964, the eighth in a family of nine children. His family has operated Ryan's Funeral Home in Bay Bulls, serving the Southern Shore for over fifty years.

Twice elected to the town council for his hometown of Bay Bulls, first in 1993 and 1997, he also sat on the board of directors for the East Coast Trail Association for five years, serving the last year as vice-president. On April 23, 2013, he was awarded the Flamber Head Award for volunteerism for years of service on the lobbying committee and the first project management committee of this group and its board of directors.

Chris spent a number of years on the Ferryland District Liberal Association and served the last two years as president. A former board member of Say No to American Garbage Group (SNAGG), an organization that opposed the importation of garbage/waste into Newfoundland and Labrador for final distribution. He is a former member of the Witless Bay and Area Conservation Group. This group's goal is to protect sea trout and salmon that visit the Lower Pond in Witless Bay, a pond made world-famous for record-sized sea-run brown trout.

On August 21/2019, he was awarded the Sovereign's Medal for Volunteers. Chris is a serious birder who has seen 337 species of birds in Newfoundland. He holds a second-degree black belt in Shotokan Traditional Karate from the Newfoundland Karate Association.

"The Bay Bulls Standoff" was his first book. Published in November 2014.

Made in the USA
Monee, IL
09 November 2021